JIM M. ⸺ɪʟᴇ

A Killer Legacy

Contents

1 - A Death

Monday, July 7, Nice, France

Security around the Palais de Justice was intense. Restaurants in the normally bustling square it overlooked were closed and police manned roadblocks on the network of streets which enclosed it.

It had been decided to bring him in by the imposing building's grand front entrance where police marksmen could have eyes on everything.

But nothing was being left to chance and when the fleet of black vans discharged their contents of uniformed officers, even Barney couldn't make out the man who had made all these precautions necessary.

Around eighteen of them scurried up the long flight of steps then crowded around the doorway, forming a barrier as one of their number was hustled inside.

Detective Inspector Barney Mains stepped back into the hallway while two officers led their charge towards an inner door.

Pieter Nel was smiling broadly despite the handcuffs, appearing to revel in the excitement after months of confinement

- and to find it hugely amusing to be dressed in a police uniform.

One scary serial killer had been ghosted safely into court, a man believed to hold secrets of the rich and famous so dangerous that many would rather he took them to the grave, ideally sooner rather than later.

Barney stood watching from across the wide marble hall as his minders peeled off Nel's camouflage with loud velcro rips as if performing some bizarre striptease act. Moments later they were marching him into the courtroom and Barney fell into step alongside his friend, Captain Jean-Luc Verten of the Police Nationale.

The court's public seats were empty apart from the final two rows on the left which were almost filled by police and lawyer types. Across the aisle from them a boxed-off area was packed with members of the press, most of whom turned sharply to check out the latest arrivals, apparently on edge.

As Barney eased his way along the front row to sit beside Jean-Luc, it suddenly hit him how much his life had changed in the past year. Having handed in his resignation at Police Scotland, he'd been drawn back into policing again largely because of the prisoner whose back he now stared at, only a few metres in front of him and separated only by the low gate of the dock.

He'd been ordered to the city to liaise with French authorities because the accused faced related charges in Edinburgh and as Jean-Luc started to explain the preliminaries in a low voice, the judges suddenly appeared from a hidden door in the rich wood panelling behind their bench.

The two black-gowned judge-assessors flanked the principal judge, who looked magnificent as he fluffed out his bright red gown and took his seat. He gave a curt nod to the clerk and stenographer seated below him, off to Barney's left.

Maybe it was the ritual formality of such events but they'd always made Barney a little tense and irrationally prone to giggling. For some reason he recalled a funeral years ago when he and his father carried the coffin of an aged relative to a hole in the ground, whispering jokes to each other and stifling their laughter like schoolkids. Happy days.

The accused seemed to find the current situation a bit silly too because he was smiling as he turned to face Barney's row.

Nel should have looked pale and defeated. But the man before him wore the kind of forever-young good looks that some people were cursed with; short fair hair in a side parting, an unblemished dark complexion and sharply intelligent blue eyes which were taking everything in. He was said to be highly cultured and to have mixed in elite circles of celebrities and politicians despite the brutish build of a weightlifter and the anonymous role of security consultant.

Today, in a dazzling white polo shirt and cricket jersey above loose, silky black slacks and matching fine leather sandals, he looked like he'd just dropped in from some society photo shoot.

Whatever was really going on behind those striking eyes, they were now sparkling with a merriment which matched the mischievous big grin now spreading across his face as he started to scan the seated police and lawyers.

Barney almost laughed when Nel suddenly formed his right hand into a mock gun, the thumb a cocked hammer, the first two fingers the barrel.

The prisoner started at the far end of the row then trained his aim on each target in turn. Jean-Luc was spared but the

3

gun's traverse stopped on Barney and now the man, having great fun, jerked his fingers to fire an imaginary shot.

At the very same instant there was a sound like a sharp snap of the fingers and someone let out an involuntary laugh.

The wide grin on Nel's face shortened. The expression began to turn sad, like a white-faced mime artist playing with emotion. Barney noticed a mark on the forehead just as the man crumpled and fell.

A woman screamed.

But Barney had heard that snap of the fingers before. He was on his feet, then into a low crouch. 'Gun! Everybody down!'

He heard someone, Jean-Luc, repeat his shout in French but he registered nothing more because he was too busy dragging the lifeless body towards him from where it lay draped face down across the dock gate.

He felt the neck while daring to poke his head up to seek the source of the shot. But there was nothing; no answering pulse from Nel and only policemen with guns drawn, bent low and scanning the empty rows.

He hadn't noticed the small gallery high above the main courtroom until now. It looked empty too with no sign of life. Apart from the door swinging slowly closed.

'Jean-Luc!' Barney pointed and the Frenchman, gun in hand, understood. He instantly shouted for the building to be sealed. Then he was on his radio, barking short, sharp commands.

But Barney knew that for the man at his feet it was all too late, the darkening pool of blood beneath his head an unnecessary proof.

* * *

4

Barney stood up as Jean-Luc approached his cafe table in the Cours Saleya. The Frenchman looked like he was ready for a fight as he barrelled his way through the chaos of traders packing up their wares after the weekly antiques market.

'All right, Jean-Luc?' A stupid question, he knew. But his friend had just come from what was probably the toughest meeting of his life and clearly needed a bit of normality.

'Well, I'm still alive, if that counts,' the Frenchman grumbled as they shook hands.

'What can I get you? You look like you could use a large beer.'

'I could, but better make it coffee. I don't have long.'

The waiter, whom Barney previously suspected of suffering from agoraphobia, must have recognised the policeman because the normally elusive character was already hovering close by.

Barney ordered two coffees. 'We must meet here more often. You seem to have influence.'

Jean-Luc nodded at the waiter's back. 'Oh, him. I put him away a couple of times. A slippery thief that one. But he has been, what do you say, *clean*, for a while. Please, sit. I have much to tell you. But first…' He dropped heavily into a chair then loosened a couple of silver buttons on his jacket and took a long, deep breath. He stretched his head back to savour the heat of the sun on his throat and face. Barney waited; the man needed this. Soon a thin smile emerged above the distinctive silver goatee. He was probably about fifty, around ten years older than Barney, but in normal times Captain Jean-Luc Verten cut a striking figure. Despite his comparatively short and burly frame, his distinguished beard and silky hair gave him a formidable presence. He was as suave as Barney was big and awkward.

The sound of coffees being placed on the table brought them both back to the present.

'Claude, merci.'

'My pleasure, Captain,' said the man, his long skinny frame bent in a shallow bow.

Barney expected him to retreat backwards out of the royal presence but was disappointed.

They tasted their drinks in silence. Jean-Luc made appreciative noises and took a second sip then paused to look around him as if just realising where he was. He was sizing up people at neighbouring tables and then the blank-faced stallholders dismantling their temporary homes, mechanically wrapping and packing away into battered boxes all the stock which had failed to convince and which would have to wait for another chance in some lesser market in the mountains or back here, on stage yet again, next week. The Frenchman replaced his cup and nodded to himself as if having made a decision. Barney felt something coming and at last his friend faced him.

'Barney, thank you for being so understanding. You know what it's like. But I'm fine now. And as I said, I have much to tell you.'

'OK, Jean-Luc. Hit me.'

'Ha! I won't do that. But you might prefer it if I do. You see, I not only want to bring you up to date; I also have a proposition for you.'

Barney instinctively moved back in his chair. In his experience, when policemen said they had a proposition, it tended to be less of a proposition than a legal requirement.

The Frenchman laughed. 'It's not that bad. Honest. But wait. I'll come to that.'

He then proceeded to outline the meeting he'd just left at police HQ. He wasn't being blamed directly for the shambles in court that morning; he hadn't been personally responsible for security arrangements. But it had happened on his patch and he had played a key role in the arrest and interrogation of the victim, therefore becoming central to the whole process leading to today's disaster. Plus, they always needed someone to blame.

'But that's life,' he suddenly said with an exaggerated Gallic shrug. 'It comes with the job. Of course they are as concerned as I am about the shooting, how it could possibly happen and who was responsible. But it wasn't the murder alone which concerned them. It was also the problems it might cause.'

Barney was puzzled. What could be more important than a man being executed in public view in the middle of a courtroom?

'Yes, I know,' Jean-Luc said, holding up his hands to stop the questions he must have read on Barney's face. 'But let me finish. You see, there are two angles to this. Yes, there has been a serious breach of security. And yes,' he said, shaking his head in wonder, 'it looks as if the killer may have had inside help. That is going to be my first priority when I go back. But there were some very senior people at this meeting. And this is where you come in.'

Barney was nodding slowly, as if he had a clue what was going on, while asking himself why the hell the French would have any need of a Scottish cop when they would have their hands full with the media frenzy which was bound to surround this case.

He was still trying to take it all in shortly afterwards, as he made his way past the Opera House and tourist shops then up into the huge open space that was Place Massena. The heat was horrendous and he was glad of his new broad-brimmed straw hat but he was sweating profusely in the supposedly lightweight suit he wore for court and he chose to linger at the square's fountain despite the groups of noisy tourists posing for photos in front of the towering statue of Apollo. He slung his jacket over his shoulder and savoured the brief respite offered by cool, damp air.

There were no velo-taxis standing on the square's chequerboard paving. Besides, he always thought better when he walked and so, having braved the gauntlet of selfie sticks, then the crowds seeking shade under the porticos, he headed up the bustling main shopping street of Avenue Jean Medécin, making for the relative cool of tree-lined Boulevard Victor Hugo. Even the tram seemed to be labouring in the heat as it whined past him on the long, gradual incline towards the Place de la Republique.

If he'd understood correctly, the plan was for Barney to be seconded to the Police Nationale for up to six months to help in the aftermath of the assassination. Nel had been well known within the large British ex-pat community, having worked for one of their most distinguished members, and it was a community which was already distinctly twitchy after a series of break-ins and torchings of mainly unoccupied holiday homes.

Barney knew that the region was the most right wing in the country - and that simmering resentment against wealthy incomers had recently boiled over into demonstrations and violence as more and more Brits swapped the not-so-brave new world of Brexit Britain for a better life in the sun.

According to Jean-Luc, the powers that be had previously

agreed just such a scheme in principle with a UK government keen to restore relations with France. But it was today's audacious murder that had forced their hand. Off the record, he'd said, local politicians feared an exodus of foreign home-owners who currently paid exorbitant extra taxes for the privilege of owning a home in paradise. But they were even more worried that the resulting instability would boost the chances of a right wing takeover in upcoming elections.

Barney laughed out loud as he walked, just as he'd done a little earlier when Jean-Luc outlined the proposal.

The Frenchman had looked confused. 'I have said something funny?'

Barney then explained: 'Sorry Jean-Luc. It's just that I originally handed in my resignation because I'd had enough of all this political bullshit. Now you're saying you want me as a glorified public relations man for six months - all because some politicians are shitting themselves about their approval ratings.'

Jean-Luc had thought for a moment then said: 'Maybe so. But on the other hand, we have an excellent canteen.'

By the time Barney turned into Rue Gounod, he'd made up his mind. If Edinburgh were going for it, he would give it his best shot.

The ancient little lift was closed for maintenance and as he mounted the last flight of steps to his rented studio flat on the top floor, he knew he should crash out on the fold-down bed. But It wasn't every day that you saw a man shot in front of you and then faced the uncertainty of a completely alien new job. He was buzzing. And he still had to decide whether to renew the lease he'd taken out almost a year ago in the first flush of resignation freedom.

The cool shower was a lifesaver. He changed into shorts and a t-shirt then took his laptop and a cold beer out onto the balcony. The joy of his wide north-facing terrace, as big as the flat itself, was the escape it offered from the cloying heat which radiated from every building and every pavement like one great storage heater. There was even the whisper of a breeze today as he took a first sip then almost emptied the glass.

His laptop sat in front of him on the small, glass-topped table. He had a lot of research to do if he was going to be of any use in his new persona. But first he had a phone call to make. She answered on the third ring. He could hear the familiar sound of water lapping against the hull before she spoke and he instantly saw her on the *Bonnie Fechter* in the glorious bay of Villefranche-sur-Mer only a few miles away to the east.

'Oh, so you've finally got round to calling me, have you?'

He laughed. She'd given the little yacht its name because that's how her beloved late mother had always described the young Shona. Her mother hadn't been wrong.

'I assume you've heard then?' he asked.

'What, about the court? About how my man was within a few feet of a murder and did his usual stupid stunt of diving straight into the line of fire?'

'Aye, well it wisnae quite like that. You know how they always exaggerate.'

'You still might have called. I *was* worried, you know.'

'I'm sorry. It all got a bit busy, then I had to hang about for ages for my turn to be interviewed. But listen, everything's fine. I've just got back home after meeting Jean-Luc. I've got lots to tell. Are you coming in or going out?'

'In. Just mooring up.'

'Great. Is it OK if I come round later?'

'Oh well, I don't know. Let me think. Don't be bloody stupid! Get your arse round here, pronto!'

He smiled at his image of her, survivor of a bleak Edinburgh westside slum, daughter to an ex-junkie single mum, a fighter with a God-given genius for computers who built an online empire which made Shona Gladstone one of the richest women in the world. Yet still the same sassy wee lassie. And he loved her dearly - a fact he'd only discovered during the traumas of what the press had ended up calling the Major-Minor Murders, the case which had got him all fired up again about policing and which ended today with Nel's murder.

He risked telling her that he might be a couple of hours, that he had work to do, but he promised to tell her everything later. He just about got away with it. Besides, he was already opening his laptop and thinking of the searches he wanted to get through.

The first found reports of the most recent fire attacks in the area. It turned out that one of those had been close to Shona's villa in Villefranche and a second, four days later, had been not far from there, up on Mont Boron overlooking Nice.

The police had attributed both to extremist protesters. That hadn't been difficult. There were Anti-Brit slogans and French flags crudely daubed on the outside walls of both.

The property on Mont Boron was the holiday home of a British hedge fund owner. It had been virtually destroyed but the bullish owner was quoted as saying: *An Englishman's home is his castle and nobody's forcing me out of it. I'm going to build back, bigger and better.*

Barney shook his head. Sometimes you just couldn't protect

people from themselves. He even felt a twinge of sympathy for the genuinely disgruntled locals who were faced with such arrogance. By all accounts, they had seen not only the biggest and best properties of their beautiful region snapped up by foreigners but a veritable invasion which had pushed up prices all round. Now even modest family homes in decent residential areas were beyond ordinary working folk who'd had to move further and further out into the suburbs.

He'd ask Jean-Luc for the case files. He needed to understand the mindset not just of the locals but also that of the ex-pats whose brows he was apparently expected to mop.

Next, he acquainted himself with the structure of the Police Nationale force. He remembered how a French officer attached to Police Scotland was given the runaround by his tosser of a minder. In Nice, the mickey-taking might well be topped up with more than a little resentment. He wanted to at least know what he was walking into.

He would then compile a list of all the main English-speaking organisations and social groups in the area. His likely new brief may well turn out to be a totally shit job but he would knuckle down and do it to the best of his ability. That was his thing, or *his curse*, as he called it.

2 - Canned Heat

Jean-Luc had a splitting headache but he knew that it was going to be a long night, that it had to be. Until today, all he'd had to worry about was his ongoing investigation into last year's $30 million art heist at the Musée des Beaux-Arts. It looked like they might even be about to make progress, with rumours circulating that the thieves were trying to fence some of the paintings. But now, here he was, sitting in the Commandant's office, part of a team tasked with not only catching a diabolically efficient killer but with salvaging even a vestige of the force's reputation. The fact that they would have nervous politicians breathing down their necks throughout was just an added bonus.

'Right', said Commandant Christian Garnier, as he thumped his desk with a great hock of a fist, fixing each of the six officers in the eye then returning to stare directly at Jean-Luc.

'So, Verten, tell me what the hell happened and how come you've landed us all in the middle of a right fucking shitstorm.'

The Captain had been here before and knew his boss's style, which had all the grace of one of the lumbering great bulls the man's family had bred for generations.

'Well, as you know, sir, I can't speak to security arrangements in the court...'

'Yes, yes, *don't look at me, it was the other guy.* I've heard it all before. But this was your baby, you broke him, charged him and got him into court. So don't tell me you didn't bloody well know what the arrangements were.'

'No, of course I knew about the arrangements, sir. They were good. Quite impressive, actually.'

'Impressive? You're not trying to butter me up are you, Verten? You know I oversaw the planning.'

'In fact, sir, I would go so far as to say that you had thought of everything. But then, as we know, some things can never be planned for. I'm only saying that if the plan had been carried out efficiently, nothing could possibly have gone wrong...' Jean-Luc looked across at the two plain-clothes officers seated at the far end of the desk, his eyebrows raised.

Young Fleur Dupont seemed to sense that her senior partner wasn't going to answer, despite Jean-Luc having agreed a joint approach with them beforehand. She cleared her throat. 'Unless certain officers were either criminally incompetent... or just plain criminal. Sir,' she said.

The Commandant, his jowls quivering as he swung round in his chair, was aghast. 'Dupont! What the hell are you suggesting? That someone under my command could have actually connived to let the killer in?'

'And out, sir. With respect,' she added when her senior kicked her foot while appearing to admire the room's decor.

Jean-Luc picked up the ball. 'Commander, at this stage we can't rule out these two unpleasant possibilities. But I hope to know more later this evening. A more intensive study of the upstairs area is underway and I now have the names of officers who were assigned to guard it.'

He looked around at his colleagues. 'And if it pleases you sir,

I have a car waiting.'

The Commandant fluttered a hand by way of consent.

'Thank you, sir. I'll give you a full report at the earliest moment.'

'Fine, fine, Verten. But you'd better take Dupont with you. Since the pair of you seem to have been in cahoots already.'

The last thing Jean-Luc heard as he closed the door behind them was the Commandant shouting: 'Right, now, I want a complete briefing on who was where and when and I want diagrams and a video presentation for upstairs as of right now!'

The Captain looked at Fleur Dupont and winked. 'Pity we couldn't stay for that, eh?'

In the short journey to the Place du Palais de Justice he refrained from asking why her boss seemed to have lost his tongue in the meeting. There were enough internal politics and personality clashes in his own department. But he knew he had one of the best in this young up-and-comer. Dupont may be inexperienced but as the daughter of a retired cop of renown she'd had to work harder than most to prove herself. He looked forward to finding out if what he'd been told about her was true; that as well as a keen brain she had also inherited her father's allergy to bullshit.

They were back in the square in no time but it was only when they were climbing the long flight of steps to the court building that he appreciated how much older he was than his new assistant. He could sense her almost breaking into a run to be inside and working.

The officer on the door knew Jean-Luc but insisted on checking his superior's identity. 'Pity you weren't here earlier,' said Jean-Luc, passing inside.

'I was,' said the guard. 'But it was the buggers guarding upstairs who cocked up.'

Jean-Luc did an about-turn. 'You know your colleagues who were on duty?'

The man, with a good twenty years of service and good food under his straining jacket buttons, seemed to back off. 'No, never seen them before. Different unit. But whoever they were, it was them that fucked up. There's no way anyone should have been able to get up there. They had to have been sleeping. Or whatever. But what they definitely were not doing was their bloody job. So now we're all in the shit!'

Jean-Luc nodded sympathetically and thanked the man before continuing toward the foot of the stairs where Fleur Dupont waited with two uniformed officers. He fully took her in for the first time, her short jet-black hair and strong, somewhat swarthy features matching her trim black trouser suit; the only permitted hint of personality an open-collared white shirt peaking out from the fastened jacket.

The two uniforms, a young man and an older woman, subjected them both to identity checks and body scans.

'Bit late for all this isn't it?' Jean-Luc's plucky colleague suggested. She got a pair of surly looks and a muttered *just doing our sodding jobs* from the man. She pretended not to notice. 'So were you the ones on duty earlier?'

The man looked to his partner to reply. She made a face like a snarl. 'No, they've apparently given their statements and buggered off... Beg your pardon. Gone off duty, ma'am.'

Dupont nodded then joined Jean-Luc as he mounted the stone steps. 'Yes, I've seen those statements,' he told her in a lowered voice. 'We need to speak to those guys asap.'

At the top, they found themselves alone in a tall, wide

corridor, curved like that in a theatre but with not a drop of colour on its floor or walls.

'Forensics have cleared the place so we're OK to go in now,' he said, pulling a document from inside his jacket and opening it in front of him as they walked the short distance to the balcony door.

She smiled. 'So you already have a diagram?'

'First thing I did. Like the man said, I needed to know who was where and when.' He pointed at the plan. 'See, two officers just there, where we were stopped just now and two on the second set of stairs at the other end. And they say this door was definitely locked, with the only keys held by the officer in charge. It was only when these guys ran up the stairs after the shooting that they found the door was no longer locked.'

She studied the plan then leant her head back towards the corridor's far wall. 'So, unless I stand like this, the curve of the corridor means that I can't be seen from either end.'

'Good point,' said Jean-Luc. 'Let's keep that in mind. Now, the balcony.'

But she was staring at the ceiling, at a small access hatch.

Jean-Luc noticed. 'Yes, this would have been a possible hiding place but I think we will be able to rule it out because we had marksmen in the roof space keeping an eye on the square.'

He turned the handle and the door opened.

He hadn't expected the narrow balcony itself to offer any revelations and at first glance it didn't. A series of wooden pews were ranked on either side of the steeply descending aisle, their varnish yellowed with age into an institutional sterility which made him shiver.

Jean-Luc stood in the doorway, looking straight down into

17

the well of the courtroom below, just as the shooter must have done.

'So what's your theory, Dupont?'

He had to give her her due. She was working the challenge hard. At last she spoke. 'Well, let's see. If everything we've been told is true, then we're talking about an armed killer so clever than he managed to get into a heavily protected court building, past officers at the foot of the stairs and then got into a locked room, shot someone in the head from, what, thirty-five metres, then calmly walked out of the building with what was most probably a rifle of some sorts - all without being challenged or even seen.'

He gave silent applause. 'Very good. You sum up our problem nicely. And I note that you started with the correct qualification: *if everything we've been told is true.* But until we go down that road, maybe there is more we can do here. For instance, if you're right about the weapon having been a rifle, then even assuming the killer somehow got in and out without being noticed, how could he - or she - had done so carrying a rifle?'

She seemed to pick up on his attempt at a rhetorical question.

'You mean unless he never actually carried the rifle? Unless it was already here? Unless he left it here?'

He shrugged. 'It's a theory. But if it's correct, then where could it have been left in the first place and where is it now?'

She thought for a moment. 'I don't know, but assuming it's metal, then why don't we scan the whole place with metal detectors.'

'Bravo,' said Jean-Luc. 'That's the first thing I asked to be done. Sadly, they found nothing.'

She grimaced but didn't give up. 'So if it was left here, it had to have been left in something metal.'

Jean-Luc threw his head back. 'Bloody hell. I'm wasting my time here. Yes, that's exactly the conclusion I came to. But I've had a lot longer to think about it.'

She paused. He was looking at something behind her. She turned. Fixed to the corridor wall were the most mundane and disregarded of familiar objects; two big red fire extinguishers.

She had her latex gloves on before him. She peered at the tops of the canisters and tentatively tried to turn each in turn. Nothing happened, so she took a closer look at the longer one and tried again.

'Shit! Sorry. It moved. I was terrified it would explode or something, but look, the top's loose.'

Jean-Luc moved in. 'OK, but be careful now. Let's have it down before we go poking about inside.'

She quickly had the extinguisher standing on the floor, leaning against her legs. The cap with its attached black tube and trigger came away in her hands. She laid it at her feet and looked inside. 'There's something there!' She drew her pencil torch and shone it inside the cylinder. 'Yes!' she almost screamed. Barrel and stock. 'We've got it.'

'Well done,' he said quietly. 'Now we've got something to work on.'

Jean-Luc was privately delighted, partly with the discovery itself and partly with the fact that he had found a brilliant young officer who could be a massive help in solving the case. He didn't expect the gun to yield much. Someone who had carried out such a clinical hit was never going to leave their fingerprints plastered over everything.

No, their best chance was to focus on finding whoever

helped the killer get in and out. They were looking at the possibility of one or more corrupt officers on the day of the shooting. But the killer had to have got into the building beforehand, which is why he asked Dupont if she fancied a bit of overtime that night.

'I'd like you to come back here later and have a word with the night staff. Did they notice anything unusual the night before, anyone hanging around, that sort of thing. Play it by ear.'

He got the reaction he was hoping for. Not the long face of so many officers these days but a refreshingly bright and happy one. 'That's great, sir. Leave it to me.'

But Jean-Luc's smile faded as they left the building. However the killer had managed it, they were still left with the big, unavoidable question. Why would anyone go to such trouble to carry out an execution in the most heavily guarded and public place imaginable? Unless that was the whole point. Such daring said: *We can hit anyone, anywhere, whenever we choose.* But Jean-Luc had to take that to its logical conclusion. For it also said: *the police are powerless to stop us.*

3 - Double Take

Tuesday, July 8

Barney wasn't to know it when he knocked on Jean-Luc's office door and was surprised when he entered to find the Captain sprawled on his couch and trying to keep his head raised long enough to see who'd dared to wake him.

'Sorry Jean-Luc. I'll come back.'

'Eh, quoi? Non. C'est bien. Come in.' He swung his stockinged feet round and let them fish for shoes.

'Late night, eh, my friend?'

'The first of many, I fear, Barney.'

But even having just woken up in crumpled trousers and shirt the man looked good. He swept back his silver hair, inflated his great barrel chest then stretched as he shuffled around behind his desk.

The Scotsman put down the two large black coffees and a bag of croissants he'd brought from the canteen.

'Ah, we'll make a Frenchman of you yet!'

'Aye well, I believe that might be what's about to happen. I got confirmation last night. I'm to stay here, like you said. So, I guess I should say: *Reporting for duty, sir,*' he joked, saluting in the French style.

Jean-Luc laughed. 'At ease, Mains. Bet you never thought you'd end up working beside me when you left your police force.'

'Ha! It actually turned out that, technically speaking, I'd never really left the force. I handed in my resignation, right enough, but thanks to our incredibly efficient personnel department, I was only listed as being suspended without pay until I signed a non-disclosure agreement. Then it turned out that they'd lost another Detective Inspector and were so hard up that they made me an offer I couldn't refuse.'

Jean-Luc laughed. 'This kind of efficiency; it's the same here. But sometimes bureaucracy works in our favour, yes?'

'Aye, makes a change,' Barney said as he pulled a chair across.

'But you're glad that you're still a detective?'

Barney reached for a croissant. 'Time will tell, Jean-Luc. Time will tell.'

The Frenchman had made short work of a croissant and was savouring the day's first gulp of coffee. He leant back in his chair. 'And so, I have things to tell you. First, my bosses have set it all up with Edinburgh. It'll be good to have you here. You'll have my former assistant's desk there and come and go as you please. I have a special pass for you, just to say you are working with the knowledge of the Police Nationale. You can't arrest anyone, obviously, but if you have any problems, let me know.'

'All good, Jean-Luc. I've been doing a bit of research and unless you have other plans for me, I thought I'd have a look at the two local arson cases.'

'Sure, Barney. I had much the same idea. I'll have the case files brought to you.'

They sat quietly for a moment, pleased with having set the ground rules for his stay. But he couldn't help but ask. 'So, how's the Nel case going, then?'

The Frenchman grimaced and nodded, which could have meant anything. 'Oh, a little progress. A little. But much to do.'

Barney sat silently long enough for Jean-Luc to feel obliged to say more. 'My friend, you will appreciate that we must keep a certain gap between our jobs. All I can tell you, between ourselves, is that we found the gun. Our technical guys are trying to see if there is any more to learn from it.'

'That's great, Jean-Luc. Great work. Em, where did you find it, if I may ask?'

'Ha, I see that I am in your interview room. But all I will confess to is that a young colleague found it within the court building, hidden inside an empty fire extinguisher. And now, as you say, inquiries are continuing.'

Barney smiled, trying to calculate what that discovery might imply, while noting that his friend didn't volunteer any more.

He rose. 'Ach well, I can only wish you the best of luck and get my Scottish butt into gear.' He carried the last of his coffee over to the desk which would be his new base for the next six months. Jean-Luc was immediately on the phone ordering the necessary case files while Barney checked out his new accommodation. The top drawer in the grey-veneered chipboard desk had a phone book and a laminated list of internal numbers. There was also a menu for the canteen. *Only the French would see that as essential information,* he thought. Of more immediate use was a supply of office equipment and a smart new desk phone. He took off his jacket and draped it over the back of his chair, making a mental note to shop for some proper office clothes fit for a Nice summer.

He pulled his laptop out of its leather case and placed it in front of him. Jean-Luc had left a note which gave him the necessary codes to access the network and internet at *guest* level. He called up news reports of yesterday's events and found why Jean-Luc might be a bit chary about sharing. His friend's mugshot was everywhere, under headlines baying for heads to roll. The horror of the shooting and the incompetence which allowed it to happen made a common theme across the media. He'd been there before and while he was happy not to feature in the coverage, he was also itching to get involved in the investigation.

The arrival a short time later of the two arson files told him that this wasn't to be, so he got stuck into them, pausing only to wish Jean-Luc good luck as the Frenchman left the office.

When he started to read, it looked like police reports were much the same the world over; short, factual and incomplete. So, with his French in reasonably good shape these days, translation shouldn't be a problem.

The first incident report referred to a fire at Hollywood, Avenue des Sapins, Villefranche-sur-Mer.

Officers despatched after blaze reported by residents. Fire brigade in attendance.

Residents, Mr and Mrs Fitzwilliam, only occupants, standing at safe distance in nightclothes.

Minor damage to utility room and kitchen at rear of property.

Exterior walls at rear daubed with slogans "Brits Out" and "Allez France."

Neighbours canvassed but no-one saw or heard anything.

No structural damage found. Occupants safely returned. Inquiries continuing.

An image of a pro forma from the fire brigade was the only other document. It had the usual cursory ticks and scrawled signature. They'd attended, nobody died and they left. An unspecified accelerant had been poured on the back wall.

The second incident report, dated four days later, wasn't much more informative, even though it resulted in near destruction of the Mont Boron mansion of one Charles Taylor-Smith.

Again no-one saw or heard a thing and the building had been well ablaze by the time the fire service was alerted.

Same rough slogans on two of the outside walls.

The fire brigade's report this time offered a little more. Several seats of fire had been identified within the building, with an accelerant, suspected to be petrol, having been applied to groupings of combustible materials. *Probably just money,* Barney thought, as he closed the file and lifted the phone.

Jean-Luc had cleared it for him to get one of the force's electric pool cars. He had all the necessary documents to drive in France but the man on the phone from the garage said he needed something else which he couldn't understand. No big deal. He knew he could take a number fourteen bus up Mont Boron for his first visit and from there walk downhill to Villefranche for the second.

The bus trip, which he'd taken several times on painting expeditions, was always a thrill, particularly the harum-scarum last section where bus drivers liked to work off their city centre frustrations by putting the foot down on tight turns. The view over the city was to die for, but not just yet.

It was still warm when he was left at the little bus shelter terminus, but not as ferocious as yesterday and clouds were building up over the mountains in the north. He consulted the map on his phone and found his way to the property.

They'd done a good job. There was little left of the roof and the blackened walls still bore the rough graffiti of protest. A digger driver emptied his latest load into a skip. Two workmen threw their own meagre contributions in behind.

One of the huge ironwork driveway gates was already open and Barney walked straight in. The shout was almost immediate. 'Oi! You! You're not allowed in here.'

English. Very. The voice's owner was picking his way awkwardly through the rubble, cutting a quite comical figure, Barney thought, in his grey suit and tie, brown city shoes and a yellow hard hat which was tilted like it might fall off at any moment.

'Do you not understand the Queen's English, man? I said you're not allowed here.'

He was of medium height, medium build, with no discernable features. A nightmare in a line-up. What he did have was a lot of attitude and Barney was enjoying himself, just standing there, smiling pleasantly.

'What the..?'

'Police, sir.' He flashed his new card. No-one ever looked.

The man opened his mouth to speak but didn't.

'Just need a few words with whoever's in charge here, sir. And you would be?'

'Oh, right. Yes. Of course. Sorry.'

He was what the British called *well-spoken*, the product of a privileged education. Which didn't make him a bad person. Though it didn't rule him out either.

'Your name, sir?'

He fumbled in his inside jacket pocket. 'Burton-Tate. Rufus. Here.'

He was right enough. That was what it said on his passport. Though Barney had never met anyone less like a Rufus.

'I'm overseeing things here for Mr Taylor-Smith. He's back home in England at the moment. Coming back out tomorrow. Lucky you caught me, actually. I just dropped by unannounced to give these guys a kick up the arse. You know what these bloody immigrants are like. You have to keep on top of them or they'll spend the day sunbathing.'

Barney looked at the two wiry, dark-skinned labourers standing sullenly behind the skip in worn clothes, their heads down. He tried to imagine them lying back on beach towels with cocktails in their hands. He failed.

'You live here, sir?'

'Yes, yes, along at Antibes. A lovely part of the world. Moved here a couple of years ago.'

Barney nodded reflectively. For wealthy westerners, becoming an immigrant was a lifestyle choice.

'Bit of a mess here, sir. The owner's planning to rebuild, I believe. Bigger and better.'

'Yes, my office is drawing up the plans as we speak. Architect. Here. My card.'

'Thank you, sir. Just wanted to have a look for myself. But while you're here, can you tell me if this was the only incident here or if the owner's had any other trouble? Or his neighbours?'

'To the best of my knowledge, em, officer…?'

'Detective Inspector, sir. Mains.'

'Well, Detective Inspector, no, I don't know of anything else. But, as I said, Mr Taylor-Smith will be back tomorrow. Maybe you'd like to contact him then. He'll be stopping at the Westerling for a bit.'

Barney smiled his gratitude. 'I'll do that, sir. I'll leave you in peace now. Let you crack on with cracking the whip, eh?' He winked and left. He was barely twenty metres away when he heard the man shouting at the workman. *Come the revolution,* he thought.

His route down to the main road between Nice and Ville-franche was cut in great serpentine sweeps to lessen the suddenness of the descent. The views along the mountainous coast towards Italy were breathtaking from each successive level, whenever he could see them between luxury villas.

When he reached the main road he thought to carry on down the long flights of steps to the idyllic old harbour at La Darse but he was on duty and knew that the property he sought was on higher ground.

It was a short walk and he spotted a beat-up old Mini in the front yard which he hoped meant someone was at home, so he pressed the bell on the tall stone pillar and waited. Moments later, the oblong length of metal gate slid quietly off into the bushes to his right. No questions from the speaker box by the bell. Just: *come on in, set a fire and leave.*

All the activity seemed to be at a secondary entrance off to the left of this squat Seventies slab of the once-modern. The door was open but he knocked on it anyway and someone, probably a man, shouted from far inside: 'For God's sake, just come in.'

It was what Barney reckoned might be called an ante-room to match the exterior's anti-architecture. Today it was a waiting room because three people were seated on a bench along the facing wall. Someone said to take a seat, that she'd be here in a minute. So, amused, he did.

Then he gave the three people sitting across from him a

closer look. They seemed to be checking him out too. And yes, he really was looking at Marilyn Monroe, Charlie Chaplin and Albert Einstein. *Just another day in paradise,* he thought.

A woman he took to be the lady of the house, elegant in a long, vanilla-coloured dress and pulled-back blond hair, was wafting a slender vape at head height as she made an appearance.

'Thank you so so much everybody for coming, if you could all just come through for a moment, we'll get you signed up for tonight.' His three fellow callers got up, mumbling various forms of thanks, and wandered inside. Charlie Chaplin didn't have a funny walk and Marilyn had a limp but it was still a sight to behold.

'My God, who are you meant to be?' Barney didn't need to look to realise that Madame was addressing him. He stood.

'Seriously, who are you? Because whoever it is, I'm afraid you're not very good.'

'I'm sorry about that, ma'am. I try my best.'

He flashed his pass. 'DI Barney Mains, ma'am. Hoping to have a word.'

'Oh,' she said, confused. She took a steadying big draw from her vape and blew the smoke up and away over her right shoulder, like a scene from an old movie. She was even dressed for the role in her flowing gown with a fancy buckle at the waist, a long pearl necklace and make-up worthy of a Hollywood studio. Hard to tell her age but he guessed at around forty.

'Um, what is it about? It's not the bloody cats is it? It's not my fault. It's Roman. He lets them run wild, you know.'

'Not the cats, ma'am. I take it I'm speaking to Mrs Clarinda Fitzwilliam?'

She confirmed the fact but still seemed distracted as she signalled for him to follow her inside. He wondered why she'd never acquired a hyphen like everybody else around here.

The three lookalikes were standing around a small table to sign sheets of paper, watched by a casually-dressed, skinny young man sitting behind. Possibly Roman, he of the impatient shout.

'It's for our party tonight,' she explained. 'Just a bit of fun to break the ice.'

She laughed a shrill, nervous-sounding laugh and led the way further inside, to an enormous room which he thought must extend to the back of the house, where the fire had been. The walls were festooned with all sorts of posters and memorabilia from *movieland.* But she only took him as far as two huge white leather sofas with overly-wide arms. The couches seemed to be squaring off against each other across a contested coffee table holding the winner's prize of a bowl of fresh fruit. His contender was as uncomfortable as it looked.

'Now Inspector, Mains wasn't it?' she asked, sitting across from him and for an instant a lot sharper than her act.

'The fire, ma'am. I'm just here to find out anything I can about the fire. And whether you've been subjected to any other such incidents either before or after. And to let you know that we're doing everything we can.'

'Oh, I'm sure. I'm sure. The police here are so lovely. And how wonderful to think that we've got our very own English Inspector here too. Oh, you must come to the party. Seven p.m. To whenever. You must. They'll love you.'

He had long ago stopped bothering to correct people regarding nationality and since it appeared that the fire had been dismissed as a minor incident in her busy social calendar, he was unlikely to overstay his welcome.

Barney had the distinct impression that there was a lot more to this woman than her performance suggested. But he reckoned there was no more to be learned here today and when she rose after a few minutes of pleasantries and extended her right hand he didn't object. They shook and she led the way back out to the door, insisting loudly that she'd see him later.

Then she fluttered back inside, leaving him to stand in wonder at the sight before him as the lookalikes clambered into the battered old Mini. He'd never forget the image of Marilyn Monroe driving off with Albert Einstein in the passenger seat and Charlie Chaplin in the back, looking puzzled as he gave a sad little wave goodbye.

* * *

Jean-Luc said it one more time. 'I'm giving you the chance to tell the truth right now. You tell me what really happened and I promise, I'll put in a good word for you.'

But Lieutenant Pierre Martin just continued to stare at the wall. According to him no-one passed him or his colleague at the stairs yesterday morning. They'd raced up to the balcony corridor the instant they realised what was happening. Nothing and no-one was there, other than officers from the other end of the corridor.

Jean-Luc hoped that the man's partner, just out of his probationary year, might eventually prove a more amenable subject but so far, he too was adamant - as were their counterparts who had guarded the opposite staircase. Two of these four had to be lying. But so far, whoever pulled their strings had either made them too rich or too scared to talk.

'So, are we finished? I can go?' Martin asked. 'I'm not supposed to be here today, you know.'

'Oh, of course, we wouldn't want a little murder to spoil your leisure time. Away you go.'

Jean-Luc waited for the door of the interview room to close before turning to his young protégé. 'Well, Dupont, he's the last. What do you think?'

'Sorry sir. I'm not much use. As far as I can tell, all four are innocent. Which I know they can't be.'

'Don't worry about it. I can't tell either. We need to look into their backgrounds, what they do in their spare time, friends, finances. But we'll start with that later. Meantime, I want to get it all written up. I didn't expect the gun to yield much. I had more hopes of the canister. But nothing. I didn't have time to tell you earlier, but that extinguisher's not the one registered as being serviced six months ago. So someone's managed to replace it with the dummy during that time. The court maintenance staff are looking into who had access but I wouldn't hold your breath.'

'No, sir. We're not having much luck with the court staff, I'm afraid.'

'Don't worry about it, Dupont. That official you saw last night said nothing out of the ordinary happened before the incident, didn't he? The cleaners signed in and out as usual and you remembered to take his logbook into evidence, yes?'

'Well, yes sir. It's just that…'

'It's just what?'

'Maybe I'm looking for something that isn't there. But the man just didn't seem comfortable.'

'Dupont. There are two ways to go in such a situation. You

either decide he was just twitchy because he's not used to being quizzed by the police at night and worried he's going to be blamed for something he didn't do. Or you go with your guts. What's it going to be?'

Dupont stared into the middle distance for a moment then looked up and with the gravest of faces said: 'Guts, sir. I'll see him again.'

'Good. It might be a good idea to get his boss to phone him to say you're going to be paying him another visit. If you're right, a little advance pressure may help.'

As they left the interview room and started towards their separate offices, he said: 'Speaking of bosses, how are things with yours?'

She didn't exactly roll her eyes, but he could see that there was a problem there. 'He's not a hundred per cent delighted with me being seconded to you but upstairs have approved it, so no sweat.'

4 - Auchtermuchty Man

Barney knocked and opened the office door wide enough to peer inside. 'Come in, Barney,' Jean-Luc shouted. 'No need to knock. It's your office too. Although I wanted to have a word with you about that. How would you feel about it if you did a bit of hot-desking with a plain-clothes colleague for a bit? Just until we can squeeze another desk in. Good, I knew you wouldn't mind.'

The Scotsman smiled and put his bag of new clothes beside the coat stand. 'Got myself some better togs,' he said. 'More in keeping with my high office.'

But Jean-Luc only grunted, seeming not to hear, and continued squinting into his computer screen as he typed. He made a final emphatic stroke then sat back in his chair, apparently satisfied.

'Sorry, Barney. Just firing off a quick message. So how did it go? Did you get to meet our lovely British neighbours?'

Barney sat heavily into his chair and sighed. 'Well, they weren't all lovely. Though I did get to meet Marilyn Monroe.'

He then gave his friend a rundown of his experiences earlier, ending with his invitation to the party that evening.

'Why don't you come along? Could be interesting.'

'Thank you Barney but Monique would kill me. I didn't

make it home last night, so whenever I finish here I'm driving straight home to Tourrettes.'

Barney pictured the lovely Monique and understood Jean-Luc's priorities.

'Totally understand. Tell her I was asking for her. I mean give her my love. Ha, bloody language.'

'I will, I will. You must come up again soon.' The Frenchman paused, seeming to reflect. 'You didn't want to take the car I laid on for you today?'

Barney explained about the garage needing some other document or whatever. Jean-Luc raised his eyebrows and nodded deeply several times. 'Indeed. Leave them to me.'

The Scotsman twigged. The garage had been playing funny buggers. *Better get used to it,* he thought.

There was a knock at the door. The young woman clutching a stack of folders and a laptop to her chest saw Barney and hesitated.

'It's OK, Dupont,' Jean-Luc called. 'You've come to the right place. Barney, meet your *hot-desker*, probationer Fleur Dupont.

Barney moved the phone to make space and she thanked him as she put down her load. They shook hands and Dupont looked around.

'It's OK, you can use my seat,' Barney said, rising. 'I'm just off. Bit early. But working tonight.' He grabbed his shopping bag and opened the door.

Jean-Luc called after him: 'Give my love to Marilyn!'

* * *

With the famous Shona Gladstone on his arm at such glamorous events they would normally be pounced upon by all and sundry but she'd insisted on going incognito in a short blond wig and without the sparklers. She may have dressed down but Barney thought she still looked like a million dollars in her light grey trouser suit and low heels.

The young man from earlier introduced himself as Roman and invited them to help themselves to a glass of champagne. Charlie Chaplin, uncannily real in his disguise, said hello as they entered and Barney could see that he was curious. The Scotsman put him out of his misery by leaning over to explain who he was.

'Ah,' said Charlie. 'I wondered. Because you don't look like anybody I know.' He stuck out his hand and they shook. 'Real name, Jack Thomson. All the way frae Auchtermuchty.'

Barney laughed. 'Is there no escape?' He introduced Shona as his girlfriend and the three of them had a good old chinwag about places and events back home in Scotland.

Jack, or Charlie as Barney kept calling him, had joined the Army straight out of school but very soon realised the error of his ways and swapped the range for the stage. He'd been an actor for a long time, did the Edinburgh Festival Fringe for years, went on tour to provincial theatres in England, ending up in London, where he started struggling to find work. Like many in the profession, he was taken by the drink and things were tough for a few years. He couldn't remember how he ended up in the South of France but he found it much easier being a bum here, even in winter.

'Then one day, I was lying on the beach with a couple of cans and this gorgeous blond turns up. Gracie - that's Marilyn over there - says: *you know you're a dead ringer for the great Charlie Chaplin?* Well, a couple of people have said that before and I used to ham it up with the funny walk at parties. But Gracie, she says I can make money out of it. And well, here we are. So many bored rich folks around here, we're in great demand, don't you know.'

He stopped then and started to look uncomfortable. Barney looked around and noticed the lady of the house quickly turning her gaze away.

'Anyway, I'd better move about and mingle a bit,' Jack said. 'They don't like us enjoying ourselves too much. But maybe we can catch up later.' Then he was off, hirpling across the room, happily twirling his cane.

Shona said: 'What a great guy. We must meet up. Bet he's got some stories.'

Barney agreed but now that he'd taken the time to look around he noticed that the place had filled up quite a bit and he had to remind himself that he too was being paid to mingle.

Clarinda Fitzwilliam, resplendent in a fluffy pink chiffon number, solved the problem. 'Ahhh, Inspector. So glad to see you enjoying yourself, and your lovely partner. You must meet my husband, Peter.'

The husband was not what Barney expected. Shorter and rounded, he was like some Dickensian character. With a well-padded middle under his loose camel suit and chubby red cheeks, it was easy to imagine him holding court in some tavern with a glass of port in one hand and throttling the neck of a half empty bottle with the other.

'Peter,' said the man, sticking out a powerful hand. 'Good to meet you. Barney, isn't it? And your lovely lady.'

As Barney completed the introductions, he noted that even in the furthest corner of that tavern, people would hear every word of Peter's tales. In contrast to his size, he had a voice powered by bellows. The accent was surprising too; strong northern English and proud of it.

'Sorry to hear about your fire the other week,' Barney said. 'Must have been pretty scary.'

The couple exchanged a quick glance. 'Oh, not that bad,' said Peter. 'Just some toerags with nothing better to do. The graffiti was the worst. Took them ages to get off. But hey, you need drinks.'

He signalled to a serving lady and they accepted glasses of champagne. Peter turned out to have been big in the movie industry, which explained a lot. Now the closest he got to movies was putting up the cash to make them and he claimed that this suited him just fine.

'Bit of a gamble,' Shona suggested. 'Picking the winners, I mean.'

Peter beamed: 'Ah but that's what it's all about, Shona my girl. You'll never make any real money unless you're prepared to take a risk. Big risk, big profit.'

It may have been his stock answer but he seemed to swell as he looked around him at his luxury surroundings, master of all he surveyed. Shona just smiled sweetly.

'But here I am talking about high finance when I've not even asked Barney here what brings him to the glorious South of France.'

'Oh, just here on secondment from Edinburgh. It was thought that with so many Brits here now, it was appropriate to have an extra police presence.'

'Surprised the Frenchies went for that,' Peter said.

'Aye well, the jury's still out. But it's not so surprising when you think about it. I mean, we've been paying millions for extra French police to stop immigrants crossing the Channel to

England. Logical next step for dealing with British problems was to provide the personnel rather than the cash.'

Peter was nodding thoughtfully but his wife had a hand on his arm and was flicking her eyes towards the door. Barney turned to see what was happening and by the time he turned back, Clarinda was pulling her husband away towards the new arrivals. Her husband apologised on her behalf but forgot about them when he saw where he was going.

The new arrivals were three men. The closest one was an impressive specimen. In a room of fakes, he looked like the real thing. Except that from a distance, with the grey half length coat draped on his shoulders, the long blue silk scarf and tight black leather jeans, he looked unnervingly like the famous actor Morgan Freeman. He even carried himself like a film star. And the two men behind him were so nondescript all in black that they might well be the type who ran shotgun for such people.

His hosts were all over him, smiling and gesturing as he smiled thinly and scanned the room in the apparently forlorn hope of spotting something interesting.

'Is that who I think it is?' asked Barney.

'Don't know,' said Shona. 'But judging by Peter and Clarinda, it might well be. Maybe they've invested in one of his films.'

Just then Barney felt a tap on his shoulder. It was Jack and he was keeping Barney between himself and the performance at the door.

'Saw you looking, guys. Thought I'd better come over. Not who you think it is. The guy you're looking at is no movie legend. Although he *is* a legend in the South of France. That's none other than Serge Leroy, Mr Big if you like your dime novels. Got his hands in everything. Nothing goes down around here without his say-so, and that includes our Italian friends. But can't stop, I'm working.'

And he was gone, a skinny nobody with a cane, performance art.

'Well, how's about them onions?' said Barney, which had Shona looking oddly at him. 'Don't know where that came from,' he added. 'Must be one of the old man's sayings. But, shit, what the hell have we walked into?'

They watched as Mr Big and his entourage settled themselves down at a far table with the Fitzwilliams. The hosts were only there for a moment however. He seemed to make a gesture and they rose, smiling and nodding, backing away from a criminal who appeared to be their guest of honour.

'Pretty strange, don't you think?' said Shona. 'I mean, they obviously know who he is. What do you think? Is he another investor, or what?'

'Aye, the *or what* bit is what interests me. Come on, time we left. I can't be here. We can slip out while everybody's looking at the new arrivals.'

He tried to catch Jack's eye but he was busy being Charlie so they made their escape unnoticed.

It was a wonderfully clear night as they strolled the short distance to Shona's villa via local lanes which offered moonlit views of Cap Ferrat and along the coast which were as spectacular in an eerie, ancient kind of way, as those Barney had enjoyed earlier. He couldn't help but wonder what would happen here as climate change stepped up its assault on the planet. But he said nothing. The moment was too precious to spoil.

5 - Uniform Means

Wednesday, July 9

Jean-Luc looked almost affronted to find Barney in the office before him.

'Hey Jean-Luc. How goes it?'

'It goes very well, my friend. But what are you doing here so early?'

Barney waited for him to settle at his desk then started to explain about the night before.

'It was the usual sort of stuff. Bored rich folks showing off, people there to be seen, you know? Except that a wee while after we arrived we got talking to this Charlie Chaplin lookalike from Auchtermuchty.'

'Okturmuktee? This is a place?'

'Oh. Yeah, in Fife. Just up from Edinburgh. Anyway, after a bit this guy comes in with a couple of minders and the Mr and Mrs were all over him. The thing is, he was uncannily like a film star called Morgan Freeman and we thought at first maybe this was all part of the lookalike theme. But not so. It must have been obvious we were looking at him because Charlie came across and had a quiet word in our ear.'

'Charlie?'

'Sorry, Jack. He was playing Charlie Chaplin. Anyway, Jack told us who this guy was. Serge Leroy.'

Jean-Luc raised his head slowly, as if noticing Barney for the first time. 'Serge Leroy was there?'

'Yeah, apparently a big deal.'

'A very big deal, Barney. The King is never seen. This must have been very special.'

'I didn't know that,' said Barney. 'But judging by the Mr and Mrs, I knew it was at least a very big deal for them. They invest in movies so we thought maybe this Leroy guy - *The King* you call him? - maybe he was a fellow investor.'

'Ha. I suppose that is a possibility. But maybe we have to look at your hosts a little more closely.'

Barney nodded. 'Maybe so. But why *The King?* Just a straight translation of his name?'

'If that is his real name,' said Jean-Luc. 'He is thought to be Algerian but no-one knows for sure. I suspect he chose the name when he started to rise through the ranks. Even the first name. The name *Serge* originally meant servant. So we have a man who rose from being a servant to a king. He is well known to us of course. You must have criminals like this in Scotland. The devil you know is better, yes?'

Barney smiled, knowing exactly what he meant. He pictured one particular person of interest back home. Sadly, Scottish villains would never match the style of The King.

But Jean-Luc wasn't finished. 'You know, this is all we need. First it's the Musée des Beaux-Arts robbery, then we get street demonstrations against the British, their homes going up in smoke, wildfires throughout the region, an assassination in open court - and now you tell me The King is out of his hutch.

I just don't like it.'

They were saved the effort of further conjecture by a knock at the door. Barney automatically said *come in,* then winced and apologised. Fleur Dupont seemed to appreciate the humour of the situation but said nothing other than *bonjour* to her boss and then to her desk-mate.

Barney noticed a look between them and decided to make himself scarce. He knew a Chinese wall when he imagined it. He said he was away to have some breakfast but then stopped at the door. 'Sorry, Jean-Luc, I assumed I wouldn't be able to do this, but is there any chance you could pull the Fitzwilliams' bank accounts?'

Jean-Luc's head shot up. 'Yes, I agree. If they are friends with The King, we will most certainly have a look into their affairs. Leave it with me.'

Along in the canteen with his laptop for company, Barney continued his research on Leroy. There was so little old stuff online that he guessed the man had demanded its removal as defamatory. The more modern listings covered openings of hotels or nightclubs, donations to charity, all good stuff. What surprised him was that there were no clear pictures of the man, which was quite a feat these days and probably down to his entourage in black, who always seemed to be in shot.

Failing to get anything revealing, Barney switched his attention to the man from Auchtermuchty. He was much more visible. There he was in picture after picture, doing his thing at parties and shows with the rich and famous. There was even a feature article on *Jack Thomson, the man behind the cane.* To read it, a person might believe that he'd been a star of the stage back home before moving to Nice. But if he *had* been, nothing from those days had survived online. Someone, a university researcher, once told Barney that the creation of false impressions like this weren't lies but *truth management.* Whether or not Jack was a master of that dark art, Barney had taken a shine to the little lookalike and made a mental note to look him up some time.

Then he got to thinking. What if Leroy wasn't there last night as a fellow investor but as an extortionist who'd only come to pick up protection money? Perhaps fires only happened to people who didn't pay.

But then, would the boss of a huge crime empire bother to appear personally, particularly this crime boss, who went to so much trouble to remain anonymous? No, he wouldn't dirty his hands. But there was definitely something very odd about last night. He got the impression that Jack Thomson had felt it too. Maybe he should look up the actor sooner rather than later. He wouldn't be hard to find. According to the magazine article, he stayed in a famous block of flats at Parc Imperial, close to the Russian Church. A bit too far to walk in the heat but a good opportunity to see whether Jean-Luc had had a word with the garage. Barney made the call.

'Ah, Monsieur Mains, but of course. I have a car with your name on it.'

Same man, different attitude. *Thanks JL.*

* * *

The door had barely closed behind their Scottish colleague when Fleur Dupont pulled a chair up to her new boss's desk.

'I was right!'

Jean-Luc could see she'd been dying to speak to him but he held up both hands to slow her down.

'From the beginning Dupont. Calmly.'

'Yes, sir. Well, as instructed yesterday, I organised for the nightwatchman's boss to give him a call at home and say I was coming to see him. Just like you said.'

'And?'

'And he was a different man. He was all over the place. I was right! Sorry, sir. I mean it looks like my suspicions were correct. When I took the log book and started checking through the signatures, he just blurted it out. It was Saturday night. One of the cleaners had forgotten to sign out and after the murder he decided to fill in the gap himself. I have his statement here.'

She opened up her notebook and continued: '*I know it was wrong but I thought what harm would it do? Some of these people can't even write. Six cleaners and one of them just forgot. It happens. Can't remember the last time.*

'*No, I couldn't identify that particular cleaner. The agency sends us different ones all the time. They definitely all signed in. I remember. I think they were all women that night but I never pay much attention just so long as they sign in.*'

Jean-Luc said: 'You still have the logbook?'

She put on a glove and reached into the laptop case at her feet and put the book in front of him. He put on gloves before he opened its shabby blue cover and leafed to the Saturday before the murder.

'It's that one there, sir, the third one down. You see? It's just a scrawl. But the sign-out doesn't match.'

Jean-Luc looked her in the face to appreciate his good fortune anew.

'You've done well, Dupont. I'd like to think our lab boys would have picked this up once they had a good look at it. And you really should have called me with this. We just have to hope he hasn't done a runner.'

She straightened in her chair. 'That's not going to happen, sir.'

'But how can you be sure?'

'Because he's sitting in a cell downstairs. Sir.'

He couldn't help but smile.

'OK, Dupont. No need to look smug. Come on, we'll take this book with us. See if we can get him to remember anything else. Maybe he'll even recall seeing someone walking past him with a big red fire extinguisher.'

The man was a wreck. Delivered to the interview room by the custody officer, it was obvious that he hadn't slept a wink since Dupont first called on him.

Jean-Luc read aloud from the custody notes. 'Hugo Renaud, aged 51, married father of four, with nine years' service.' He looked up at Renaud sitting slumped in his chair on the other side of the table. There was no need to go in heavy. 'Do you want to see your family again, Hugo?' The man refused to meet his eyes, choosing to keep his head bowed.

'Now Hugo, you have to speak to us sometime and the more helpful you are now, the better it will go for you. So, you've explained to my colleague here how you made a little entry in this log book. I get it. A cleaner forgets to sign out, something happens and you get it in the neck. So what's the harm? I understand, I really do.

'But Hugo, my friend, in a case like this, an innocent little stroke of the pen may turn out to be a lot more. It could be aiding and abetting a murder. It could be accepting a bribe. It could be concealing the whereabouts of a felon.'

'No!' Renaud shouted, suddenly throwing his considerable

weight forward. Jean-Luc never flinched. He saw the blood-shot eyes in the loose skin of a lazy man used to an easy life, the sweat and the wild, greying hair a picture of the chaos now no doubt raging within.

'So if that's not true, tell me what is, Hugo. But you only get one shot at this, so get it right.'

The man sat back and appeared to gather himself. 'It happened like I told the girl,' he said looking over their heads. 'A cleaner forgot to sign out and I filled it in. They check now and again. Audits they call them. It's no big deal. Just keeping the book straight.'

Jean-Luc stared in wonder. Was it possible that the man could be that stupid? Or was he merely sticking to the story he was told to tell? Either way, his act had concealed a fact which could show how the killer got into the building to then lie concealed from Saturday night, before the place was stuffed full of police.

'Hugo Renaud, you will be charged with forging public records. Other, more serious, charges are likely to follow. You have the day to think it over.'

When the man had been taken out Jean-Luc turned to his young colleague. 'We need to speak to the other cleaners of course, so please set that up as soon as possible. But meantime tell me what you made of our man's performance.'

'I don't know,' she said. 'That moment when he suddenly looked defiant. I didn't think he had it in him. It was like he was saying we could do what we wanted but he would stick to his story regardless.'

Her boss nodded, smiling. 'Yes, as if he had no choice. As if someone had given him no choice. A threat against his family, or whatever. A waste of time asking him about fire extinguishers. If he's blanking us on this he's not going to cop to anything else. Maybe we'll never know when the extinguisher was switched. But whenever that was, the gallery key may well have been copied at the same time, while it was still hanging on a hook, visible to all.'

She made to speak but stopped herself.

'What is it?' he asked.

'Just to be clear, sir. What we're saying is that these six cleaners came in and only five left, meaning that the killer was in the building all the time. Meaning…'

'Yes, Dupont. Meaning that our four colleagues were telling the truth. They never let anyone past them to go up the stairs because the killer was up there already. But think, Dupont. Thanks to this cretin, we may now know how the killer got into the building but not how they got out. Damn it, we're still missing something. The killer didn't just vanish into thin air. The cops who went running up the stairs just had to have seen something. We need to go through all their statements again.'

His protégé fell into step in the corridor but he sensed a reticence. 'Look Dupont, I know what you're thinking. I gave our guys a hard time. But it was necessary. I had to test them. They don't have to like us.'

'Yes, sir. I understand.'

He wondered if she did. There was a time when he too assumed that all policemen were as honest as he was. But he had good cause to know that this was very far from the truth. She would find out soon enough.

Back in their office, they called up the statements taken from the four officers who guarded the two staircases. They saw the contradiction at the same moment.

How they never spotted it earlier, neither could explain. The officers who ran up one staircase immediately after the shooting said they arrived at the gallery door just after the pair from the other end.

But that was only their assumption. They saw a cop standing with a raised gun and just assumed it was a colleague from the other end. Exactly the same assumption the other two made.

The four officers had come within a metre of the killer. An assassin dressed as a cop.

Jean-Luc said: 'Dupont, get all four of them in here right now. I don't care where they are or what they're doing. Just get them here.'

It took almost an hour but eventually all four were squeezed around his desk, two of them in civvies, all of them looking uncomfortable.

'Now I need each of you to confirm something very simple,' he said. 'I want you to tell me if you see in this room the cop who was standing outside the balcony door with a gun.'

All four looked confused as they cast glances at each other. The previously truculent Lieutenant Pierre Martin was less so when Jean-Luc put their theory to him. He dropped his eyes then said: 'Actually, now that you mention it, I just assumed it was one of these guys. We're from different stations so we've never seen each other before. Plus there were cops coming from everywhere and it was all a bit crazy. But yeah, OK, when we ran along the corridor, there was one officer there just ahead of the others. And it wasn't either of these guys.'

'Thank you Lieutenant. Now think carefully. Can you describe this person?'

'It happened so fast but thinking about it, she was in the textbook position, you know, in the crouch, gun extended, both hands. Hair was blond, or at least fair, mainly tucked up under the cap but I can see a strand hanging down. Face? Never really took her in. White, though.'

'You said *she*. So we're definitely talking about a woman?'

'Oh, yeah, for sure. One thing I *do* remember. She had this really cute arse.'

By the time they'd put together fresh interviews with all four officers, they had a fairly good idea of what had happened. The second pair had also assumed the woman had come from the other side and the only potentially useful information they could add was that she had what looked like a small dark birthmark on her right cheek. It was just an impression but it made sense that only they would notice it because they would have seen the woman from the other side. And an assassin with a birthmark on her right cheek had to make their search a heck of a lot easier.

Now, whoever she was, they knew how the killer got into the building and could now guess as to how she got out. In the chaotic aftermath of the shooting, she simply used the camouflage of her fake police uniform to walk straight out the door. The very same ruse they'd used to get Nel into the building had enabled his killer to escape from it.

6 - Cane & Table

Back home, he'd resisted any idea of driving a glorified electric milk float instead of his beloved old sports car. But the extreme weather events tearing the planet to shreds had concentrated many minds. And Barney had to admit, after the short drive to Parc Imperial, that the little car had been amazing. It had even parked itself right outside the monumental art deco building.

He found the gardienne in the gatehouse, a lithe older woman with severely tied-back grey hair who took some persuading to share Charlie's apartment number. She actually studied his French police accreditation then called the number at the bottom to verify its authenticity. Only then did her frosty manner thaw. 'I am so sorry Monsieur, but many people come here to get these damned selfies with our Charlie. And we have to protect him.'

'So you all call him Charlie too?'

'Ha. Yes. Just here. Outside he is Jack.'

Madame Charpentier then took him along a wide corridor of marbled floor and walls to the ornate wrought iron lift that would rise to the great man's top floor home. 'He's a lucky man to live in such a beautiful building and with such lovely, protective friends,' he said.

But she gave only a short smile and a tilt of her head, then she was gone, back into duty mode.

He was alone the whole way, the lift gliding smoothly ever upwards until it slowed and clanked to a halt. She'd told him to go left to the end. Seeing no bell, he knocked and almost immediately sensed movement behind the peephole. The door swung open.

'Barney Mains? My God, what a lovely surprise. Come in man. Come in.'

He wore the paisley-pattern cravat and dark green velvet dressing gown and slippers of the off-duty thespian. But he was talking and beaming like Jack Thomson from Auchtermuchty. There was nothing fake about him, beyond his act.

He saw Barney looking. 'I know, I'm a walking cliche. But, believe me, it's so bloody comfortable, like you wouldn't believe.'

The air-con was doing its job and Barney felt the sweat start to chill. 'You don't mind me dropping in like this? You're not going out, or anything?'

'Take a pew. What would you like, something cold, tea?'

'Anything cold would be great thanks, Charlie. Shit, sorry. I'm calling you Charlie.'

'That's OK, Barney. You can call me what you want,' he said, adding with a mock-theatrical flourish, 'so long as you call me.'

Then he was off to fetch drinks, his gait more like that of a light-footed Fred Astaire than poor old Charlie Chaplin.

It was only then that Barney took in the apartment's decor; despite his host's slight frame, he was one of those people whose personality took centre stage. The club chairs had a black and white zigzag pattern, part of an enveloping art deco theme, authentic and calming. The coffee table was black with silver corners and inlay, a combination repeated in picture frames displaying richly-coloured period paintings above dressers of stunning design bearing ornaments of cute young ladies in artistic poses. Light flooded in from the balcony's double glass doors between pulled-back heavy drapes with what looked like 3D lightning strikes in silver satin.

Jack returned with a tray of glasses, a carafe of cold water and one of orange juice. There was a small bowl of medjool dates and another of cashew nuts, which happened to be a favourite combination of Barney's. He proved it by helping himself.

'Ah, you like that combo too?' Jack said. 'The locals tend to go for walnuts but I'm a cashew nut myself.'

They silently toasted each other's good taste with glasses of orange juice.

In the pause that followed, Barney said: 'You'll be wondering why I'm here.'

'A bit. I mean, a social visit is absolutely great. But you're a cop.'

'Yeah, 'fraid so. But this isn't exactly cop stuff. I'm really just hoping to be able to pick your brains.'

'Take whatever you can find, my friend,' Jack said, spreading his arms.

'I hoped you would say that. It's just that I'm trying to get a handle on what's going on here, what with the demos and the home attacks. I can get everything in the press and, theoretically, everything the police have. But I don't have the street knowledge, the scuttlebutt, what people are saying behind closed doors.'

'What, you want me to spy for you? Go undercover? What fun!'

'Ha. No, nothing like that. It's just that you recognised the King and by all accounts, he doesn't get out much these days. You also get invited to lots of places to perform and must get a good feel for what's happening behind the scenes. With the Fitzwilliams at Villefranche, for instance. What's going on there?'

Jack put down his glass and placed his hands on the studded arms of his club chair, his playful expression gone.

'There's a whole lot of stuff in what you just asked. And there's a lot I don't know.'

'Just what you feel comfortable with, Jack.'

'Well, starting with the last thing you said, I don't know exactly what's going on with the Fitzwilliams. But I do know there's something. Old Serge Leroy has never to my knowledge been at a single gig like that. Even the backroom staff were shocked when he showed up. So I don't think even the Fitzwilliams knew he was coming.'

'But they obviously knew him.'

'For sure, Barney. You saw the way they fawned over him? No, my guess is there's money involved. Maybe some movie investment or whatever. That's their thing, the Fitzwilliams.'

'But why would he have turned up unannounced?' Barney asked, half to himself. 'Unless that was the point; the element of surprise, shock tactics.'

'Well, I don't know. Can't see the King wasting his time like that.'

Barney resumed: 'But they could be in some kind of deal together? Maybe the Fitzwilliams failed to deliver and he turned up as a final warning? A final warning after a first warning, maybe.'

'The fire?' said Jack, smiling. 'You think that was Leroy, not protesters?'

Barney made a *maybe* face. 'But if he was behind that one, then...'

His host just shrugged. 'If you're thinking of that hedge fund bloke's place nearby, on Mont Boron, I couldn't say. All I would say is that it couldn't have happened to a more deserving guy.'

'You know him?'

'Did a gig there a while ago. Objectionable SOB. Treated people like shit. I might have been persuaded to light the match myself. But I'll tell you one thing. A lot of people are questioning these fire attacks. Sure, there are all these demos. Can't blame folk. But the kind of hotheads who go torching buildings tend not to be your regular disgruntled residents. Yet not one person has been hurt in all these attacks anywhere in the region.'

'What are you saying?'

'I don't really know; just that they all seem to have been pretty well planned. No-one hurt and no-one caught. Just odd, that's all. At least, that's what folks are saying.'

Barney took a drink of his orange juice. In his research online and in police case notes, he'd never seen this perspective aired. He knew he'd been right to come here. 'For someone who purports not to know very much, you've given me a lot of food for thought,' he said.

Jack, who'd displayed a keen focus throughout the conversation, now reverted to playfulness. 'Then, my work here is done. How about a coffee?'

'Actually,' Barney said, pushing his luck, 'I was hoping I could impose on you a bit more...'

Five minutes later they were out on the pavement. The

clack of pétanque boules came from somewhere across the road from his parked car. Despite his prejudices, Barney was starting to fall in love with his little battery-driven milk float. It had the retro look of an old Renault Dauphine, a model he remembered a friend working on day and night for many months to restore.

They were on the high corniche in no time and for once he managed to avoid the sense of vertigo which he previously fell victim to on this perilous stretch of road carved into the mountainside.

Jack had agreed to show him around and while no-one knew exactly where to find The King at any given time, he could at least show him previously known haunts and businesses he owned. He also seemed tickled pink at the prospect of being driven around in a new car and there being no compulsion to get somewhere for work.

The first point of interest was a rundown little stone building near a junction to the middle corniche. Barney recognised it at once. 'I've passed here before. It really stands out. A ruin that no-one's ever renovated for some reason.'

'This is where they say he started out. There used to be a big old dog which lay outside every day, a bit of a landmark, just waiting for him to come back. Allegedly, he never did, though he had someone look after the beast.'

Next on the gangster tour was a smart hotel near La Turbie, reputed to be his first venture into the legit business world. Jack suggested a stop at the nearby Trophy of Augustus, which turned out to be a still-impressive monument despite much of its stone having been repurposed by villagers since the great Caesar had battered all their forebears into submission.

But his main reason for the stop was to point out the view of

Monaco on the coast far below. 'There you go, Barney, as far as I'm concerned, the best view of Monaco this side of Space.'

Barney laughed, wondering what could have prompted such disdain for the Principality. But he preferred to live with the enigma of a great line.

Jack then insisted on one more highlight as they drove down towards the sea. And Barney was glad that he did because the nightclub and casino turned out to be a spectacular sight, cantilevered out over a vertical cliff on giant steel arms. It was said that Leroy thought it his crowning achievement, built so close to where he started and against much opposition from the locals.

But they were now close to Villefranche and Barney wasn't going to pass up this second chance of a cool drink beside the old harbour of La Darse.

It turned out to be one of Jack's favourite spots too. They ordered beers and took one of the few free tables, a metal one by the water's edge with an umbrella which gave welcome cover from the burning sun now playing spangled reflections of rippled water on basking white hulls. They had just taken welcome first sips when Barney sensed someone standing behind him. But it was his guide the visitor was interested in. 'Mr Thomson, can we do a selfie?'

The young American woman took Jack's surprise for agreement and was suddenly bent down at his side while her abashed partner hung back. She got her picture and he smiled graciously as he signed a serviette for her, which seemed to make her day.

'You get that a lot?' Barney asked.

'Only every day. Don't knock it. You worry when they don't recognise you.'

But the young woman's antics had made them the centre of attention and suddenly a Frenchman shouted from another table. 'Come on Jack, give us a show. Do the walk.'

The ensuing applause seemed to leave him no choice. He shrugged a sad Charlie Chaplin shrug and stood. He gestured with a raised right hand and looked around. An elderly man passed him a walking stick. From nowhere, Jack produced the fake moustache. Then he was off along the quayside, another man from another time, loved now as then, the applause echoing off hot stone walls.

Then he was back. He took several bows, returned the walking stick and removed his only other prop. 'Sorry about that,' he said. But Barney could see that he was aglow, that performance was fuel to him.

Barney shook his head in wonder and raised his glass.

'You enjoyed our little tour then, Barney? Was it helpful? For what it's worth, I've had a super time.'

'Thanks, man. I owe you big time. Don't know what I'm going to do with it all but I think at some stage I'm going to have to seek an audience.'

'With The King?' Jack was shaking his head. 'Well, good luck with that. But be very careful. In the meantime, I'll keep my ears open. Anything comes up about these fires or whatever, I'll give you a bell.'

7 - Brits Out

He heard them before he saw them, thousands of placard-bearing, chanting protesters.

He'd just dropped Jack back home and was heading down Boulevard Gambetta and under the iron railway bridge when the first of the procession streamed in from the left, from the direction of the main railway station in Avenue Thiers.

Barney was only three cars back from the blocking police car and so stepped out to get a closer look.

He knew that such demos were a regular part of French life, particularly in major cities like Nice. But today's was different because what they were chanting included the very clear words *Brits Out!*

He slipped around the police car and stood reading some placards. They said: *Price caps now! Fair quota on sales!* and *No More!*

It didn't seem to him like the friendliest of environments in which to start a conversation but he wanted to know more, so he joined a group of men and women with a sign saying they were from the city's Musiciens district. He had to shout, trying to explain in his as yet imperfect French that he was a visiting Brit who wanted to understand.

He could feel the hostility. One of the group, a big man

swinging a placard, shouted back. 'What the hell are you doing here, Englishman? You're not welcome.'

Barney knew that despite the anger and the noise, such demos rarely resulted in violence. But the man had detached himself from the group and was coming closer.

'I'm a cop, sent over from Scotland to help,' Barney started.

'Bloody Scottish, you're just as fucking British. Go home, foreigner!'

Barney heard voices repeating the words and felt many furious faces directed his way. Genuine mass hatred. He had to admit to himself that for the first time in France, he suddenly knew what it felt like to be an outsider.

He tried again to explain that he was here to help ease tensions between them and his countryfolk but he felt the weakness of his words. How the hell could he help solve a problem on this scale? Besides he was being shouted down by a hail of vitriol and was aware of a French policeman coming to push him back.

As he was eased back behind the police car, Barney realised he'd actually been racially abused, here, in a city and country he loved, his second home.

For his part, he'd never thought to distinguish between black and white, muslim or christian, Brit or Frenchie. To him, you were either a friend or an enemy, guilty or innocent, goodie or baddie, end of.

He suddenly felt incredibly naive, as if he'd missed something all his life that he should have known. Of course, there had been the odd incident back in Edinburgh; you couldn't live in Scotland and not know the division that religion had caused. But he'd never been on the receiving end and so he stored the memory of the man's hatred, the blind injustice of it. And the sense of what it must be like if everywhere you go you're made to feel like an outsider, a lesser being. He felt angry for all those made to feel that way.

Then he laughed to himself at the idea of anyone having so little to do that they stored up resentment of the Scots. Such types were more to be pitied. *Maybe that goes for them all,* he thought.

He felt a hand on his shoulder just then. He turned to find a tall, refined-looking woman with the suggestion of a kindly smile on her middle-aged face. There was a man beside her, a matching professional type.

'We saw you trying to speak to them.' the woman said. 'We just wanted to say that we Niçois are not all so bad-mannered.'

Barney thanked her, said he knew that this was the case and introduced himself.

They were, as he'd guessed, professionals; she a doctor, he a lawyer. They too happened to live in the Musiciens district, which boasted some of the city's most striking Belle Epoque architecture, not to mention Barney's own little rented flat.

'You have to understand their anger,' she said. 'The prices have soared in recent years. They can't afford city centre rents and so have to commute from out of town. I believe the only reason we have not seen such anger before is that our excellent tram network makes the commute so easy. But once the squatters started to occupy empty holiday homes and some of those buildings were set on fire, the sense of injustice has flared up like the wildfires.'

Barney asked what should be done but she could only shrug. 'I know what the leaders of the protests say; that it is for the authorities to reduce foreign ownership to a set percentage of properties that can be sold to them; to cap rents at an affordable level and to end the disgusting practice of allowing your richest people to buy their residency here through the so-called golden visa system.'

His faith in the generosity of the French restored, Barney thanked the woman and her husband and climbed back into his car. He decided to forego his planned visit to the majestic Westerling Hotel on the Prom. He could happily postpone calling on Mr Charles Taylor-Smith for a little longer and so, once the last of the protesters had passed, he turned left along Avenue Thiers and back towards police headquarters. He passed his elegant neighbours strolling arm and arm.

* * *

Barney could hear Jean-Luc's raised voice through the door so he decided to hold back outside. He couldn't help but hear his words.

'Look, we've got a blond shooter with a cute ass who was there before our intrepid hero cops. And it looks like she spent two uncomfortable nights on a hard bench in the gallery, having locked herself inside. And quite possibly not for the first time. Yes, I know you've dusted everything for prints but we need your guys back in there asap to do a proper, painstaking, forensic sweep. She must have left something; a hair, a food wrapper, something.'

The phone was slammed down and Barney paused before pushing the door open.

'Bloody Forensics Department!' Jean-Luc said.

'Ha, we're lucky in Edinburgh in that regard. Got a wee genius in charge.'

'Well, get your *wee genius* over here right away because I've just had to put a rocket up the fat arse of ours. But anyway, Barney my friend, how are things with you? I have the bank records for your Fitzwilliams by the way. They're in a folder on your desk. Interesting reading.'

Barney sidled round to his seat and flicked open the folder.

'You will see massive movements of cash. Although the bottom line is that it recently all moved in the wrong direction. Your friends are millions in debt.'

Barney closed the file again and sat back. 'So maybe that's the connection with Serge Leroy? They owe him big time? A movie deal flopped, maybe?'

'As you say, Barney. Whatever the case, you may like to have another word with them.'

The Scotsman nodded in agreement then hesitated before speaking again. 'Em, Jean-Luc, do you think there's any chance I could ask another favour?'

His request had seemed a good idea at the time but the Frenchman quickly shot it down. A similar check of financial records for Charles Taylor-Smith wouldn't show much, Jean-Luc said, because he wasn't a French resident and merely owned a holiday home here.

However the very request made Jean-Luc wonder. 'So you think maybe he could owe a lot of money too? Possibly also to The King? And that both fires were warnings, dressed up to look like the protesters did it?'

'Something like that,' said Barney. 'Though in Taylor-Smith's case, they literally burnt the house down so maybe there's something else going on we don't know about. Might be interesting to see what it was insured for. Fires have in the past been known to turn property into liquid cash.'

'Ha-ha! Now the insurance on a French property I *can* help

with,' said Jean-Luc.

'Sorry, Jean-Luc. I know you're kind of busy yourself. How's it going, if you can say?'

The Frenchman leant back in his chair, appearing to relax for the first time in a while. 'Well, off the record, we're making good progress. This cannot go outside this office, you understand, but I would appreciate your thoughts. You see, we have established that our shooter was a woman, possibly a blond but probably that was a wig. And possibly with a mole on her right cheek. We have no record of such a shooter on our files. We have put in a request to Interpol but it can take time. It is a pity that, with such lack of cooperation between the French and British since Brexit, that we can't make the same request to the UK.'

Barney smiled broadly. 'I'll see what I can do. Is there anything else you need?'

'No, no, I don't think so. But thank you for that. It could be a massive help. No, otherwise the picture is coming together. Dupont has found that the shooter appears to have got into the building as a cleaner then hidden until the day of the hearing. The gun, as I told you, I think, was already in the building, in a fake fire extinguisher, which is where the killer left it. And before you ask, we believe she was wearing a police uniform, which was how she got out unchallenged.'

Barney sighed. 'The same as Nel. Ironic.'

'Yes, that's what I thought. But, meantime, I have Dupont rounding up the other cleaners. I'll hopefully be joining her soon at the recruitment agency to get their statements. Maybe they can give us a better description. In fact, I'd better be going.'

Barney had been looking for an excuse to call Edinburgh and

as soon as the Frenchman left, he picked up the desk phone and called his force's headquarters.

'Allo, bonjour, eez thees Sarjong Mclucky?' he asked.

Her lowered voice told him someone else was close. 'Alright, Barney. It's OK for you,' I'm up to my eyeballs in it here. Sir.'

He smiled, picturing her chiselled young face, a slash of black eyebrow raised in that Bond-like question mark of hers.

'At ease, Detective-Sergeant McLuskey. This is work too, you know.'

'Of course, sir,' she said for the benefit of the room. 'How can I help?'

'OK, Ffiona. I get it. I'll keep it short. You'll know all about the Nel murder, of course. I just need you to run a wee search for me...'

His mobile sounded. An unknown number and a text which he could ignore while he filled her in on everything he knew about the shooting and the shooter. He visualised her scribbling notes in the ubiquitous notebook as she gave curt, professional responses for the benefit of whoever was hovering close to her in the *Eggbox*. He now had his own office in Edinburgh but Ffiona was stuck in the detectives' room, in one of the six stifling compartments which gave it the name. Though they both knew that she was marked out as a high-flyer and would soon flee the coup.

'If that's all, sir, I'll see what I can do.'

'Great, Ffiona. How about you call me back on the mobile later, when you can talk?'

'Certainly, sir. Consider it done.'

Barney ended the call and checked his phone. The text was short and to the point. 'Please call this number as soon as possible. And don't tell anyone.'

* * *

The recruitment company was close to Place Garibaldi, only about ten minutes walk away, and so Jean-Luc opted for some fresh air along Boulevard Carabacel. Dupont got up when he entered. Sitting on a row of seats in front of a wall-length mural of some Mediterranean beach scene were six people he took to be the cleaners in question. Jean-Luc sighed. This could take a while. But his bright young sidekick turned out to have done the spadework.

'If I may, sir,' she said. 'I have all the names and details that we need but I can save a lot of time if I give you a quick summary.'

Jean-Luc took a spare seat beside a cluttered desk behind which squirmed a shifty looking man with tired eyes and a two-day stubble. He assumed this was the recruitment company boss and that he was imagining his licence flying out of the window.

'Fire away, Dupont.'

'Well, the six ladies we have here are the six who for the past few weeks have cleaned within the court building. Except that one of them was off sick for two days, the Saturday and Sunday. I have statements from all six but it is this lady's which is really interesting. Madame Cortes here,' she said, encouraging a slight young women towards the middle of the row to identify herself for the Captain. 'Madame Cortes says she has no idea who replaced her.'

'You believe her, that she was sick?'

'Gut feeling? I think the timing was just too convenient but she's adamant.'

'Very well. We can bring her in and see if she might like to be more forthcoming. Now, the important bit. Can the other

66

five give us our description?'

Dupont stiffened. 'Nothing definitive I'm afraid, sir. White, fair hair, slim. No-one noticed any mole, but they don't seem to have paid much attention to her, just got on with their jobs and went home. They get put into different teams all the time, so they're used to new people coming and going.'

Jean-Luc said: 'Considering half of them probably have fake papers, they're no doubt happy just to keep their heads down and take whatever pay they can get. Which in this case means that on Saturday night they went to work with a complete stranger and never paid the slightest attention to her,' he said. 'So we're no further forward, except that your Mr Laurent is about to tell us the name and address of the person he sent in as a replacement.' He turned towards the man with his eyebrows raised. Laurent promptly sat up straight and fixed his tie in a failed attempt to look professional despite the stubble and hungover eyes.

'Em, I'm afraid not, sir. You see, even although Mr Laurent is the person who assigns squads to the public sector, he says he never put in a replacement for Madame Cortes. Because no-one told him she was sick.'

Jean-Luc stared at her, then sighed. 'So our killer merely tagged along with the others. Unbelievable!'

One of the seated women suddenly stood. 'I go now? I have child.'

Jean-Luc turned to Dupont. 'We can let the five go? We know where to find them?'

She nodded and signalled Madame Cortes to come forward. 'The rest of you can go. We may be in touch later.'

Jean-Luc stood to face the cleaner, who appeared to be trembling. 'Madame Cortes, I am Captain Jean-Luc Verten of the Police Nationale. My colleague will have told you that we are chasing a cold-blooded killer and we believe that you have met her. Now, we don't have time for games. Who told you to go off sick at the weekend?'

The woman had olive skin stretched across a face which had seen barely twenty hard years. Her lower lip was quivering, yet she stuck out her chin and spoke with surprising precision in clipped English. 'I was very ill. I stayed in bed. That is all.' She may be defiant, Jean-Luc thought, but she was staring at a palm tree in the wall mural and speaking as if reciting a prepared script.

'In which case, mademoiselle,' he said, pulling out wrist restraints, I will be taking you back to police headquarters for further questioning.'

The alarm in the woman's face was a picture, and not one Jean-Luc took pride in, but he paused and fixed her with a questioning stare.

'I can't. I must get home,' she said. 'I know nothing.'

He shrugged and reached for her wrist. She pulled away. 'OK, OK. I tell you, I tell you.'

Jean-Luc noticed Dupont with her notebook at the ready.

'I never met woman. It was man. A French man. He gave me money. He said: take your child on holiday for weekend. It will be good for baby's health. But I know what he mean. He was bad man. I know men like this.'

It came as no surprise to the Captain that her description of the man was so vague as to be useless. Dark skin, dark hair, medium build, no distinguishing features.

But at least they had confirmed their theory. They would take her in for a full statement then turn her loose. The man had given her five hundred Euros, a small fortune to her, probably the best break she'd had in her young life.

* * *

Barney looked up when they entered. 'Hey, folks. How'd it go?' Dupont looked to her boss as she took the seat across from the Scotsman.

'It's OK, Barney knows the score. Plus he's helping us. At least I hope he is,' said Jean-Luc glancing at his friend.

'Well, I've asked the question Jean-Luc but I'm afraid the shooter's description isn't much to go on and I don't expect to hear back from Edinburgh until later. Did you get anything better from the cleaners?'

The Frenchman's look said it all. 'Not a description I'm afraid, but we have at least confirmed how the shooter got into the building. Someone paid one of them to go off sick while the killer took her place.'

Barney nodded thoughtfully then checked his notes and looked up. 'Well, for what it's worth, I in the meantime have found out just how much our hedgie friend stands to pocket from the ashes. Insured for a cool three million.'

'But how..?' Jean-Luc started.

'Easy really. It occurred to me that hedgie's double-barrelled architect has been hired for the rebuild. And that he's a bit up his own arse. So it didn't take much prompting for him to start chuntering on about what a fabulous design he was going to produce, thanks to all that lovely insurance dosh.'

'Good work, Barney. So what do you want to do now?'

'Well, I guess that I need to speak to Edinburgh again and get them to do some background on our hedge fund friend. Though if we fancy him for insurance fraud, I might need you or one of your officers to bring the handcuffs.'

Jean-Luc stretched and raised his eyebrows. 'I think that either I or Dupont here will have to accompany you to interview our English friend. But let's wait to see what you get back from Scotland.'

Barney nodded. His friend had enough on his plate and hedgie was never going to be hard to find.

'Oh, and Barney. I almost forgot. You have messages. There's some journalist who's been at the front office trying to contact you, a Madeleine something. Left her card. Says it's urgent, as they always do. But much more importantly, you've been given an invitation to meet with the great Henri Aubert. His office says he'd like to see you, about the fires. Dupont took the message.'

The young policewoman raised her head, reluctantly, it seemed to Barney. 'That's really it, sir. Monsieur Mains was asked to go out and see him at his country place near Fréjus tomorrow afternoon. They didn't say much. Just that the *great man* believed he could help your investigation.'

Barney got the sarcasm. 'So who is he, this *great man*. He's not that right-wing politician is he?'

She nodded. 'The idiot who thinks he's going to be the next President of France.'

Barney looked to Jean-Luc, who gave one of his big shrugs. 'Some say he has a real chance of winning here in the south, make the breakthrough the Right have always promised. But who knows? The young, like Dupont here, think he's past it, a fantasist.'

'Well, I'm not proud. I'll speak to anyone. Thursday afternoon? Fine. I can take a car?'

'Best that Dupont drives you. It might be hard to find and

there are wildfires out there, so be careful.'

Barney looked across to Dupont. It looked like this was the first she'd heard of her assignment. She wasn't smiling.

8 - The Curse

Maitre Bridget O'Brien was as Irish as her name, the long red hair, freckled complexion and no-nonsense handshake a sharp contrast to the French norm. Her means of communication had been far from normal too; a cryptic text and a mysterious summons to this confidential evening meeting. Barney was intrigued to hear whatever Nel's lawyer had to say.

He'd found her office in a less than salubrious street towards the upper end of Boulevard Gambetta. It was a square, two-storey stone building which seemed to have survived successive high-rise building booms, a little gem with a roof garden brimming with luxuriant greenery.

The heavy old door had swung inwards before he could knock and there she stood, dressed for business in a smart charcoal trouser suit and open-necked, white silk shirt but with a generous, open-mouthed smile plastered across a strong face which belonged to the outdoors rather than a stuffy lawyer's office.

'Come away in with ye, Inspector.' To Barney it sounded north-west; it conjured happy Donegal holidays and he couldn't help smiling as he followed her inside, his curiosity to hear her story pushing aside the discomfort over his summons.

She led him into a huge office which appeared to occupy

about half the ground floor, a sizeable chunk of which was claimed by an enormous leather-panelled old desk.

The scent of good coffee wafted from a hotplate in the corner as she invited him to take one of the two leather club chairs beside a long occasional table topped with white-veined black marble which matched a looming, ornately-scrolled fireplace.

'I must thank you for coming at such short notice, Barney. I can call you Barney, by the way?' she asked, not expecting or receiving any complaint. 'But I hope you'll understand when I explain why I had to see you.'

He waited while she crossed the room then returned to the coffee table with a tray.

'But first you must have some coffee and biscuits.' It wasn't exactly a command but it was clear to him that this woman, barely forty years old, liked to get her own way and generally did.

She handed him his cup and saucer and sank back in her chair, her own cup on her lap.

'You may be wondering what a good Irish girl is doing here, defending the wicked,' she said out of the blue, a wild twinkle in her eyes. 'Well, I'm actually half French and I've been practising here for years. Inherited my grandfather's wonderful home and just love the life here. But now,' she said, her tone changing, 'I have a final duty to perform for my late client.'

Barney raised his free hand. 'Before you say any more, Maitre O'Brien, I need to say something. First, I'm delighted to meet you after what must have been a very traumatic experience for you, having been so close to your client when he was shot in court. But if you have anything of relevance to the investigation, you should be speaking to the French police

73

and not to me.'

She smiled as she put her cup down on the table then raised both hands. 'I understand. And yes, I'm aware of your own position here. But, I haven't asked you here to discuss this awful murder. As you say, it's not every day that a client is shot right next to me and although it may not seem like it right now, I was actually quite shaken up. However I have some final responsibilities towards Pieter, not the least of which is to make the funeral arrangements. He had no known relatives, you see, and he told me that the only person he had ever loved was dead.'

She sat up straight in her chair. 'Which brings me to the reason I invited you here. So, if you can just bear with me a moment longer.'

He watched her rise and stride to her antique desk where she unlocked an upper drawer and withdrew a large envelope. As she sat back down across from him, she became deadly serious. 'Barney, my client gave me clear instructions to carry out in the event of his death. He knew that certain highly-placed individuals would prefer him dead. Though I'm sure he would never have anticipated such a shocking end in such a well guarded public place.'

'Hang on. Just what is this?'

'Barney, trust me. You're here not as a policeman... but as a beneficiary.'

Barney realised at that moment that it was true; that in certain moments of shock, the jaw can drop of its own accord. He managed to form the words. 'Listen, Maitre, I don't know if this is some kind of sick joke - either yours or his - but you need to explain yourself, right now.'

She nodded abruptly. 'Of course. I understand. Just believe

me when I say that if I had any information regarding Pieter's murder I would most definitely give it to you or as you say, to the French police. I want to catch his killer as much as you do. However, all I can offer you today is one of the two documents in this envelope. I should say that Pieter Nel signed and dated them in my presence in prison. They were then sealed and have until now been locked away, unopened in my safe. I should also stress that I have no idea what they contain. All I know is that I was to contact you and give them to you.'

Barney was screwing up his face, as if that would help. 'But *a beneficiary?* Are you serious? Nel was a ruthless assassin and I had nothing to do with him other than wanting to see him locked up for the rest of his life.'

She appeared not to hear him as she tore off a red seal and pulled out a document of several A4 pages stapled together. 'Now Barney, I'll leave you to read this in peace. I hope that everything will be explained in that letter.'

He looked blankly at the document in his hand and then at her back as she moved away and sat at her desk.

He raised the letter and started to read.

Hi Barney, If you're reading this now, I guess it's bad news for me. Probably no surprise and I guess it's poetic justice for my sins. Dying by the sword and all that. C'est la vie. I've had a good innings and there's not much to look forward to.

I had been planning on getting a ghostwriter. Tales to tell. But they must have got wind of it. Nothing's private here in prison. Which is why I'm glad to have had a backup plan.

And when I found out you were being sent here for the court proceedings, it was a no-brainer. It's down to you now. You're my plan B!

Barney stopped reading to look across in utter confusion at

the lawyer sitting at her desk.

'This is crazy!' he said out loud to no-one in particular. But he had to read on.

First, I should apologise for landing it on you like this. And of course you can choose to walk away. It's just that once you hear what I have to say, I think you won't be able to do that.

In fact, I'm counting on it.

Barney dropped the letter on the coffee table and raised his voice to the lawyer. 'This is insane. You must know what's in this.'

She turned and shook her head. 'My client said it was better that I didn't know. Although…'

'Yes? Although..?'

'Although once you finish reading the letter I may or may not have a final instruction to carry out.'

Barney tilted his head and peered at her, trying to imagine what new madness lay in store. He shook his head and retrieved the letter.

It took him several minutes and when he'd finished, he read it again.

At last, he folded the crisp sheets of paper and tucked them inside his jacket. He looked across at her. 'So what happens now?'

'If you're willing to do as he asks,' she said, her eyebrows raised, 'then I'm instructed to give you this.' She held up a smaller envelope.

Barney couldn't help himself. He let out a wild, crazed laugh. 'Oh my God, this is too good! I'm trapped in an episode of bloody *Mission Impossible*. Don't tell me, the letter will self-destruct in five effing seconds!'

She rose and he noticed a look that could have been

sympathy or apology as she returned to the coffee table then handed the envelope to him.

Barney saw that this too bore a red seal. But when he saw what was written on the front of the envelope, his blood ran cold. One word: *Barney*.

He took a moment then looked up at her. 'Presumptuous,' he said, grimly sarcastic.

'He seemed sure that you'd do it, whatever it is he asks. He said you were the only man he'd trust to do the right thing.'

'Ha! Do the right bloody thing. Gets me in trouble all the time,' Barney grumbled, thinking: *the curse strikes again.*

He threw the envelope onto the table. 'Now, Maitre...'

'Bridget, please.'

'Bridget!' Barney had had enough surprises from her and needed to get back to brass tacks. Bridget, you now need to explain yourself. What the hell do you mean by that? *The only man he would trust? I mean, seriously?*'

'Barney there's a lot I don't know but I can tell you this: Pieter was convinced that the police were corrupt.'

'Well, of course he would say that. He was a killer.'

'No, it was much more than that. He didn't actually say *corrupt*. He said *rotten to the core*. That was why he needed someone he could trust. Which is why he instructed me to have you checked out.'

Barney leapt to his feet.

'Barney, please. I know. But let me explain.'

He sat down and gave his head another good shake to make the craziness go away.

'You see, he read about you handing in your resignation. And when he asked around, he heard that it was because they blocked you from investigating certain highly-placed individuals. Which was a big plus in his book. But he wanted to be sure.'

'Oh, he wanted to be sure, did he? And I passed this check of yours, did I? OK, don't bother. I guess I did, more's the pity.'

'Look, Pieter knew that he was on borrowed time and he told me long before his arrest that he had been building up a *treasure trove* to leave behind. He never said what it was and I didn't want to know but it was clear that it wasn't actual treasure but a cache of information, something he obviously thought of great importance. Beyond that, you presumably now know more than I do after reading his letter.'

'That may or may not be true. But if you knew Nel's story you would be suspicious too. For instance, he told you that the only person he'd ever loved was dead. But I bet he didn't tell you that I was involved in that death.'

She shook her head. 'Barney, I can understand your suspicion. But he never blamed you for that. You didn't pull the trigger, after all.'

Barney's head dropped as he tried to take this in, to believe that Nel held no grudge against him, was not setting him up for some twisted kind of revenge. Besides, he tried to reason, the letter tied in with everything she'd just told him and Nel had been right about one thing: once he'd read it, he would have no choice but to follow through.

But he'd had enough for one evening. He needed time to digest all this. He needed space, out of this claustrophobic office and into the fresh air, where he could think. Only then would he decide what to do about the contents of the sealed envelope he now picked up and slipped into his pocket alongside the letter.

He stood and shook her hand. She seemed to be trying to

78

read his face, but it had become the blank, deadpan expression he usually wore for the world. 'It's been… interesting,' he said. 'I'll let you know.'

And then he was out the door and into the real world where serial killers don't leave bequests to policemen and policemen don't accept impossible missions from killers.

* * *

The walk down Boulevard Gambetta was surreal. In his pocket, he had a letter which Nel claimed would lead to a Pandora's Box with headline-making revelations. And in the sealed envelope lay the key to that box. If it was all true. If Nel wasn't setting him up from the grave, leading him into a trap and waiting to greet him on the other side with a great big smile on his face.

Yet here in the easing heat and softening light of evening, cars cruised by, people sat smoking and drinking at pavement tables while others boarded buses to go home and some waited while their dog did what it had to do. He was in sight of the familiar metal railway bridge when he heard a shout from across the road. It took him a moment to understand. But it was Jack himself, aka Charlie, waving at him like a shipwrecked sailor. Barney grinned. The neon-lit wine bar was a siren call.

Jack had had a few and was in good form. He stood, none too steadily, and introduced his friend with a theatrical flourish. The lovely Marilyn Monroe, aka Gracie Jones from Plymouth, England.

They had a bottle of red on the table and the moment Barney sat down, a mature lady delivered an extra glass, which Jack promptly filled. 'What a coincidence. We were just talking

79

about you, about our little trip. What fun it was.'

Gracie still looked the part that she played but she was out of character tonight, appearing more watchful and thoughtful than the original. But then, maybe the real Marilyn wasn't so dumb either. Gracie had a weird mid-Atlantic accent, whether through having lived in the States or having lived too long as a doppelganger. Either way, Barney took an instant liking to her.

As the evening light imbued the street with muted colour and calm, he let the ordinariness of the setting wash over him, like the world was still the same as it had always been. He suddenly became aware that he'd emptied his glass.

Jack laughed. 'I guess you needed that.' He picked up the bottle to give him a refill.

'No thanks, Jack. I think it would be safer if I ordered a large beer instead.' He sat up in his chair and stretched his back, letting out an involuntary groan.

'Alexander,' said Gracie.

'No, it's Barney.'

'No, I mean the Alexander Technique. Best thing for a sore back.'

'Oh, is that where you balance books on your head and walk over hot coals or something?'

She giggled, suddenly ten years younger, like Marilyn. 'Ha, I've not tried that one. No, when you're out walking, try imagining a space behind your head and just let your head move back into it. You'll be amazed.'

Barney's beer arrived and the conversation stayed light as the performers discussed various gigs they'd done together, the outrageous lies they'd told drunken guests about their characters' lives, the great and the good they'd seen behaving badly.

'It's OK for guys like Jack here,' Gracie said, cutting the reminiscences short. 'If he keeps himself in shape, he can carry on being Charlie for a long time to come. But everyone has only one picture of Marilyn and let's face it, I'm already struggling to match it.' She ignored the men's protests. 'It's only a matter of time before I start to look like some corseted bloody drag act. Then how do I pay the bills?'

Jack leant across, his chair tilting dangerously, put his arm around her shoulders and squeezed. 'Then you'll come and live with me, my precious, and we'll have the time of our lives. Our wonderful, glorious lives.'

She gave him a heavily sceptical look and pulled away, causing Jack to teeter on the brink of disaster until she gave him a push and he rocked back to upright, spilling not a drop of his wine. They laughed uproariously and Barney joined in, applauding Jack's performance, which the performer acknowledged with several curtain-call bows. Barney noticed the unappreciative looks from three Frenchmen at the adjacent table who looked like they were all too familiar with such loutish British behaviour.

When things calmed down, Jack tried to be sensible by asking how he was getting on with his inquiries. But Barney's mind was far away from the trivial matter of two house fires and he gave a non-committal answer.

'The reason I ask is that I was talking to a couple of people and for what it's worth, *da wud on da street* is that our lovely local hedge fund owner is in deep shit.'

Barney gave him a tell-me-more look.

'I mean, serious debt. Maybe enough to inadvertently spill petrol all over the place and drop a match.'

Barney nodded. 'Very interesting, Jack. You wouldn't happen to have the names of the people who told you this, I suppose?' He got a shake of the head and continued: 'Well, thanks, Jack. That's something that I might just tie in with something I'm looking at. You wouldn't have anything on the Fitzwilliams by any chance, would you - or even the small matter of who had Pieter Nel killed?'

'Pieter Nel? The guy shot in court? God, no. And not something I would want to know anything about.' He checked the glasses. 'Anyway, time for another bottle. And Barney, are you sticking with the beer?'

Barney emptied his glass and nodded. 'Yeah, best stick to this. One for the road.' When his phone went off, he knew who it would be.

'Shona, darlin'. Really sorry. I had to work and I just forgot.' The clink of glasses seemed to contradict him and he pictured Shona laughing in her Villefranche villa.

'No problem, big man. Just you enjoy yourself. We'll catch up tomorrow.' Some partners might have an edge to their voice in the circumstances but not her; he knew that she valued her own freedom too much to ever be possessive.

He was still smiling as he put his phone away.

'Ah, I know that look,' Gracie said.

* * *

By the time Barney opened the door of his top floor flat his body was demanding sleep and his mind was telling it to stop being so ridiculous.

He hung up his jacket, refusing to look at the contents of the inside pocket as he retrieved his phone. There was a missed call.

'Sorry, Ffiona. Not too late am I?'

'Hi Barney. No problem. Having a night in. But listen, I thought you were only down there to hold hands with flaky ex-pats. How come you're on the Nel murder?'

'I'm not. Just a favour for Jean-Luc. Any luck?'

'Afraid not. Not much to go on. And besides, if *she* was wearing any sort of disguise, she could just have well be a man, couldn't she?'

The same thought had occurred to Barney. 'Fair point. Didn't cause any problems did it, you running the search?'

'Actually, no. Bizarrely, they seemed quite pleased that you were helping the French. All very weird. But weird's the new normal here, these days.'

'Tell me about it. But, Ffiona, I know you've no doubt got a lot on but can I ask one more teensy weensy favour?'

Silence.

'Ha! I knew you wouldn't mind.' He then gave her the background on Charles Taylor-Smith and his fire insurance windfall. 'I'm told he's in serious debt and if that turns out to be true…'

'I get it,' she said. 'OK, I'll see what I can do tomorrow. Unless you want me to go back into the office right now?'

He smiled. She was allowed to be sarky. 'No, that's OK. Crack of dawn'll do.' He might have asked her about the office, her caseload, her life. But he was tired and neither of them was good at small talk, so he was happy to be able to end the call at that.

Besides he needed to get back to worrying.

9 - Connections

Thursday, July 10

Barney toyed with his coffee, noticing that Jean-Luc was otherwise engaged with his head down over his keyboard. The Frenchman appeared to have slept about as well as Barney had, which wasn't well at all.

All Barney had to do was wait for his phone to ring, get confirmation from Ffiona and then the pair of them could pay Mr Charles Taylor-Smith an early morning visit at the Westerling. Which is why he shouldn't have been startled when his phone started ringing then cursed when hot coffee spat out onto his hand.

'Ffiona! What a nice surprise. Didn't expect you this early. It can only be, what, seven-thirty with you?'

'Morning, sir. Yes, just in. But I have that information you asked for. Got a lot on today so I called a friend in financial crime last night and he gave me enough to go on.'

Barney shook his head in wonder. She'd only been based in Edinburgh for about a year but had built a network bigger than he'd ever had. No wonder they'd marked her out for great things. All he said was: 'OK, great. Shoot.'

'Well, I'm just about to email you but basically, he confirmed what you suspected. Big rumours in the City, liquidised assets, serious debt. When all his pals were cleaning up after Brexit, it looks like he managed to keep picking losers. But it'll all be in the email.'

'That's excellent, Ffiona. I'll look out for it. Thanks again. Sorry for dropping it on you like that.'

'I am only here to serve, o master.'

'Ha! Well, you dun good. Have a great day.'

The groan he got in response said the day might not be so great for her. But Barney now had what he needed and as he ended the call he saw that Jean-Luc had raised his head.

'Ffiona. She's just confirmed it. Hedgie's up to his neck.'

Jean-Luc seemed delighted. He shut down his computer and rose. 'Right then, Barney. Are you ready to visit one of our finest hotels?'

'Ready and willing. Let's go.'

Barney had always wanted to see inside the Westerling. Lifting a fraudster at the same time would be the icing on the cake.

They found their man in the foyer. 'I don't bloody-well believe it! Someone burns down my house and you come to arrest me. And with a damn Scottie in tow, to boot.' Charles Taylor-Smith was not pleased. And he didn't care who in the hotel's opulent marble interior knew it.

'Now, sir,' Jean-Luc said, calm yet firm, 'I'm sure that as a guest in our country you will agree to come along with us to answer a few questions in connection with your unfortunate fire. You are not under arrest, merely helping the police with their inquiries.'

The man was big and powerful but he was also overweight

and judging by the red tide now washing upwards from his neck he suffered from high blood pressure. Barney thought it must be hard to look indignant when you're wearing a silk safari suit. But Taylor-Smith finally seemed to realise his theatrics were wasted on the implacable Captain. Instead, he gave a hard shake of his jowls then barged between the two policemen and stomped off towards the door.

The doorman, professional despite his theatrical, multi-coloured costume, calmly took in the situation and wished the hotel guest a friendly *bonne journée*. The agitated Englishman only grunted then seemed to realise he would have to wait on the pavement. All he could do was to angrily shift his considerable weight from foot to foot while looking left and right along the palm-lined Promenade des Anglais, as if his limo was late.

'This way, Monsieur.' Jean-Luc had had his driver wait in a side street and Barney thought their passenger would be well advised to take a good long look around along the magnificent palm-lined Prom. The chances were that he would be deprived of such beauty for a long time.

It was only as they reached the junction, the Englishman leading the way as if he was in charge, that Barney noticed a taxi pull in to the hotel's impressive entrance. He did a double take when he saw the passengers get out. First, Peter Fitzwilliam and then, accepting his helping hand, his good lady wife, Clarinda.

So that's why hedgie was in such an all-fired hurry to get the hell away from the hotel. He was meeting the Fitzwilliams. Curiouser and curiouser.

He tapped Jean-Luc's arm and nodded in their direction. 'And *that*,' he said, 'is the Fitzwilliams.'

The Frenchman grinned. 'Your other rich friends? Ha! The plot thickens, eh Barney? But first, let's get Taylor-Smith back. We will speak to them later.'

Barney felt that old tingle as he climbed into the car. Now what would link the Fitzwilliam fire to hedgie's insurance fraud four days later? Normally the question would be intriguing, but Barney had been banking on a quick result, with the French police taking over prosecution of Taylor-Smith, leaving him free to tackle his *mission impossible.* 'Sod it,' he said out loud.

'Everything OK, Barney.'

'Eh, oh fine. Sorry. Yeah, let's go.'

Jean-Luc got Taylor-Smith processed and safely tucked up in the cells to await his lawyer then suggested that they head straight back out to call on the Fitzwilliams in Villefranche. 'They've probably gone straight back home. Must have been a nasty shock to hear that their friend just left with the police.'

Barney agreed.

Half an hour later, as the sun beat down from a pure blue sky, they pulled up outside the squat box of a building.

* * *

Peter Fitzwilliam looked crestfallen at the sight of a French police car at his gate and as he let them inside, the movie man seemed even smaller than Barney remembered. Clarinda tried a bright welcome for her unexpected guests. 'Oh, what a lovely surprise,' she trilled. But she appeared to then read her husband's face because her smile broke and her worry showed through.

Barney did the introductions but was happy to sit back and

87

let Jean-Luc take the lead. They both knew it wouldn't take long and it didn't. Jean-Luc explained that their hedge fund friend was currently helping police with their inquiries and wondered if they could throw any light on the recent fires at their two properties.

Clarinda gamely tried to bluff but Peter took her hand as they sat close together on the facing white couch and said: 'Darling, it's no use, I'm afraid.' He then turned to Barney and said they wanted to call their lawyer.

The Scotsman tried not to look surprised. 'Well, you've asked for a lawyer, so I imagine my colleague here won't be able to question you too much in the meantime, but for what it's worth, I think it would do you no harm at all if you were to co-operate and at least tell me why you'd arranged to meet Mr Taylor-Smith at his hotel today.'

The couple exchanged a worried look. Then Peter said: 'Well, obviously it was best that he wasn't seen here.'

Barney sensed in the momentary pause that Jean-Luc was as confused as he was but he played along: 'No, of course. But I think it would count in your favour if you were to explain how you came to be involved with him.'

The couple stared into each other's eyes, seeming to ask the same question of each other, while Barney bit his tongue and hoped he had said the right thing.

'OK,' Peter Fitzwilliam said at last. He turned to face the Scotsman. 'OK, I'll tell you everything.' His wife hung her head to focus on the clasped hands wrestling each other in her lap.

'I want to make it clear right from the start that we had nothing whatsoever to do with the theft itself.'

Barney thought *what the hell?* but said: 'I understand. Go

on.'

'Well, you may not understand but investing in movies is a high stakes game and I'm afraid we made a couple of very bad bets. Which put us in, em, shtuck. Financially, I mean. That's why meeting Pieter Nel at the party seemed heaven sent.'

Barney sensed Jean-Luc tense and tried to displace his own shock by nodding his head, as if he knew exactly what the man was talking about.

'Well, to cut a long story short, we knew that Pieter had a bit of a reputation and somehow or other he seemed to have found out about our predicament. So, as I say, one thing led to another and a couple of days later we had a meeting with him and came to our agreement.'

Barney fought to stay calm. 'That agreement being?'

'Well, that we would take the paintings, of course. Turn them into cash, fence them, as you would say. We've got many very wealthy friends in the States, you see, people outside Pieter's circle, who wouldn't ask too many questions.'

Barney was struggling. 'The paintings?' He cursed inwardly when he saw the man's confusion.

But Jean-Luc had seen it too. 'Yes, yes, we know,' he said. 'The paintings from the Musée des Beaux-Arts last year. We know Nel carried out the heist but not what he did with the paintings.'

Peter Fitzwilliam turned to his wife with a rueful grin on his face. She looked up and responded with a hopeless shrug.

He explained: 'That's the problem, you see. He says they've all gone up in smoke.'

'Taylor-Smith? So he was in on it too?'

'Yes. He's a friend. Was. He was holding on to them until we could get them out of the country. But then, the fire. And according to him, they're all gone.'

'But you don't believe him?'

The man swung his head from side to side. 'Well, we don't really know for sure. It's just such shit timing. But to tell you the truth, I'm kind of glad it's all over. We're movie-makers, not crooks. Wish we'd never met that damned Pieter Nel, rest his soul.'

The silence stretched as he put his arm around his wife and she sobbed quietly into his shoulder.

The two policemen exchanged a guarded look. 'Right,' said Jean-Luc, standing. 'I must thank you for being so co-operative. You will appreciate that I now need you both to come to the station to make formal statements. Your lawyer can meet us there.

* * *

Back in the office the two policemen sat at their desks, coffees in hand, staring blankly at each other. Then Barney said what they were both thinking. 'Well, that was some fucking morning.'

'Unbelievable,' said Jean-Luc. 'It looks like your case and my case have suddenly got married. We've solved the gallery heist and maybe given me a motive for Nel's murder. And we've probably solved both of your fires.'

Barney waited for the explanation.

'Bear with me,' said the Frenchman, 'but the King would be furious if some outsider carried out a heist like that on his patch. And he wouldn't allow a bunch of clumsy amateurs to get away with the proceeds. His reputation, his authority, would be trashed.'

'So you think he found out about Nel and the Fitzwilliams?'

'It's a theory. He might not have had Nel's name at first but he would surely have heard if someone was trying to move such hot property. A little fire to concentrate the minds of a couple of upstart incomers called the Fitzwilliams would be nothing to him.'

Barney was nodding. 'And as we know, the Fitzwilliams would roll over and cough up Nel's name without too much trouble. But what you're suggesting is that Nel's murder was all about the King asserting his authority? That the theft gave him a motive for having Nel executed, simply for operating in his exclusive domain?'

'As I say, Barney, it's a theory. But it sounds just like the man to choose the most public and difficult of settings. He would have meant it as a clear warning to others, proving that he's still the King and that he can get to anyone, anywhere, any time he choses.'

'So what about the paintings? If you're right that the King knew all about them, and that he wouldn't let a bunch of Brits hold onto them, then Taylor-Smith had lost his chance to make some serious cash. Leaving him no option but to torch his mansion for the insurance money. And at the same time get the Fitzwilliams off his back by claiming that the paintings went up in smoke too. Mmm, good theory.'

But Jean-Luc seemed to be less convinced by his own argument. 'The problem is that this doesn't explain why the King turned up at the party.'

Barney thought for a moment. 'Yes, you're right. It must mean that he was still trying to squeeze them for the paintings. That he believed the Brits were all trying to con him. That they'd stashed them somewhere out of his reach, for later.'

'Mmm,' said Jean-Luc.

10 - Merde Happens

It was a tried and tested technique, apparently as familiar in France as it was in Scotland. First, separate the suspects and then alternate the interviews until one coughs up something useful against the other. In this case, Barney was effectively only an observer but it was an education to see Jean-Luc in action.

True, the Fitzwilliams had been easy meat. Even with their lawyer in attendance, they seemed relieved to tell all, or virtually all.

In their formal statements they failed to repeat their admission that they knew about the robbery in advance. Their lawyer had presumably advised them that they could deny setting up the heist with Nel on the basis that the only person who could contradict them was lying in the mortuary.

But they were sticking to their claim that they handed all eight paintings to their hedgie pal. The juge d'instruction could surely be convinced to charge them with handling stolen goods.

Just where Serge Leroy, aka the King, fitted into it, they wouldn't say, claiming that the godfather of crime in the region had merely been a surprise guest at the soirée attended by Barney. Jean-Luc felt sure that their story would change in time.

But now it was again Taylor-Smith's turn. Jean-Luc had obviously had enough of the man's dismissive manner. The ignorance of his English lawyer hadn't helped. 'Look, you have two choices. We know the fire was set deliberately, so it was either started by you for the three million in insurance money or it was the work of Serge Leroy as punishment for your fencing the proceeds on his patch. So what's it to be?'

Barney appreciated the leap Jean-Luc was taking, trying to unsettle the Englishman, and spectated from his seat alongside as the exasperated suspect rolled his head back and stared at the ceiling. But his lawyer was now whispering to him and Taylor-Smith took on a look of cunning before finally responding.

'Well, Captain, it seems that I should be frank with you and confess; confess that I'm the victim in all this.' He waited for a reaction. Getting none, he flicked a look at his lawyer then continued. 'Right. This is what happened. The first I knew of any artworks was when friends of mine approached me about some paintings they wanted to sell.'

'The Fitzwilliams, sir?' asked Jean-Luc.

'Em, yes. You knew about that, did you?'

'Oh yes, we've had a long chat with the Fitzwilliams. They're sitting right next door.'

The hedge fund owner looked less sure of himself. 'Oh, OK. Well, you'll know this then; that they wanted me to help find a home for these bloody paintings.'

'And for you to hold them, all eight of them, in your mansion?'

'Ah well, that's what they wanted. But of course, I couldn't have anything to do with such a thing.'

'You're saying you never received the paintings?'

'No, God, no. The place lay empty half the time. Why would I want a bunch of supposedly valuable paintings lying around? And as for me supposedly torching my own place for the insurance cash... Well, come on. Would I? Really? No, I had nothing to with it. I have no idea who did it. Presumably these bloody nationalists who want us all to piss off and leave them in peace.'

'So you also deny any knowledge of, or connection with Serge Leroy, also known as the King?'

'Absolutely. Never 'eard of 'im.' He seemed pleased with his posh attempt at a Cockney accent and sat back as if that ended the story.

'In which case, Mr Taylor-Smith, I will end the interview here and resume later. I should advise you and your lawyer that at this stage in the proceedings it seems likely that you will be charged at least with handling stolen goods to the value of many millions. Further charges in relation to insurance fraud may well follow.'

Jean-Luc rose. Barney paused to enjoy the suspect's discomfort then followed the Frenchman out of the interview room.

In the corridor, Jean-Luc was matter-of-fact. 'That's fine for now, Barney. We'll get more later, once they have time to stew. They'll sing like canaries.'

Barney smiled to himself as they walked back to the office, vaguely registering the sound of the hedgie's protests as he was led to the cells.

Fleur Dupont was on the phone as they entered, her face screwed up in concentration, her pen scribbling on a notepad. She hung up. 'DI Mains, that was the hospital. They've just had a woman admitted who is asking for you. Quite badly hurt. But conscious enough to give them your name.'

Barney felt the blood drain from his face. *Shona!* But that wasn't the name Dupont gave him. No, not Shona but Bridget.

'Shit! I'd better get over there.' Barney was almost back out of the door before thinking to add: 'A friend. Must be bad.' he said, worrying that Jean-Luc might remember the lawyer's name from court and feeling like a shit for his deception.

Then he was gone, knowing that this must be connected to last night's meeting at the lawyer's office. Which got him thinking that someone might also know about Nel's poison chalice, Barney's unwanted legacy.

The velo-taxi got him to the hospital in minutes. By the time he found her private room, he'd been prepared to see a very different woman to the striking red-haired specimen he'd met the evening before, but he couldn't even recognise the patient beneath the bandages and tubes.

'Shit, Bridget, you poor thing.' He pulled a chair to the bedside and gingerly took her one free hand and held it between his. She managed only a dry groan. 'It's OK, you don't have to talk now. Just get better.'

But the lawyer was having none of it. 'Barney…' She was struggling but was apparently determined. 'I need to warn you. Two men, big, older guys. Last night. Heard them downstairs. Saw them at the safe. Attacked.'

'OK, OK, take your time. I get it. Someone has got wind of Nel's will. Someone who must be scared shitless about what it contains.'

She tried to nod but froze with pain.

'It's OK. I understand. You wanted to warn me. If they know about it then they might well know that I've got what they

96

want. Don't worry, I'll be careful. But Bridget, can I ask if they got into the safe?'

'Safe empty. Barney, sorry. Can't remember if I told them anything.'

He patted her hand: 'It doesn't matter. I'll assume they're on to me and I'll be prepared. All you have to do is get better and get out of here.'

She was failing from the effort and was almost asleep when she said what sounded like: 'Promise. Just get the fuckers!'

The best thing about hospitals is leaving them and Barney was glad to get back out into the sunshine and the everyday sounds of people and traffic. He found himself walking back towards headquarters, the questions spinning around in his head.

It couldn't have been a coincidence. They had either followed him to Bridget's office or were already staking it out. Probably the latter, he thought, because she, not some irrelevant Scots cop, was the obvious link to Nel. And if Nel was right in his letter that someone must have found out about his plans for a ghostwriter, then they might reasonably have assumed that his lawyer held his secrets. But they never acted until they saw Barney at her office. So it was his visit which sparked the attack. Maybe they panicked because they thought the British police would beat them to those secrets. Whoever the hell *they* were!

He felt that he was no further forward by the time he reached base. Except that he now knew he had to be careful. Whoever these guys were, they didn't mess about and if they showed no mercy in attacking a lone woman lawyer then the chances were that they were acting for an equally ruthless boss, one who had power and would do anything to keep it. As Barney entered the secure police headquarters he also realised that because of his subterfuge, he couldn't ask for Jean-Luc's help. He was on his own. *Great,* he thought.

He was still distant when he entered the office. The two French officers looked up, concern on their faces. 'What? Oh, right. Yes, she's fine. Well, not fine but she'll live. Nasty accident but she's in good hands. No worries.'

'That's good Barney,' said Jean-Luc. 'We were worried. But now we can move on, yes? You don't need some time?'

Barney muttered that he was fine as he waved a dismissive hand.

'In which case, there is still time for you and Dupont here to keep your appointment. With Aubert?'

He'd totally forgotten. 'No, of course. Fine. Ready to rock.' What he was thinking was: *Shit! This is all I fucking need.*

What Dupont was thinking, he couldn't tell, but he reckoned it was probably something along the lines of: *All this action going on and I'm stuck with a bloody Scotsman who doesn't know his arse from his elbow and now I've got to babysit him while he meets an old tosspot of a politician with delusions of grandeur.*

She sent Barney a comradely smile.

He responded with a tilt of the head and a raise of the eyebrows which said: *Shit happens.*

11 - Mister President

The drive to Aubert's place near Fréjus hadn't started well. Dupont had snatched the car keys off the garage hook and said: 'I'll drive.' To Barney's continuing surprise, she then drove impatiently, without a word, all the way through the western outskirts of Nice. And only once they were cruising on the motorway did he choose his moment to break the ice.

'Look, Dupont. Fleur. I know you're not happy to be lumbered with me. But you have to take that up with your boss. I didn't ask for this, any more than you did.'

She sighed and glanced across. 'This Aubert. He's a waste of time. He's just an old man living a fantasy that he is going to be the next President of France. Why we're doing this I have no idea.'

'I get that. But he asked to speak to me and Jean-Luc said I should go. He apparently has information about these home attacks.'

She shook her head. 'If he has anything useful to say, he can tell the Police Nationale and not a…'

'Stupid Scotsman?' he suggested.

'I was going to say a British policeman with no authority in France.'

Barney laughed. 'Well, I'll settle for that.'

She suddenly slowed to match the reduced speed limit on a steep downhill section near Cannes and the changed pace seemed to help her mood.

All the vehicles around them suddenly dropped their speed too, as if everyone was under the command of the same sci-fi movie director. 'This'd never happen back home,' he said. 'You French are so obedient.'

She flashed him an angry look. Then she laughed, seeming to have picked up on his needling sarcasm. 'Not so obedient. Just not stupid. Break the limit here and it's an automatic fine.'

'Oh, that's alright then,' he said, then resumed watching the world go by.

It wasn't a long drive but by the time they arrived, Barney felt they had at least achieved a mutual tolerance.

The sat-nav led them up a dusty track to a grand old farmhouse. A blue and white flag hung limply from a flagpole as if wearied by the heat. Four men in shirtsleeves were playing pétanque on the gravel in front. Two of them broke off and ran to either side of the car. They were wearing guns in shoulder holsters.

Dupont had her window down and was showing her police ID card to one of the men, a heavy-jowled type with greying hair above a sun-dried face. The face nodded and its owner opened her door. Barney smiled at the second armed man now peering through his door window. He was a lookalike for his chum. He stepped back and gestured for him to get out. Was it Barney's imagination or did the man recognise him?

He had no time to ask because the man they were there to meet had appeared at the farmhouse door.

'Mr Mains. How good of you to come all this way to see me. That's OK, boys.'

If the *boys* had perhaps seen better days, their boss cut a fine figure despite Dupont's caricature. Old he may be, but he didn't look it. Henri Aubert's wavy silver hair framed a virtually unlined, almost youthful, face and it was giving Barney the warmest of smiles. The man was tall, with broad shoulders from which the jacket of his casual fawn suit loosely hung. As he strode towards Barney, he looked to have the gait of a man half his age, whatever that was. When Barney went to meet him, Aubert's grip was strong, his look compelling.

'A pleasure to meet you Monsieur Aubert,' Barney said, conscious that Fleur Dupont appeared to have been sidelined. He turned to introduce her but his host had an arm around Barney's shoulders and was leading him to the side of the house.

'Come Barney. See my beautiful garden. It's always easier to talk outside under the sun, is it not?'

He had the accent of someone who could speak perfect English but preferred to smooth it over with mellifluous French slurs. Barney thought *Aznavour.* What he said was: 'Where I come from, we're more likely to be running inside, out of the rain.'

The Frenchman laughed. 'Ah, but Scotland is a beautiful country. I know it well, your malt whisky, your golf courses. You are very lucky.'

Barney nodded politely. For him, golf was a good walk spoiled. And judging by the fabulous grounds around the ageing farmhouse's rustic exterior, his host appreciated the freedom of the great outdoors too. 'You have a beautiful place here. But is there any reason you've not invited my colleague to join us?'

Aubert raised his shoulders and spread his hands as they

strolled down a palm-lined path towards a small fountain. 'I don't like to be rude but Barney, I wanted us both to be able to talk freely.'

Barney waited for him to continue but he merely signalled for them to take the two metal folding seats beside a fountain, beneath the welcome shade of old vines. The Scotsman remembered what he'd read about the man online. He'd made his money in shipping and then grown it into a fortune on the world's stock markets.

'Please,' said Aubert, waiting for his guest to sit first. From behind the house a man appeared unbidden with a large trayful of refreshments. He set the drinks down between them on a roughly-carved block of stone while the feeble flow of the fountain struggled against the relentless sun.

'Thank you, Paul. We'll help ourselves. Barney, we have white wine, a rather nice one, some orange juice and some iced tea. Which would you prefer?'

'Well I'm afraid I'll have to pass on the wine. But I've become a big fan of iced tea. And though this is all very pleasant...'

'You want to know exactly why the hell I've brought you here. Of course.' Aubert poured himself an orange juice before continuing. 'Well, as my secretary will have said on the phone, it is about these bothersome fires and house invasions that have plagued my region.'

'And particularly the two fires I'm investigating?'

'Actually, no. I mean, this is what brought you to our attention. But there's a much bigger picture.'

Barney squinted at him. 'You'll have to explain.'

'Look, I'll lay my cards on the table. I don't know how much you know about the Avance Party and our path to winning the next election here. But this catalogue of incidents has the potential to do us great harm, because everyone is assuming it is we who are behind it all.'

'And it's not?'

Aubert put his right hand on his heart. 'I swear, no. You see, we believe we will win at the ballot box - *fair and square,* as you say. Why would we want to destabilise everything and frighten people into voting the same old way they've always done?'

Barney thought for a moment. 'But surely by targeting the hated incomers you'd gain votes, not lose them.'

'But only from the *extreme* right,' said the Frenchman. 'And that's not our territory any more. No, the immigration issue is a problem everywhere and must be tackled but I'll have nothing to do with these idiot slogans like *Brits Out.'*

Aubert took a swig of his drink then put his glass down and leaned in towards his guest.

'During your career, have you ever known a series of incidents like these fires and protests which have resulted in not one injury or death? You see, they're being careful to make it look like a popular uprising and that's what it's becoming. But they're making very sure that no-one's hurt because that would make people stop and think.'

'Your point being?'

His host laughed. 'I like this Scottish directness. My point, as I believe you already understand, is that such widespread crimes can only be possible if they are co-ordinated by a massive organisation with its tentacles throughout the region.'

Barney looked away, apparently scoffing at the very idea, even though it was an explanation he had himself been resisting. His tactic seemed to have worked because Aubert now sharply extended both hands, the fingers stiffly spread, imploring, his face now lined and blotchy, showing its age. 'No, no, listen! The logic is inescapable. Who has a finger in every pie? Who has the authority to order such a campaign? Who, tell me, would benefit most from chaos here, a breakdown in law and order?'

Barney had been asking himself the same question but it seemed that they had come to different conclusions.

Aubert leaned back, smiling as if he had the answer to life, the universe and everything. 'Why, criminals, of course.'

Barney tried not to show surprise. 'Which in this neck of the woods could only mean one person, Serge Leroy.'

Aubert shrugged and spread his two hands, palms up, meaning: *You said it!*

Barney wore a face of exaggerated disbelief. 'So, let's see if I've got this right. You're saying that Avance has nothing to do with these attacks and that it's all down to the King. And all the King's men, presumably.'

'I know you are kidding me, Barney. But you now see why you, as the man investigating these attacks on our poor British cousins, need to know what's really going on?'

Barney dropped his head, momentarily taking in the proposition that, with Nel's *mission impossible* already weighing heavily on his mind, he might now have been handed the challenge of nailing criminal royalty.

And he'd thought his job here was going to be boring.

He managed to push both thoughts to the back of his mind by the time Aubert abruptly signalled that their meeting was over and beckoned one of his *boys* to escort Barney back to the car.

But his host had a parting shot. 'Just be aware, mister policeman, that whatever you are told about us by anyone

- anyone among the living or the dead - nothing will stop us on our road to power. Our great destiny will not be denied.'

As he was led back towards the car, Barney mused on these words. Was this what Aubert had really brought him here to say? Had the apparently suave politician exposed a scarily messianic side because he feared Barney in some way? What a strange phrase - *the living or the dead.* Did Aubert somehow know about Nel's legacy? Was it two of his *boys* who'd attacked the lawyer? Maybe the man who'd seemed to recognise Barney earlier was one of them, having seen Barney at Bridget's office. Maybe.

His minder left him in sight of the car without a word. Barney had been sent on his way. And the stony face on the young policewoman who awaited him inside was no comfort. She never said a word as he climbed in beside her but he could see that she was furious with him for excluding her from the meeting. She promptly proved the point by sending the gravel spitting behind them as she spun the wheels and took off toward the main road.

Barney braced one hand against the dash and tried to anticipate the next manoeuvre. It was her angry silence which was the hardest to take, however. Which was why the sound of his phone ringing soon after they joined the eastbound motorway came as a welcome diversion.

'Barney, Jean-Luc. It sounds like you're in the car. I take it Dupont's at the wheel?'

'Yes, no sweat. She's having a great time.'

'Oh, OK. Well, I just wanted to update you. Your hedgie wants to make a statement. And I thought if you're on your way back, you might want to be here for that.'

'Thanks Jean-Luc. That's good of you. But just carry on. So

long as we get a result, I'm happy.'

'No problem, my friend. I'll let you know how it goes later.'

When Barney ended the call, he looked across at Dupont. 'I don't know how much you heard but that was Jean-Luc and he says you've got to protect me with your life. So I'd really appreciate it if you would stop driving like a maniac.'

Dupont seemed to relax and slowed down. 'I'm sorry. That bastard Aubert just riled me.'

He offered a sympathetic smile. The best she could manage was a sharp nod before turning her focus back to the windscreen, which at least allowed Barney the peace to think about the bizarre meeting he'd just left. So Aubert, the supposed firebrand of the right, wanted everyone to believe he was all sweetness and light, while all the bad things in the world were down to the King. Not members of a police force which Nel had reckoned was *rotten to the core*.

As the road began to rise, he could see the far hills through her window. A wide sweep of the landscape was engulfed in swirling dark clouds of smoke, their undersides aglow.

He became aware again of the pleasant smell of burning wood which he now remembered had also hung in the air at Aubert's place. He thought about the devastating impact these damned wildfires must be having on the region, on forests, on villages, on lives. There had already been several deaths. And most probably there would be more.

Just then a low-flying aircraft appeared from the right, somewhere towards Antibes, heading straight for the hills. It had to be one of the constant flights of water-bombers which scooped up tonnes of sea water then hauled their cargo inland to dump it on the advancing enemy. They were all that lay between the heavily-populated areas and devastation.

12 - Lot to Digest

He knew he probably should have dropped in to see Jean-Luc but it had been a long day and he didn't need the guilt of maintaining his pretence. Dupont didn't complain when he asked her to drop him at Nice Gare, where there would be only a little time to kill before the next train to Villefranche.

Within half an hour, he was strolling along the seafront of his favourite place in the world. He half expected to see Shona mooring the *Bonnie Fechter,* having just returned in time for dinner after one of her regular sails around Cap Ferrat. But the little yacht was unattended on its mooring and he calculated that she must have made it back home to the villa by now. He thought to go straight there but he was enjoying too much the calming effect of the still water to tackle the steep climb through the village and so claimed one of the quayside tables which hadn't yet been set for evening meals. He ordered a large beer and merely sat there, thinking of absolutely nothing.

The cold liquid was just what the doctor ordered and as he put his half-empty glass back on the table, he pulled out his phone. 'I have a table at the waterside and they're just about to set it for dinner. Any chance I could tempt you down?' She shrieked something about him taking her for granted and called him some choice names. All of which he took as a *yes* and in no time at all, his empty glass replaced by a chilling bottle of white, he saw her striding along the seafront towards him in a plain white summer dress with a little yellow bag over her shoulder. Her outfit showed off the tan on her slim body. And she was blond again.

'Hi, big yin,' she said, as she reached up and gave him a big kiss.

'Hi, wee yin. Lookin' a bit gorgeous, by the way.' He gave her a hug.

'Hey, steady on. I've not had my dinner yet.'

'Ah well, you've come to the right place.' They sat and he poured. 'Here's lookin' at you, kid.'

Shona had indeed been sailing. Around the Cap. Not much wind though, and it had all been a bit too tame for her. Back when she'd just settled here and learned to sail, she'd deliberately bought a small yacht because she wanted to feel the power of the wind - while being able to handle it on her own with a minimum of gadgetry. And despite her riches, the *Bonnie Fechter* had become her most prized possession.

'The good news is, we're about to get some weather coming in. So maybe we can get out together sometime soon?'

'Count on it. As soon as I can get away.' Barney said. A waiter delivered the grilled squid starters he'd ordered and they tucked in hungrily.

'I'm sorry, big man. I never asked. How have you been getting on?'

He said it was a long story and she said she had all night. So he gave her chapter and verse; the lawyer, the letter, the envelope, the stolen paintings, the attack on the lawyer and then his afternoon with a man who expected to become France's next president. He even mentioned the persisting impression that one of the president's men had recognised him. As if sharing the thought would explain it.

'And the envelope? You've given it to Jean-Luc, right?'

'Well, not exactly.'

She dropped her cutlery on the table. 'You're not serious. You're carrying it around with you? Even after this lawyer woman was nearly killed. Are you mad?' She broke off when she became aware of the waiter hovering at her side.

'There is a problem, mademoiselle?'

'Oh, no, no, everything's fine and this is really lovely.' She ate a mouthful to prove it and she waited until the man left.

In a lower voice, she said: 'Are you crazy? The woman who gave you it is almost killed and you go walking around with it as if nothing's happened? You've got to speak to the police.'

'Shona, come on. I'm careful. The thing is, according to Nel the police are corrupt to the core.'

'But not your friend. Not Jean-Luc.'

'Listen, I'd trust Jean-Luc with my life. But he would have to report it and I can't risk someone higher up trashing the whole thing.'

She sat back, reading his face. She could always tell. 'And besides,' she said knowingly, 'you've already opened it, haven't you?'

'Well, yes. I had to really. When I was at the railway station.'

She sat up straight. 'And?'

'And it contained a key.'

'God's sake, Barney. It contained a key. That's it? A key to what?'

'Well, that's the funny thing. I recognised it at once. I had one just like it when I first came here, before I had somewhere to live. I took a locker at the station.'

'And don't tell me, you've opened the box.'

'Yeah, Pandora's got nothing on me, ha!'

'Never mind laughing, you bloody nutcase. What was inside?'

'Bit of a let-down, really. All I got was a cryptic note written on rice paper which Nel actually told me I had to swallow once I'd, er, digested the contents. Which, before you ask, simply said that what he called his *treasure trove* was stowed somewhere safe. In some ruin above Saint-Jeannet. Le Castellet it's called.'

'I know it,' she said, surprised and enthused. 'Great area for rock climbing.'

'I was afraid you'd say that. You know what I'm like with heights. But whatever Nel has in store for me, it's in that ruin.'

She tilted her head and peered into his eyes. 'Please, tell me you're not going there on your own.'

He thought about how to put it to her but there was no easy way. 'Shona, Nel specifically left that key for me for a reason and I just can't risk this stuff being buried by one of Jean-Luc's crooked colleagues.'

She said nothing and they wordlessly finished the remnants of their starters. The plates had only just been removed when she threw her serviette on the table. 'Right! You don't like heights and you don't know your way around Saint-Jeannet…'

'Absolutely no way. Sorry Shona but you're simply not coming and that's an end to it.'

'Look, Barney, all I'm proposing is that we drive up there tomorrow. I point you in the right direction and you go off treasure hunting.'

He smiled a grudging smile. 'Listen, Shona, I don't want to spoil a nice night by arguing, so can we just leave it until later?'

Their seafood platter arrived and the impressive spread got the kind of reaction the previously-concerned waiter seemed to appreciate.

She started to reach for an oyster but paused. 'So you're going to manage to eat this alright, are you?' She had a mischievous look on her face. 'I mean, after all that rice paper. You did eat it like he asked, I take it?'

He dismissed the idea with a shake of the head. 'Och, that only happens in spy movies. I chucked it in a bin.'

She laughed and they tucked in. He was never going to admit that he actually did what they do in spy movies. Or that he'd had a niggling feeling at the railway station that someone had been watching him do it.

13 - The King

Friday, July 11

Mornings had never been his best time and when he finally stumbled onto the terrace, the coffee was cold.

The sun however was already hot and Barney stood by the terrace's big round table for a moment, arms extended in supplication to the life-giving rays. 'Why didn't you wake me?'

'I tried. You were dead to the world.' He slumped into a chair and as if by magic, Hermione, the maid, appeared and put a fresh coffee pot in front of him.

'You know, I could get used to this.' He told Hermione she was a lifesaver then leaned over and gave Shona a peck on the cheek. 'And you must be..?'

'Aye, that's me, the lassie from last night, you drunken sod.'

'I resemble that remark,' he mumbled as he poured his coffee, reassured by the sight of her naturally dark hair; it helped dull his nightmare image of her as a blond policewoman pointing a sniper's rifle straight at him, while two of the president's men applauded from the court balcony.

'Well, now that you've honoured us with your presence,

sire, I have news. If you have a wee look out one of the front windows you will find that we appear to have a couple of visitors. Sitting in a car outside, in the shade.'

'Shit,' he said, looking round, as if he could see anything from there. 'Don't tell me Jean-Luc's running a taxi service now.'

'Well if he is, I wouldn't complain. At least you'd be safe. You need protecting from yourself.'

He let that one pass, preferring to concentrate on attaining full consciousness. Not much later, proof of life was the cleared platter of pastries and an empty coffee pot.

'Right,' he said, standing. 'I'm off to get dressed for the mountains. What do you suggest?'

'Knowing you, I'd say a crash helmet and medical insurance.'

'Ha, very funny.'

Once upstairs, Barney found his phone and checked the time. Still only nine-thirty but he knew Jean-Luc would be wondering where he was. He dialled the office number.

'Barney, I hope you've had a good night?'

'Hi Jean-Luc. I'm sorry. I was totally shattered yesterday and just headed straight to Shona's. Which I guess you figured out.'

'Figured out? No. What do you mean?'

Barney paused. 'Oh, nothing. Just thought you would have realised, when I didn't appear. Sorry, I should have said.'

'That's OK, Barney. But will you be in soon?'

'Actually, Jean-Luc, unless you need me urgently, I wasn't planning to be in until the afternoon. I wanted to speak to the staff at the Fitzwilliams' place and as it's just along the road...' He hated lying to his friend. But how could he explain that members of his beloved Police Nationale, perhaps friends,

113

could be subversives? And for all Barney knew, there might be two of them sitting outside right now.

But Jean-Luc seemed unconcerned. 'It's OK, Barney. I'll see you later. I'll let you know how we get on.'

'Sorry?'

'Oh yes, you don't know. I'm seeing the juge d'instruction this morning. After Taylor-Smith's confession. We're throwing the book at him.'

Barney cringed. How could he have forgotten to ask about hedgie's new statement? He wanted to say something but he just couldn't. He'd started in a lie and he had to follow through. 'Oh, that's great news,' he said. 'I'll catch up with you in the office.'

'Yes, my friend. I look forward to it. And to hear how you got on with Monsieur Aubert. Dupont was not happy that he showed her no respect.'

'I'm sorry about that, Jean-Luc. It was out of order. But I'll fill you in later.' Barney had never felt like such a shit.

Back downstairs, he rejoined Shona. 'Well, Jean-Luc clearly didn't know anything about those guys outside. So God knows who they are. But Shona, you know, I've been thinking. We're talking about going up to Saint-Jeannet to collect whatever *treasure* Nel stashed there. But what's the point? I mean, I can't hand it over to the French police and it's pretty clear from our minders outside that someone wants me to know that they're right on my tail. So, say I go and get my little bequest. What then?'

Shona looked confused. 'But whatever it is, you've got to go up there and get it at some stage.'

'Yes, but why now? Look, whatever Nel's left for me, it's not gold but information; information that he claims will name names and uncover corruption and wrongdoing on a grand scale. No, there's absolutely no point me bringing it back down here and then having to guard it from all comers. First, I need to have a way to get the information out, out into the world.'

'Such as?'

'Well, don't quote me, but the press have their uses.'

'The press? Seriously. Who the heck can you trust in that parcel of rogues? Why not just fire it out, whatever it is, on social media? Let the whole world see it.'

'Ha! I know the internet has been good to you, Shona. It's where you made your disgustingly huge pile of dosh. But the chances are it would be taken as a hoax and brushed off by the guilty as a pack of lies. Though more likely it would just sink like a stone in the morass of information overload out there. No, it needs a reputable source. There might be a way. But I need to think it through.'

'Well, Barney, my darling man, get thinking. And if we're not going into the hills, what do you propose to do right now?'

He thought for a moment then smiled. 'I'm going outside to introduce myself to our guests.'

She was horrified at first but then she grinned. 'Well, I'll say this much: it's never dull around you.'

Barney stood, leant over and kissed her on the lips. 'Shona, darlin', that's the best thing anyone's ever said to me. But now I've got to be dull and boring and get dressed for the office.'

He was ready to go half an hour later, resolved to facing Jean-Luc but unsure how he was going to play it. First however, he was looking forward to taking the initiative by confronting the two men outside.

Their car was an old Merc, possibly vintage, in highly-polished black and chrome. It was pointing towards him in the exclusive street, which was lined not only with trees but also security cameras. The ever-alert electronic eyes let the wealthy sleep easy and did no harm to Barney's self-confidence as he prepared to confront two men, possibly the thugs who brutally attacked the lawyer.

They saw him coming. And through the windscreen, Barney could tell that these were not ageing heavies like the neanderthals he'd seen at Aubert's place but fit-looking young black guys who might be twins.

The driver's smile flashed as he casually opened his door and got out. Tall, athletic, twenties, in a white polo shirt, grey shorts and flip-flops. Not Barney's idea of a strong-arm man.

'Bonjour, Monsieur,' said the driver, 'Comment allez-vous?'

'Good, I'm doing fine, thanks. But you seem to know me and I don't know who the hell you are or why you're sitting outside my friend's house.'

'Forgive me, Monsieur. I am Stefan. Pleased I meet you, Monsieur Mains.' His English was laboured but his manner unsettlingly charming in a moment when Barney remained ready for trouble.

'Pleased to meet you too, Stefan. But you haven't answered my question.'

'Ah, Monsieur. I am sorry. We have been sent by our boss to invite you for tea.'

Barney thought for a moment then laughed. These were the nicest thugs he'd ever met.

'Well, that's helluva kind of you, and him. Assuming your boss is a *him?*'

'Mais, oui. Pardon. Yes, he is Mr Leroy.'

The name hung in the air. 'You don't mean Serge Leroy, by

any chance?'

The young man was nodding, the sparkling smile gone, his handsome face serious.

'And if I choose not to take tea with the King today?'

Stefan spread two enormous hands wide. 'Non, non, you come or not. You free. Boss say take you where you want to go.'

Barney turned to look back at the villa. He waved to Shona to say everything was OK.

'Since you have been such a gentleman, Stefan, it would be churlish to decline. So, let's go. Your boss is a man I really want to meet.'

The rear bench seat of the car was as luxurious as the exterior suggested. Barney sank deep into the green leather and enjoyed the smell of proper wax polish. It was almost a disappointment when, after only about five minutes, they pulled up in front of an impressive low building. Stefan's lookalike opened the back door. He wasn't a twin but together they'd make a strong guard at basketball.

This was Leroy's casino. Barney remembered it from when Jack Thomson gave him a conducted tour of the King's haunts.

Stefan alone showed him inside. He gave a friendly wave to the concierge. 'Visitor for Mr Leroy,' he said as he loped easily across black and white chequered marble towards the gothic, wrought-iron door of a lift. It seemed a bit excessive for a building of only two storeys but as Barney now realised, excess was something else, other than crime, that the owner seemed good at.

His guide said he would be there when he was ready to leave then left Barney to travel up on his own. The old iron and glass door took its own good time to close, then there was clank of engaging gears and a slight jerk as the wood-lined cabin began its leisurely flight.

His first sight of Serge Leroy, the King, was his rich brown leather sandals, fawn woollen slacks, then simple, loose white shirt and finally the rough map of a face, deceptively familiar because of its likeness to Morgan Freeman's.

The door slowly opened. 'Mr Leroy. An unexpected pleasure.'

Barney took Leroy's almost imperceptible nod and tensing of the mouth as the great man's version of a welcoming smile. Whatever. He wasn't here to like him. Besides, Leroy had already turned to presumably lead Barney towards the terrace.

The Scotsman thought he was by now used to the spectacular coastal views of the area but now he felt the urge to actually gasp. The terrace wasn't a terrace but a glass shelf. Far below his feet were jagged rocks. He felt his legs go weak and he cursed his fear of heights, forcing himself to look straight ahead, even though little comfort was to be had in the nothingness of deep blue sky and dazzling sea.

Leroy spoke for the first time. 'Ah, but there is a chilly breeze out here, Mr Mains. Perhaps we should sit inside.'

Barney led the way, wondering if his host had spotted his discomfort and whether this was the most considerate crook he'd ever met.

The tea was served by a clone of the basketball guards as they settled just inside, facing each other across a square table of heavy oak with tree trunks for legs. The chairs were comfortable tan leather but upright, more for business than leisure.

'I see you looking at Louis. You're wondering if we breed clones here.' The man said it like a fact. 'If you were to stay, you would see more. I sponsor a team, basketball. It keeps them out of mischief.'

The man was still strongly reminiscent of the great film star but more fixed, harder. The stained mahogany skin was cratered and riven with plough lines. And the voice: it didn't speak; it ground out words like gravel under a miller's wheel, deliberately, one by one. And yet its timbre seemed to reverberate around him, as if his vocal chords were powered by an internal amplifier.

'But Mr Mains, that's not why you're here.'

'True,' said Barney, shaking himself out of his observations.

'You're here to look after your countrymen in these troubled times.' This time he did smile, tightly. 'And yet you find yourself investigating some of them. And then visiting the poor Ms O'Brien in hospital.' He paused when he saw Barney's surprise. 'Bear with me. You see, I believe there are those who want to blame me for everything that's going on here. The fires, the protests and maybe even the attack on your friend the lawyer.'

Barney raised his head. 'Look, Mr Leroy. Or should I address you as Your Majesty? I don't know how the hell you know all this. But from what I understand, if I was looking for a suspect for just about any crime in this neck of the woods, I'd probably be looking at him right now.'

A flash of anger seized Leroy's face. But it was momentary and he resumed his slow, considered tone.

'I understand that you are a policeman and think as a policeman. But think it through. Forget about the stories about my past. I'm a businessman now. A major player in the economy here and totally legal. So, tell me: why would I want to stir things up, create chaos, destabilise the whole system?

No, I like things just as they are.'

'Ha! You remind me of someone else I just met. Someone who insists he wants stability too.'

'You mean, Aubert?'

Barney gave him a look.

'Yes, I know you went to see him. I may seek a quiet life but I do like to keep up to date with what's going on in my home area, particularly when a strange new policeman goes rambling about in it.'

'Rambling about, is it? Look pal - sorry, Mr Leroy, since we're being all nice and civilized here - I want you to tell me what you know about these missing paintings.'

'Paintings? You mean the ones stolen from the museum? But nothing. I know nothing about them.'

Barney grinned. 'You, who like to know what's going on in his home area, or *domain*, should I say? I saw you *keeping up to date* when you paid a visit to the Fitzwilliams' place. Pretty cosy you all looked too. Did that little fire put them straight? Did they hand over the loot? Or do you want me to believe that you let those paintings go up in smoke in another fire four days later?'

Leroy had both hands up but Barney was in full flow.

'And I have to wonder what you made of the theft in the first place; some outsider daring to rip off the museum without so much as a by-your-leave from the King. Is that why you had Nel executed? A punishment? A warning to others?'

'Mr Mains,' he said, the amplifier cranked up just a little, 'I think maybe our meeting is at an end.'

'That's as may be. But answer me one thing. Why did your men attack the lawyer, Bridget O'Brien?'

'I'll say this one more time: I'm a businessman, not a thug.

It was that incident which attracted my attention. Someone believes that your Ms O'Brien has something they want and naturally, I would like to know what's so important. That's why I had a couple of my boys at the hospital.'

'Where they saw me. And you put two and two together.'

Leroy nodded.

'And at the railway station? That was your men watching me?'

Again a nod. 'Mr Mains, I don't know why, but I believe you are in danger and I wouldn't want anything to happen to you.'

'Until you find out what it is they want? Right?'

Leroy only shrugged.

'But you know who it is?' Barney asked.

He raised his eyebrows, instantly ploughing deep furrows across his forehead, 'I have my suspicions, as you would say.'

'And they are?'

He smiled. 'Well it could be Aubert. I don't know why, before you ask. Or it could be a lot closer to home. But now. I think I've said more than enough. It's time for you to leave.'

Leroy rose, leaving no doubt about it. He led the way to the lift and pulled open the door. He didn't shake hands but gave a short nod. 'A pleasure, Mr Mains.' The door closed on his final words. 'Stay safe.'

And Barney was gone, mulling over that phrase he had used; *it could be a lot closer to home,* and wondering: *whose home, his or mine?*

14 - Kumbaya, Baby

Commandant Christian Garnier, in contrast to his first name, had never in Jean-Luc's experience been known to exude the milk of human kindness. And today, as the Captain gave him the news, all the man projected was pure bile.

'What do you mean bloody *nothing*?' he bellowed as he stood up behind his desk. 'What the hell is this bloody Scotsman doing, going off to interview Aubert in the first place? He's here to do as he's bloody told and investigate a couple of piddling fires. Now he's wandered off the reservation and had a cosy chat with one of the most prominent politicians in France. Would you kindly tell me what the fuck is going on?'

'Sir, Monsieur Aubert's office made the invitation. Said the gentleman had information relating to these two fires DI Mains is investigating.'

'And?'

'And as I say, sir, I haven't had a chance to receive his report yet.'

'Not had a chance? You mean you've been too busy doing his bloody interviews for him while he's off on a jaunt, stirring up who knows what kind of shit. Find out what the hell happened at that meeting and let me know straight away. And for God's sake, put a leash on this bloody Mains guy!'

Jean-Luc paused at the door. 'Yes, sir. Thank you, sir.' He didn't quite click his heels but he hoped his sarcasm might bother the oaf.

'And cut the crap, Verten. You need to decide which side you're on here. You're way too chummy with this guy. You like the Brits, don't you? Even though they're taking over your whole region. Their politicians, journalists, all spouting off about how Brexit's put the *Great* back into Great Britain - spouting off, that is, from the comfort of their French holiday homes. Well, chances are that a few more of those homes are going to burn.'

The Captain closed the door softly behind him, wondering if he'd heard correctly. So he had to decide which side he was on? Really? He's always thought policemen were on the same side. Something to do with an oath to uphold the law.

But the Commandant had been right about one thing. Jean-Luc had been left to look pretty silly, having taken over Barney's case when he was supposed to be hunting an assassin. He needed to see Barney. And soon. On the way back to his office, he pulled out his phone and called. His friend's voice asked him to leave a message.

'Barney! Don't know where you are but I need to speak to you right away. We need to talk. So give me a call as soon as you get this. And yes, as your delightful expression has it, the shit has hit the fan.'

Dupont looked up as he entered. 'How'd it go, boss?'

'One guess.'

She frowned. 'I heard he wasn't too happy about our trip to Aubert's place yesterday.'

'Don't you worry about that, Dupont. It won't reflect on you. It's my arse in a sling for covering Barney's case while he

123

was meeting Aubert.'

The young cop seemed to think hard before speaking again. 'Sir, I hope you don't mind me asking, but how well do you know DI Mains?'

'What? No, no, Barney's an excellent policeman. This is on me. And for what it's worth, I've only known him about a year but I'd trust Barney with my life.'

The unworthy thought had however crept into his mind in the time it had taken him to walk from the Commandant's office to his own that Barney had inadvertently landed him in it and wasn't making things any easier by going AWOL today.

'But Dupont, what are you up to?'

'Well, I was going to see if I could get anything more out of Renaud, the nightwatchman, but he seems to be avoiding us. I'll catch up with him sometime. Oh, and I got the personnel file on our four officers. Nothing of significance and really pretty irrelevant, now that we know they weren't involved, but I can log all that into the file. And if you have anything else, I can get it into the system while you're busy.'

'No, that's OK, I'll top up my own notes when I get back. Just you do your own thing meantime. I've got something to do that's long overdue.'

It had been two days since Jean-Luc had given Forensics a roasting on the phone and he was in just the right mood to repeat it in person.

The scientists occupied a cellar complex with no natural light, which in Jean-Luc's eyes was appropriate since they had shed precious little on his case so far. He took the stairs and was nicely warmed up by the time he pushed open their door.

'Ah, my favourite Captain.' The sibilant voice was that of the corpulent Pascal Roubaix whose whispered tones had long ago earned him the unflattering, though accurate, nickname *The Snake*.

'I doubt that, old Snaky. But you'll be my favourite boffin if you tell me you've finally turned up something I can use.'

'Ah well, patience, my boy. I was just finalising my report and you'll have it before the day is out.'

'Try the *minute*,' said Jean-Luc.

The big man gave a hissing laugh, causing his hydraulic swivel chair to vibrate dangerously. 'Always in a hurry, that's you Verten. Good science takes time, you know.'

'The headlines, now. Give.'

'OK, OK, hold your ponies.' Roubaix felt around on the littered shelf which served as his desk before snatching up a coffee-stained blue folder. 'Right, here we are. Now let me see...'

Jean-Luc knew he only farted about like this to annoy him but he bit his tongue.

'Ah, yes, here we are. You will see that the notes are extensive. But for you, Captain, I have produced a very simple summary.'

'Get on with it man.'

'Would you like me to read it? Ah, right. I see that you do. Well, first of all you asked us to do a thorough sweep of the court balcony. And as I thought, we missed nothing first time round. Well, unless you count a very old chocolate wrapper and a fairly recent date stone, medjool variety, 63 per cent moisture, I believe, no recoverable DNA.'

Jean-Luc leant over to read the page. That's it?'

'Captain, really.'

'OK, OK, get on with it.'

'Well not a lot else, I'm afraid. No human traces there or in the corridor or even on the fire extinguisher, as we said first

125

time round.'

'And the weapon?'

'Ah well, there you're in luck. We subjected it to a full chemical screen and came up with faint traces of a substance on the upper edge of the rifle stock.'

'You came up with a substance? And this substance is... what?'

'Well I wouldn't get your hopes up too much because it just looks like some kind of make-up, perhaps originally in the form of a cream.'

Jean-Luc put a hand over his mouth, focusing on what the significance of this may be. With so little to go on, he had to make something of it.

'And that's it? You can't give me the brand or anything. Or is that hidden away in the notes?'

'Impossible to narrow it down to an individual brand but my guys reckoned it was something like the kind of stuff used as a foundation. Though you'd have to actually read the report to get the detail.'

The Captain stuck out his hand for the file.

'Oh, it should really go straight to your office. I can have it sent up later.'

Jean-Luc snatched the folder and turned, annoyed that the man had got to him. 'You'll get your reward in heaven, Roubaix. But I wouldn't hold your breath.'

He then turned to climb back out of the depths, the folder gripped tight in his hand, the questions already forming in his mind. A useless old chocolate wrapper and a date stone. The fresh stone might merely confirm their belief that the shooter camped out on the balcony. But the make-up on the rifle stock; that could be something. Well, of course, if the shooter was a woman… But no, assume nothing, he scolded. It only meant that make-up could have been transferred from the shooter's face during the recoil of the shot. Or that it had been there before the shooting and was totally irrelevant. But whether through desperation or belief, he instinctively knew that he was on to something.

Dupont seemed to pick up on his changed mood. 'Something good, boss?'

He distractedly opened his computer. 'Em, don't know yet. Forensics. The Snake has finally got off his fat arse and produced a report. Nothing definitive but it's something.'

He then filled her in on his haul: a wrapper, a stone and a smear of make-up. It sounded even less than it had a few minutes earlier. But he opened the blue folder and started into the detail.

'Sir, do you want me to pick up the digital copy and put it into the case notes?'

'Good idea, Dupont. Then you can cast your eye over it too and tell me if you see any good news, anything at all that makes these three crappy leads into something we can use.'

* * *

Barney had his minders drop him off at the hospital and told them to wait, though he reckoned that's what they'd probably been told to do anyway, if only to tail him afterwards.

She was a different woman, sitting up in bed, the turban of bandages gone, her luscious red hair expertly brushed to conceal any evidence of her head injury.

Maitre O'Brien seemed to enjoy his surprise. 'Now that's how I want a man to react.' The music of her west coast lilt made him smile.

'Well I must say you've made a remarkable recovery.'

'Ach Barney, don't go and spoil it. Just go with your gut. I look absolutely effing gorgeous.'

'My very thoughts.' he said, gallant hand on heart. 'But Bridget, we need to talk.'

And they did, for what may have been twenty minutes or so, until a nurse came in and gave them both a tongue-lashing. But not before Barney got what he came for.

'OK, you've found me out, Barney,' she'd finally confessed. 'Yes, between you and me, I knew what was in the envelopes. And yes, you're right. Pieter already had his plan B as he called it. That *B* only turned into Barney when he heard you were coming back to Nice. It was going to be *B* for Bridget. But he didn't want to put me in a potentially dangerous position, so he had me set it up for you.'

'Well thanks for that.'

'You're very welcome,' she said with a deferential smile.

'So you know exactly what Nel has left me?'

She shook her head then winced with pain. 'Absolutely not. All I know is the same as you. Except that I know he would never trust a safety deposit box. He reckoned the police would be into it the moment he was gone. And he thought the security in banks generally was a complete joke.'

'So that's it? The whole truth?'

She nodded deeply but carefully.

Barney made to leave. 'One more thing, then. When you were attacked, have you remembered yet whether you told them anything?'

She screwed up her face. 'The thing is, Barney, I've been trying to remember and I'm sorry, but I just can't. For all I know, I told them everything. Or maybe I passed out before I said a word. I just can't bloody remember.'

'OK, OK, don't fret about it. The fact that a lot of people seem very interested in me suggests that it's still all to play for.'

That's when the nurse appeared and chased Barney out of the room.

The basketball boys were slouching in the shade of a palm tree as Barney escaped into the bright light of day. But suddenly two people were standing in his way. He saw his tall protectors start towards them. But one of the pair, a woman, was speaking. 'It's OK, Mr Mains. Press.'

Barney now saw the camera her colleague held and signalled to the basketball defence that all was well. 'Now you don't point that thing at me. Alright?'

The photographer, a thin, nervous type, seemed to shake his head and nod at the same time.

'And you are, Miss?'

She pulled a wallet from the satchel bag slung over her shoulder and produced a card. It said: *Madeleine Johnson, European Affairs.*

She struck him as different from the British hacks he'd met previously; more considered, thoughtful. She had a squarish, upright stance in her light brown trouser suit and sensible shoes. She had short dark hair that she didn't seem to care about and a pale face bereft of make-up. Probably in her early thirties, she wore a pleasant, open smile, one which failed to mask the determination in those strong-boned features and jutting chin.

'Maddy,' she said, offering her hand.

They shook and the Scotsman resumed: 'Pleased to meet you Ms Johnson, but I'm at a loss as to why you've stopped me.

And I don't know anything about European or any other type of affair.'

She gave him a knowing look which said: *Yeah, right,* then started her pitch in what turned out to be an American accent. East coast, he guessed, maybe refined New York City. 'Detective Inspector, I know why you were sent here and I know your role has turned a lot more interesting, not least in view of Mr Nel's murder.'

'Nothing to do with me, Maddy. I'm purely in the mopping brows business, nothing too exciting. Now, if you'll excuse me...'

She didn't move. 'DI Mains, Barney, it wouldn't do anyone any good for us to fall out so soon... Look, I know that your priority just now will be Nel's murder - and I was hoping to ask you a couple of questions about that - but we're here too because of the anti-British protests and these two fires you're investigating.'

Barney leant his head back, curious to learn how much she knew. 'Carry on.'

'Well, before we left London we did some research on the owner of one of those properties, the one owned by a certain Charles Taylor-Smith. And to cut a long story short, it looks like his fire might not be what it seems.'

'And?'

'And we've found that he's in serious financial trouble and has one heavy-duty insurance policy on the house.'

'Thank you, Ms Johnson. That's very interesting. We will of course take note of what you say. Now, if you'll excuse me. I have to get back to the office. Brows to mop and all that.'

'But Barney... I have questions.'

'They'll have to wait, I'm afraid.' He walked around her and was half way to the car when she called after him. 'Please give our best wishes to Ms O'Brien, Detective Inspector.'

He almost stopped but kept going, muttering under his breath: 'Well, you've not wasted any time, have you?'

The boys dropped him off at police HQ. He could no longer put off seeing Jean-Luc and when he stepped into the office he found the Captain sitting alone, hunched over his keyboard. Barney sensed an atmosphere.

'Hey, Jean-Luc, how's it going?'

His friend seemed to bite back a response. 'So you have spent a profitable morning, I trust?'

'Em, not really, actually. Bit of a waste of time. Well apart from one thing. But I'll tell you all about that in a moment. More to the point, how's it going with our favourite hedge fund owner? Oh, and by the way, I just saw his architect, Burton-Tate, Rufus to his friends, leaving the building.'

Jean-Luc shook his head as if getting rid of an annoying fly. 'Wanted to see Taylor-Smith. Instructions for plans or something. He could only see his lawyer, of course. But Barney, all this is fine. What I need to know is what happened when you met Aubert yesterday.'

Barney sensed his friend was under pressure and immediately recited chapter and verse, even touching on the politician's accusation against the King. Jean-Luc said not a word until he finished. Then he asked: 'So did Aubert have any evidence that Leroy was responsible for the fires?'

'Absolutely not. Just a pretty wild accusation.'

'Yes, well, I didn't think your meeting would produce much of interest but there are those in the building who need to know these things.'

Barney felt his conscience prod him. The one potentially

useful thing he'd learned was that it might just have been Aubert's men who'd attacked the lawyer. But he couldn't mention the lawyer because... because he was a lying shit.

Instead, he offered Jean-Luc a bonus, the contents of his subsequent meeting with the King.

'For God's sake, Barney. First you meet this man who wants to be President and the next day, you're having tea with the King. What is going on?'

'Well, don't ask me, Jean-Luc. First, we've got this right wing politician wanting me to know he has nothing to do with the anti-Brit protests, that he's not really a right-winger and just wants everyone to live in peace. Then, we get the King, your criminal mastermind, saying he knows nothing about a major art theft on his patch, or the public execution of Nel. And like Aubert, all he wants is everyone to live and let live. Kumbaya, baby.'

Jean-Luc usually enjoyed the Scotsman's odd turn of phrase. Today, he just looked tired. Barney was on the verge of telling him everything, to risk putting him in an impossible position, but the Frenchman suddenly got up and trudged to the door. 'Later, Barney,' was all he said.

Silence filled the empty room like an accusation. Barney hadn't felt this low for a long time. Lying to a friend was hard. But there was no time to dwell on it. He had to do something, anything, to find a way out of this mess.

He took the journalist's card from his pocket and copied her details into the search bar. And instantly, like a helping hand from above, he dared to believe he might have found a small chink of light. With growing hope at each new page, he followed the woman's career.

Madeleine Johnson was something he hadn't met before: a

serious journalist, one who'd worked on some of the biggest European stories of recent times.

There was that investigation into the shocking growth in billionaires' wealth since the Covid pandemic hit, while the financial system let them dodge tax by hiding their cash offshore. Then she shared a byline in a report on the Pandora Papers, said to be the biggest ever leak of offshore data, which revealed the financial secrets of the rich and powerful.

Barney sat back, suddenly wondering how Nel's mysterious offering could ever measure up - and questioning whether his hoped-for saviour would even be interested.

For if she was the answer; the one person he knew who could get Nel's legacy out into the world, then his worries could be over. He could tell Jean-Luc everything. The lawyer would no longer be in danger. And neither would he. The promised land of a normal life beckoned.

That's when he started to worry. First he had to set up a meeting with the journalist. Then all he had to do was go and collect his bequest. And dodge whoever wanted it as much as he did: crooked cops, all the King's men or all the President's men. It surprised him to realise it, but Barney was buzzing again.

15 - "Accident"

He had made good use of his time while he still had the office to himself. First, he called the journalist. She surprised him by not being surprised. 'Hi Barney,' she said, then waited. He didn't give any detail, merely suggesting that they meet, that he might have something of interest for her. They settled on her hotel, that afternoon.

Then he knocked up a report for Jean-Luc on his meeting with Aubert, then another on his audience with the King. He then decided to knock up a third file, but one which he would hold back meantime, to present to the Frenchman the moment he felt free to do so. It was a note for Jean-Luc's eyes only, summing up his impressions and speculating on who might have been up to what.

This last note could have gone on forever; the possibilities were endless. But the exercise enabled him to clarify his own thinking. By the final paragraphs, he had come to the guarded conclusion that it had most likely been two of the President's men who attacked the lawyer after seeing Barney leave her office. So, Aubert must have assumed she had information that could hurt him, information which he would do anything to suppress.

The King, on the other hand, was Mr Cool, like he knew

a lot more than he was saying. But curiously, not about the lawyer. It was only her attack which sparked his interest.

Barney's final paragraph suggested that it was still possible for Nel's killing to have been ordered by anyone amongst the rich and powerful who felt threatened by whatever knowledge he'd been about to share with his ghostwriter. But why would they choose such an impossibly difficult time and place in which to carry out the execution? No, just as Jean-Luc had suggested, the King was most likely their man. He had not only punished Nel for daring to conduct an unauthorised heist on his patch but had also sent out a dire warning to others.

Barney wanted to write just one more sentence. But he couldn't, because it would require him to question the degree of corruption within the police; whether they were partners in crime with the King, or the President, or were playing their own hand. And that was a whole can of worms he preferred to open when he and Jean-Luc could talk it through, man to man. So that sentence would have to wait until he collected his legacy and passed it on to Madeleine Johnson.

Meantime, feeling like he'd done a good job, he decided to go for broke and make a long-postponed call.

'Good afternoon, sir.'

'Mains. About bloody time. And it's still morning here.'

Good old Eagle-eyes; the Assistant Chief Constable never let you down, even at the end of a phone more than a thousand miles away in Edinburgh.

'Sorry, sir. Been a bit busy here of late. Just thought I'd alert you to latest events before I send over my formal report.'

'Yes, yes, fine. Carry on.'

Barney then gave what he thought was a particularly good wrap-up on the tale of miscreant Brits who'd sought to make millions from the proceeds of art theft and a spot of insurance fraud.

'Aye, aye, good work, Mains. Just so long as you're not caught up in this Nel business.'

Barney could just see the greying eyebrows gather as his boss's eyes narrowed, his prominent beak confirming his unusually accurate nickname, his bird-of-prey looks a match for that special skill of his to verbally eviscerate.

'That's all down to Captain Verten, sir. I'm just looking at processing the Brits, working out the formalities.'

'Yes, yes. Well you're good at that sort of stuff, Mains. You can do that. But what about all these bloody fires? These attacks on the properties of decent, hard-working folks. What are you doing about them?'

'Top of the agenda, sir. Now that we've explained these first two incidents, I'm starting to look for some sort of pattern in the others. Though, I don't know if you're aware, but there are pretty widespread wildfires going on here right now which might confuse the issue a bit.'

'Och aye, Mains, they get that all the time down there. A good summer and wee fires will pop up all over the place. Nothing to do with deliberate fire-raising. That's what you need to be looking at. Not some burning bushes out in the country.'

'Yes sir, indeed. You're so right.'

'Well, get busy then. Get that report across, pronto. Then get out there. You're supposed to be protecting your countrymen. And ideally no' arresting any more of them. Right? Am I right?'

Barney detected what passed for humour and gave the necessary amused assurance before his boss ended the call. All in all, that had gone well. Now he could bring his notes together and send over his report, which should be enough to keep Edinburgh off his back for another few days.

It ended up taking a bit longer than he thought but he was almost finished when his mobile rang.

'Ffiona! What a nice surprise. Just been talking to a friend of yours.'

'I know. That's why I'm calling.'

Barney could hear the clink of glasses. So this wasn't official business. Ffiona had nipped out to the Leonard Lounge to make this call.

'Interesting,' he said. 'Tell me more.'

There was a pause and he pictured his very professional sidekick, tucked away in one of the more private corners of the pub, taking a long swig of her white wine, like she really needed it

'You wouldn't believe how weird he's become.'

'Trust me, he's always been like that.'

'No, no, he's worse. You know when you finished talking to him? He came straight downstairs, said you'd been on and asked me how much I had on the go. Whether I could wrap everything up quickly if necessary.'

'Because?'

'Well, he didn't exactly say, but he ranted on about the chaos going on in the South of France. Said you were doing a grand job but were - excuse me, his words - *a bit stretched.* Barney, I think they're talking about sending me to join you.'

Barney gave a loud laugh. 'Well, Ffiona. I'd be very glad to see you. It's a hard life, but someone has to do it.'

'It's OK for you. You wouldn't believe how busy it is here, with you away. The guys will go ballistic if I leave too.'

'Ours is not to reason why, Sergeant. Besides, things are

getting a bit interesting here. Might do you no harm.'

'That's all very well but I just don't think old Eagle… the ACC, is thinking straight. You know he's retiring next year? Moving to the South of France?'

Barney choked. 'You're kidding me! Bloody hell! That's all we need.'

'Yeah, well, the grapevine says he's sinking all his money into some luxury pad somewhere…'

'Ah,' said Barney. 'Hence his interest.'

'Exactly. But that's not all. It seems that he was instrumental in you being posted to Nice. London sent a circular round all the forces and he put you forward like a shot. The first UK officer to ever be posted to France, they say. All because old Eagle-eyes wants to protect his investment and damp down - sorry - all these fires. And then you go and get involved in this big art theft, arrest prominent Brits, just adding to the chaos. As he sees it, I mean.'

'And now they think I've got more than I can handle.'

'Something like that. But look on the bright side. If it carries on like this, you could soon end up with your very own police station down there.'

The call left Barney sitting quietly for a moment, digesting everything Ffiona had just told him. He could understand why the ACC would have a direct interest in what was happening in the South of France but he now recalled what the right-wing politician Aubert had told him; that many of Britain's elite too had second homes here. Maybe poor old Eagle-eyes was being leaned on too.

So no pressure then, he thought.

* * *

138

Jean-Luc thought Dupont looked positively flustered as she approached him in the corridor. 'What's the problem? What's going on?'

'It's Hugo Renaud, sir. The doorman who covered up the shooter getting into the court building.'

'Yes, I know who he is. What about him?'

'Sir, I've just heard. He's dead!'

'Shit! What happened? But wait, not out here in the corridor. Into the office.'

Barney was lounging back in his chair, the back of his head resting in hammock hands, but the Scotsman immediately sat up when they burst into the room.

'Hi guys, what's up?' But it was obvious that something urgent was was on the go, something that didn't concern him. He quietly rose and slipped out the door, just as Dupont started to speak.

Jean-Luc saw Barney's police ear picking up on what she said. How much of the fast French he understood was unknown but the Scotsman probably got enough to know that a man, the doorman from the court building, had been killed. He might even have picked up that he'd died in a road accident, a hit-and-run.

Alone with a breathless Dupont, Jean-Luc knew that some-one had decided the man was too unreliable to risk letting him live, that Monsieur Renaud must have known more than he'd let on during his interview.

'Merde! Why didn't I keep him locked up? But, Dupont, we've got to throw everything at this. We need all the CCTV footage all round the crash area. No doubt a stolen car but you never know,' he said.

Then it struck him. 'Wait, if they've silenced the doorman,

what about the cleaner? She was bribed to let the killer take her place that night. Dupont, get right on that. Find her and bring her in. She needs protecting. Assuming, please God, that she's still alive.'

* * *

Barney had fought the urge to hover outside the door. His nose was bothering him. But he was a policeman, a professional. So he didn't hover too long. But he had heard enough to confirm what he suspected, that an important witness had been the victim of a hit-and-run. And by the way they were talking, it had been no accident.

He suddenly felt very tired, like he was living two lives. He needed some time out before his meeting with the journalist, so when he started walking along the corridor he just kept going and minutes later found himself out in Boulevard Dubouchage.

There was a rare breeze as he absently took in the grand buildings on either side, until he came to the bustling junction with the tram-only shopping street, Avenue Jean Médecin. He had no plan, but he couldn't resist crossing into his favourite street in the city, Boulevard Victor Hugo, where the towering plane trees with their camouflage trunks could always calm a troubled mind. Finally he tore himself away, turning left down busy Rue Meyerbeer towards the Prom and his favourite little bistro.

It was seriously hot on the south-facing seafront and he was glad of the parasol over his pavement table as he took his time over a cold beer. The tourists were here in force, most of them on their way to the beach clutching all sorts of paraphernalia to help them lie about doing nothing all day. He just didn't get it.

He checked his phone. Time had somehow kept moving on and he would soon be due for his meeting.

Her hotel was close by. It wasn't the glorious Negresco facing the sea but one of the more affordable ones a couple of blocks back. Even though it was in the shade, the hotel's doors were wide open to any breeze that was going. She seemed to be getting the benefit as she sat alone in the lobby reading a newspaper, oblivious to his presence.

'Anything good?' he asked.

'Ah, Barney. How good to see you. Oh, nothing special, just keeping in touch.'

'I suppose some people still like the paper version.'

She shrugged. 'Progress they say. Everything's on your phone.'

'Ha! You know, you don't seem old enough to sound like me.'

She gave a short laugh. 'But as someone once said: *I'm not young enough to know everything.*'

He smiled. 'And as you know, that someone was none other than our Peter Pan man.'

She looked at him as if for the first time. 'You know J.M. Barry?'

'Not really. As far as us police are concerned, culture's something that grows on cheese.'

She laughed but then stood up. Her stance said what Barney wanted to see. Time for business. She never spoke, merely moved towards a lift which had sad doors of sliding metal.

Her room on the second floor had a view of a nondescript building across the way but was blessedly air-conditioned.

She offered something from the fridge, which he declined while looking around for a chair.

'Take the one at the desk,' she said. 'You only get one chair at this price. I'll sit on the end of the bed.'

He thought to be gallant but by then she was already sitting and so he did as she said and pulled out the chair.

'So, Barney, I know what it must have taken for you to contact me and believe me, I know you've got a lot on your plate at the moment, so it's really appreciated that you've agreed to talk.'

Barney froze then jerked up straight in his chair. 'Shit! The ghostwriter. It's you, isn't it?'

She looked ready to deny it but her shoulders relaxed. 'Guilty as charged, officer, I'm afraid.'

'So that's why you're here. You know Nel's the story and you want me to get it for you.'

'Well, I wouldn't put it like that, Barney, but in a way, yes. You see, I've spoken to his lawyer a couple of times and I know that he wanted to get a lot off his chest. It was going to be a great book, I believe. But as you know, someone important must have got wind of it and couldn't afford to let it all come out, whatever the hell it was.'

Barney paused. He took time to look around the little room, registering the standard characterless paintings, tired floral drapes, a kitsch Med scene which covered the wall behind the bed.

'Are you aware of that other famous Scottish expression: *maybes aye, maybes no?*'

She looked puzzled. 'No, but I suspect you mean... that I may have it wrong?'

'Like I say, maybes aye...'

'Maybes no. I get it. So you have someone specific in mind?'

'That, Maddy, is another story. Not what I'm here for.'

'OK, fair enough. But you'll keep me in mind?'

'Hard to forget. But come on. You're meant to be grilling me or whatever it is you do.'

She seemed to make up her mind to drop the question of Nel's execution. 'Right,' she said, 'this is what I know. Pieter Nel asked Bridget O'Brien to find someone who would help him write his memoirs. We'd met somewhere before, way back, Bridget and I, and she knew the kind of stuff I do, so she got in touch. I had to go through her, so I only got the headlines; that Pieter had information about corruption in high places. All very vague but Bridget believed him and I trusted her judgment. Besides if all I got out of it was *The Confessions of a Killer,* then I could live with that.'

'OK,' Barney said, nodding several times, calibrating. 'So you know nothing about Nel's stash, his *treasure trove,* as you might say?'

'There was a hint. But no, not really.'

'Well, if I'm to believe what Nel told me in a letter, it does exist. And I know where it is.'

She eased back and raised her head. Barney knew the chill which was surely now running through her. It was the moment when you knew you were on to something, something big. She started to speak but he held up a hand.

'No, I don't know exactly what it is. But I believe it exists and it looks like I'm the lucky guy who has to go and get it. Having said which, as far as I'm concerned, you can have it the moment I do.'

She was puzzled again. 'You don't know what it is? You don't want to investigate whatever allegations it makes?'

'Look, you never know. Maybe that's the way it'll go. But first, we have to get it all out into the open. That way, it can't be hushed up. Whatever the hell *it* turns out to be.'

She looked at him oddly, a half smile playing on her lips. 'Tell me Barney, just between ourselves, why you're doing this. I mean, if you know where it is, why don't you just tell the French police and let them go and get it. Then it can all come out.'

He gave a long, pained look. He wanted to tell her that he simply couldn't trust the French police. He couldn't do that but he felt the answer he gave was at least partly true; that Nel's last wish had been dropped in his lap, imposing some kind of moral obligation towards a fellow human.

What he didn't say was that he himself had felt the dead hand of those privileged few who were able to close down sensitive investigations; those members of the so-called elite who thought themselves above the law and who might now be held to account.

'On the other hand,' said Barney brightly, 'it might just be a total crock of shit!'

They looked at each other and laughed.

All that remained was the detail. He would fetch the treasure tomorrow, then they would meet back here immediately afterwards and she would be all set up to get everything out onto safe servers, far away from harm. It seemed to them to be a good plan.

'One last thing,' Barney said. 'You've got a photographer with you, but just so we're clear: I'm invisible in this. I don't exist. OK?'

'OK. But maybe then you should just tell me where it is…?'

'Well,' said Barney, apparently pondering, 'I suppose I *could* tell you…'

'But then, you'd probably have to kill me, right?'

* * *

Barney knew that one of the very best things about living in the centre of Nice was the wealth of possibilities for eating. But he also soon realised that he didn't like to sit in a restaurant on his own and so, if he wasn't with company, he tended to drop into one of his favourite places for a carry-out. Tonight, in his shoebox of a top-floor studio flat, he gorged himself on an enormous four seasons pizza and splashed deep red wine from a bottle which seemed unlikely to survive the night.

When he phoned, Shona didn't hesitate. All he'd had to say was that he was going hiking in the hills first thing in the morning and could she recommend a decent guide.

She would pick him up at five. Then they'd head straight to Saint-Jeannet and be there long before Barney's watchers had even staggered into the shower. What could go wrong?

16 - Treasure Hunt

Saturday, July 12

Another Saturday morning in the office when he should be back home in the hills tending to his bees. Jean-Luc was in a surly mood. And it wasn't made any better by reading Barney's reports. It looked as if they were on the same page in thinking that the King was most likely responsible for Nel's murder. Proving it would be another matter - unless they could find the shooter. But today was about going through CCTV footage of the fatal hit-and-run. He had help from the boys in traffic and just had to hope the cameras had picked up something for him to work on.

Dupont came in just then and her young face wasn't bright. 'Bonjour,' she said. 'But I don't know if it is.'

'Sit down first, Dupont. There's a coffee there for you.'

The young officer obeyed but didn't drink. 'Sir, I was everywhere last night. There's no sign of her, Madame Cortes. She's just vanished off the face of the earth. The employment bureau, her fellow workers, her neighbours, her child's school… nothing. The pair of them are gone and for all I know, they've been taken out too.'

'Now, now Dupont. We can't jump to conclusions. Remember that she was given what to her was a small fortune and told to take her child on holiday. And until we have a report of a body turning up, we have to assume that that's still a very real possibility.'

She appeared unhappy but to Jean-Luc that was a good sign. It showed she cared.

'Now, make yourself useful. Nip along to Traffic and keep an eye on our boys going through the recordings. Find me something!'

Alone again, Jean-Luc re-opened Barney's report on his meeting with Leroy. The King seemed to have given Barney a hint that the Scotsman may not have picked up on. But at least Barney, in producing his extremely good report, had thought to record the phrase and it was a phrase which Jean-Luc now noted in a separate file on his phone. *It could be Aubert or it could be a lot closer to home.*

* * *

She was on the dot. He, less so.

'For heaven's sake, Barney, you should be raring to go.'

'Not so loud, Shona, for God's sake. Just help me find my whatsits, you know the thingamies…'

'I'm guessing, *boots*?'

'Aye, smart arse. Boots.'

'In the car. You left them at the villa, along with everything else, last time.'

Barney managed an emerging look of comprehension.

'And you might want to put these on,' she said, handing him his hiking shorts. 'We don't want to scare the goats.'

When they finally got downstairs, Shona pointed at the little red electric car across the road. She slipped into the driver's seat before he could object. 'You don't mind, do you? I never get a chance to drive these things.'

He just smiled and thought: *Yeah, neither do I.*

He remembered the route to Saint-Jeannet from the last time he visited Jean-Luc at his home above nearby Tourrettes-sur-Loup, a memory which reminded him how guilty he'd been feeling last night about keeping things from the French policeman who had become his friend.

He knew Saint-Jeannet was a picturesque village just this side of Vence but he'd never been. And once they'd negotiated the outskirts of Nice he decided to relax, enjoy the drive and try to feel like a normal human being again, for a while.

They breezed up the side of the Var, but the river was only a trickle in an immensely wide expanse of white stones. Barney thought to check his phone. There was a message last night from Jack, aka Charlie. He liked the little man and almost managed a laugh when he read the message.

Hey Barney, me old mucker, I'm inviting you to come and see me smash the Frenchies at their own game. It's Sunday evening, at the pétanque club across from the flat. Nineteen hundred hours. Big match, lots of money at stake! Be there or be square.

They passed the turn-off to Carros and the road began to steepen. He remembered the swift succession of steep uphill bends which then followed, though today it felt like his chauffeur du jour was enjoying them more than he was. He looked across and she was a picture of excited concentration. Everything to her was a challenge.

It sounded like his actor friend liked competition too. Whether Barney would ever again be able to enjoy an evening as normal as watching a pétanque match was another matter.

He wasn't sorry when they had to slow down through the sleepy village of Gattières and knew he could now enjoy a long flat section with some splendid views to the left, back down the Var to the city and the coast far below.

A final turn-off, then a sharp climb to Saint-Jeannet, followed by a hairpin bend which took him by surprise but which Shona seemed to take as a special treat as she slung the car round at speed. A few short sprints, then they were easing into a huge charging station in a public car park at the foot of the village.

'Wow, they've really improved these things. That was fun,' she said as she put the car in parking mode and looked at him.

'Simply super,' he said. He got out and started to unload their equipment. He slipped on his rucksack then lifted hers.

'Bloody hell. What have you got in here? You're not thinking of going camping are you?'

She laughed. 'No, not this time. Only some extra bits, just in case. Though we probably won't be needing them.'

As they carried their hiking poles up the slow incline of the road into the village, Barney suddenly became aware of the looming presence of the famous Baou, a fearsome rocky outcrop immediately behind homes built by people he assumed would rather look the other way.

'That's where we're going,' she said, as they paused at benches on the village's public terrace beside a hotel bar.

'I was afraid of that,' said Barney. 'But remember, there's no *we*. You show me the way and then you skedaddle.'

Barney filled his lungs with the pure mountain air. Then he looked over the terrace wall and saw the sheer drop. He staggered back in surprise, but then steadied as he took in the panorama below; the lush fruit trees in the gardens immediately beneath, the green slopes dotted everywhere with white villas and deeply blue swimming pools, the faraway sea seeming to float as it sparkled. He felt free.

She seized the moment. 'So you reckon you'll be OK with the heights, then?'

He pushed his hands through the loops on his batons de randonnée, ready to go. 'Aye, nae bother. Lead on, Macduff.'

It started as the most pleasant of early morning rambles up the narrow streets of the village to a small chapel and car park where the road changed to a track and then a narrow trail through trees. The birds were silent and the only sound came from the background trickle of the river down to their left. He wondered what all the fuss was about. This was a walk in the park. Even the ubiquitous smell of smoke had gone. The fires had never reached this area and with no wind forecast, they weren't going to come any closer today.

A hint of the next phase came as the trail took them beneath an enormous tilted cube of solid rock. Then he saw two climbers half way up the cliff face to his right. 'Strewth, who the hell gets up at this time in the morning to go climbing?'

Shona just looked at him as if he was stupid.

'Aye, OK Shona. I meant: *who else.*'

A short distance on, she stopped. 'Right, this is where we start going up. There's nothing to worry about. It's perfectly safe. Just watch out for the fine gravel. It's easy to slip and lose your footing. Oh, and it's best if you just focus on your feet rather than what's behind or to the side of you. All we need to do is follow this trail.'

'Don't worry about me. I'll be fine. But you're saying that this trail takes me straight there? Then you can leave me here, like we agreed.'

'Look chum, I never agreed anything. And I'm taking you all the way.'

Barney knew how she could be but there was no way he was putting her in danger. 'Shona, you're staying. And that's final.'

'Absolutely,' she said as she turned and started to climb.

He shook his head. Well he'd tried.

She called back to him. 'Best to stay well back in case I send some stones down.'

At first it was no problem. The path snaked left and right, finding the easiest way up. Only once did he dare to stop and look around. He almost lost his balance. There was a sheer drop off to the left. He went back to focusing on his feet.

'OK back there?' she shouted.

'Fine, fine. No problem.'

But the climb got steeper, the ground more slippery, and at times he felt no shame in sinking to all fours. But her advice had been good. *Keep the heid doon. A message for life,* he mused, taking his mind off the precarious situation for a moment.

Suddenly he came to a sharp turn and the incline eased. He dared look ahead. The vegetation had changed from poor scrawny survivors clinging to rocks to dense, tangled undergrowth. And there standing waiting for him was his intrepid guide, a beaming smile on her face.

'What kept you?' she shouted.

'Very funny. Are we there?'

'Near enough. Just a stroll from here. Well done, Barney. Proud of you.'

A few minutes later they clambered on to the grassy top and found themselves at the ruins.

She said: 'It doesn't look much from here but if we'd come

up the easy way, you'd have got a great view across the valley.'

'You mean there's an easy way, for God's sake?'

'Too long and boring. Much better going direct. But we can go back that way if you like.'

He grunted. 'Come on, now that you're here. You can help me find this damn thing.'

The description from Nel which he had shared with no-one seemed to have no relation to what was before him. But once he worked out their position in relation to the sun he could make sense of the dead man's directions.

He recited out loud. *'From the big white rock to the south, look north to the tallest part of the ruin and walk straight towards it.'*

She spotted what must be the white rock and started leading the way. 'What next?'

'Let me think. He said *when you can't go any further, you're facing a stone wall. There are three reddish stones in a rough triangle. Pull out the one on the left.'*

They found themselves approaching what seemed to be the wall in question. The ground was flat, the grass thick. There were the remains of a grand fireplace in the wall. Someone had lived, loved and probably died here.

'OK,' he said. 'Here goes.' The stone was about eight inches square and, judging by its weight, almost as deep. But using both hands, he was starting to work it free. At last he could let it drop to the ground. He reached into the dark hole and was up to his elbow when he started feeling about. It made him think of the times his father had taken him and his brother guddling for trout. He remembered the terror of that first foray, forcing himself to put his hands under a rock, feeling his way blindly into the unknown, fearing what he might touch - then the electrifying shock of that first contact with a wild creature. This time there was no panicked fish; just a small box that fitted in his hand. And he was pulling it out.

'Well there you go. That's what it's all about,' he said, relieved and disappointed at the same time. It was just a little tin, one that once held pastel sweets. He hoped that what rattled inside wasn't one of the original residents. Nel's last joke.

But it was a memory stick, an anonymous little store of data in a plastic case which was a killer's legacy to the world. And now Barney had to deliver it.

He was aware of her watching his normally passive face for a reaction. 'You seem disappointed,' she said. 'Did you expect more?'

'I guess I did. Don't know why. Guess I would like to think that there's more left. You know, after.'

She laughed. 'Well, it's better than a pile of ashes.'

He joined in, enjoying the sudden release of tension. Now all they had to do was to get back down, give it to the journalist and get on with the rest of their lives.

That was when they heard the sound of heavy boots grinding the gravel on the track below. They looked at each other.

'Could just be hikers,' she said.

'But might not be. Best not to hang around. Where's that easy way down?'

'OK, but we need to be quick. Otherwise we might be in sight of whoever it is.'

They pulled the rucksacks tight on their backs, picked up their sticks and ran back to the path. But they were too late. Barney saw them first, two men looking straight at them. And one of them was raising a rifle.

'Shit! Come back Shona.'

They clambered back into the ruin and threw themselves

against Nel's wall.

'Bloody knew I shouldn't have let you come!'

'Oh, shut up about that. I'm here. The question is what we do about it.'

Barney looked at her. 'Well I'm open to suggestions. Don't suppose Nel left any other little presents behind the other two red stones do you? Something actually useful, like a gun?'

She slipped off her rucksack and unzipped the big front pocket. 'Don't need one. I've got this.'

Barney looked at the gun in the hand then into her eyes. 'Seriously? You've been carrying that the whole time?'

'It's my security blanket. As you know, someone with my kind of money can attract some pretty unsavoury characters, so this little equaliser goes with me whenever I'm exposed. And I had a feeling we might just need it today.'

'Well, just this once, I'm glad you brought it. But what now? I suspect it's no match for a rifle.'

'No but I only have to fire it to let them know they can't just walk in here and do what they want.'

Barney heard voices. The men were approaching the ruin and were making no effort to conceal the fact. 'Now might be a good time,' he said.

She grinned and stepped out. He saw her take aim, the gun in two hands, the arms fully extended. She knew what she was doing. It was a small gun but the echo from the rocks and the mountains went on and on. The men slipped and scrambled in their haste to escape. One dropped his rifle and Shona fired again, sending a spark flying close to the weapon. The man grabbed it and ran for his life.

'Well, that was pretty impressive,' said Barney, trying to sound like this sort of things happened almost every day back home.

She grinned. 'I knew those lessons would come in handy sometime.'

From where they stood, Barney could see that they had a wide angle of vision across the flat of the promontory. The downside was the downsides, the precipitous cliffs all around except to the north. 'Unfortunately, unless we can climb over the ruin and find a way out that way, it looks like we have a bit of a stand-off,' he said. 'Any more suggestions? I don't want to have to call the cops but as a last resort…'

But she was reaching into the main compartment of her rucksack. She pulled out the last thing in the world that Barney wanted to see: a big coil of rope.

'In the name of the wee man, what the hell else have you got in there? A fridge?'

She managed a short laugh. 'No, just some food and water. This little beauty is much more useful.'

As well as the rope, she also had a suggestion and Barney didn't like that either. She wanted them to abseil down the western face to a ledge which would take them to the north unseen. There they could join one of two trails, the one back down to Saint-Jeannet or the longer one, all the way round towards Vence.

'Vence is a lot longer but it's easy and we can probably hitch a lift once we reach the road. Safest option. We'd be visible for a bit on the Saint-Jeannet trail.'

Barney had long ago accepted that he had an inherent fear of heights. It was an involuntary thing. Which was why he couldn't prevent the tremor as they stood at the edge of the cliff.

He was to be anchor man, playing out the rope to lower her

down to the ledge. Then she expected him to tie his end of the rope to a rock and simply slip down to join her. It was so ridiculous that he actually laughed. But it had to be done.

The first part went surprisingly well. He was encouraged to hear her call after only about eight metres of rope had played out. He could do this, he told himself. Then he turned to the rock they'd agreed on and tied the rope to it, double knotted.

As she'd instructed, he turned to face the ruin with the rope in both hands and running between his legs. He then backed towards the edge, got down on his knees and slowly, so slowly, pushed his legs out and let his body slide over.

He'd once done a charity parachute jump. He'd been in a numbed panic when he slid out of the plane. But he recalled now how he had simply done what had been drummed into him. The panic was over in a flash and suddenly he'd been floating like a feather on the air. It had been a joyous experience until the planet rushed to meet him. Today, he daren't think beyond the training she'd given. He was now trusting his life to the carabiner, the small circle of metal through which the rope ran. And to his amazement he found himself slipping in slow motion downwards, playing out the rope inch by inch, beginning to feel a tentative sense of control.

He sensed her hand on his back, heard her reassuring words. He felt the ledge and planted his feet to push himself upright. He sensed that she was containing her excitement; this was no time to be jumping about. She told him to look only at the cliff and to crab-walk after her. It wasn't far at all, she insisted. She'd done it lots of times.

He thought she was lying. But he also knew that fear had its uses. It was there to save the organism. He told himself this repeatedly, accepting that he was petrified but knowing that this terror was directing all his physical and mental abilities towards this one simple task; to get to the other end. And he did. It was an anti-climax because he suddenly found himself standing on grass and realised that Shona was now behind him, which would be impossible if they were still on the ledge. He dared look round and she threw her arms round his neck. 'My hero! I know how difficult that was for you, Barney. You're a total star!'

Only then did he start shaking. She made him sit down and eat a sandwich. He then greedily drained a bottle of water. They seemed to be facing west now and he took a deep breath of the breeze blowing straight into him.

With the breeze came the familiar smell of woodsmoke. It was a wonderful smell but it was one which he had come to hate because it brought only death and destruction. For them however, it was now only a matter of joining the path she'd described and walking all the way to lovely Vence. He was already thinking that they should leave the hire car at Saint-Jeannet, just in case their visitors were waiting there. After all, he could use his card to hire another vehicle in Vence and pick up the original one later.

He was still working out the logistics when she put her hand on his shoulder.

'Barney, I think we'd better get going. I don't like that smoke we're smelling and there's a bit of wind there now which wasn't forecast. Best not to hang about.'

She explained that the route basically formed a big leftward horseshoe around a deep valley, so they'd end up on the steep downhill road into Vence. The only slightly difficult bit was a ravine of large boulders where they'd have to be careful. Otherwise a cakewalk.

157

He sprang to his feet, a new man. 'I like the sound of cakewalk. And walk. And cake, actually. Let's go.'

But after more than half an hour of fast walking they still hadn't reached the apex of the horseshoe. Barney suddenly stopped. The smell of smoke was getting stronger. 'Shona, you mentioned a big valley. Would there happen to be water in that valley?'

'There's a river but I don't know how much water will be in it at this time of year. Best not to count on it if we have to find a way out.'

They carried on, making good time on the flat, even surface. They eventually came to a pretty wooden bridge across what in winter would be a proper river. Today is was a small stream, ironically called a *burn* in Scotland, as Barney couldn't resist thinking.

He could now see the smoke in the air. It was moving into them from the right. With any luck, they could hurry onwards, heading south in the direction of salvation and the sea. But it was getting bad. They were both coughing. He scrambled down to the stream, where he pulled off his t-shirt, took out his spare from the rucksack and soaked both in what little water there was. He carried the dripping shirts back to Shona, tying one around her head and other around his own.

'Come on,' she said. 'That boulder slide's next. We get up that and then it's plain sailing. We can even run if we have to.'

The boulders made it hard going. Each step had to be carefully chosen. A misstep and an injury simply could not be contemplated.

The shirts over their noses and mouths were making little difference. And now it seemed that they would have more to contend with than this treacherous obstacle course and the thickening smoke.

For now they could hear it; the snapping and the roar. The fire was moving on the breeze. Straight for them.

'Keep going Shona. We're going to make it. Remember we can run once we get to the top.'

Looking at the seemingly endless jumble of boulders still ahead of them, he was beginning to doubt they'd ever get the chance to run.

They just had to get ahead of the fire's path. Either that or they had to get lucky, pray that the breeze would shift and carry the advancing, crackling wildfire away to the north, to pass safely behind them.

Above the roar of the fire he thought he could hear another noise. It was like the drone of an engine. What was it? They were choking badly now and they could only keep going because the boulder slide was in a sharp cleft which meant that some of the smoke was passing over their heads. But the going was still agonisingly slow and his chest was tightening.

Now he was sure, however. That was definitely an engine. Maybe a bulldozer? Could they even think of rescue? No, not a bulldozer. A plane. Barney feverishly thought how he could signal to it. But how could he, with a thick layer of smoke between them and the sky?

Then the sky was torn apart with a terrifying scream as if the hounds of hell had been set on them. The heavens opened and Barney was struck by something big and heavy like a punchbag. He was hurled onto the rocks. He lay stunned for he couldn't tell how long. He came to, pleading to have been spared a serious injury which would mean certain death. He couldn't see Shona and in a panic he scrambled to his feet, all thoughts of injury forgotten.

There she was, just ahead, stirring awkwardly. *Thank God!*

'Shona! Shona, are you alright?'

She was getting slowly to her feet. 'I don't really know. I think so. But what the hell just hit us?'

Barney looked at her. She was soaking wet. Then he realised that he was too.

He lifted his head and laughed. She looked at him as if he was crazy.

'Shona, you know what just happened, don't you? We've just been water-bombed. One of the wildfire planes. It dumped tonnes of seawater on the fire and we just happened to be in its path.'

She looked at the water on her skin in wonder and licked a forearm to confirm the salty taste. 'Well I'll be damned. But hey, Barney, that's still a big fire and we still need to get out of here.'

'You're right. Let's go. But look, the air ahead seems a bit better. We're going to make it.'

Just then he heard the engines of another aircraft approach from the same direction and then what sounded like another, further away. They looked at each other. They didn't have to speak. They just carried on up the ravine, one careful step after another.

The smoke hadn't entirely gone by the time they reached the top. But they could see that the worst of the fires were now behind them, towards Saint-Jeannet and further inland. Far ahead of them, towards Vence and the sea, the air seemed to be clear. Barney reckoned the planes were on a mission to form a buffer between the town and the wide open spaces of the scrubland. He and Shona had managed to reach that buffer zone just in time. And now they could watch from a safe distance as plane after plane moved in from the east.

He looked back at the inferno that lay behind them. 'Do you reckon those guys have made it out OK?'

'Don't give a damn,' she said. 'They shoot at us, they can take their chances.'

He knew she was right. He also knew that those men would have eventually discovered the rope and realised which trail they'd taken. If they'd followed, the chances were that they were now directly in the path of the flames.

17 - Mister Policeman

He knew something was wrong the moment she answered. He'd promised to call Maddy, his journalist saviour, as soon as they were returning to Nice. She was supposed to be ready and waiting in her hotel room to fire off Nel's treasure to various secure newspaper addresses across Europe.

But as Shona guided their replacement rental through the airport traffic, he somehow sensed that the journalist was not alone. Her first faltering words confirmed his worst fears. 'Barney, I'm sorry…'

That was as far as she got. He visualised someone snatching her phone. 'Ms Johnson is real safe, copper.' A muffled voice. A Frenchman with poor English, one who had learned all he knew from gangster movies. 'And she stay like this if you do what I say.'

Barney grimaced. He turned to Shona and pointed to the kerbside. 'We need to pull over.'

The voice in his ear: 'Yes, mister policeman, you must be careful.'

Shona looked suitably puzzled as she killed the engine outside a supermarket. Barney smothered the phone on his chest. 'Someone's got Maddy.'

'Shit!'

'Yeah, bastards! But wait…'

The man on the phone was speaking. 'Now, mister police-man, you know how this works, yes? You give me what you get from Saint-Jeannet, I give you your friend. Deal?'

'Look, sunshine. I don't know who the hell you are or whether Maddy's safe. Plus I don't know what the hell you're talking about.' Barney could only try a weak bluff, play for time, try to remember whoever it was who'd also called him *mister policeman.*

'Not smart, copper. You get text. Do what I tell you. Or I hurt your friend, bad.' Then he was gone.

Barney dropped the phone in his lap and sunk his face in his hands. 'Shit, shit, shit! This cannot be happening!' Then he took a huge breath and turned to Shona.

'It looks like someone knows what we've got and he'll only release Maddy when he gets it. I need to think…'

'Well, Barney, think quick. there's a couple of policemen coming our way and we have to move.'

They reached Maddy's hotel ten minutes later and went in together. He asked reception to call up to her room. It was only when Barney saw the shock on the pretty blond receptionist's face that he realised how bad they must look. Being fired on by bad guys, scaling a cliff and being caught in a wildfire can mess up your hair something awful.

'Sorry,' he told the young woman, 'we're been orienteering and not had time to get spruced up yet, ha!'

She looked uncertain despite her finishing-school posture and perfect make-up. 'Monsieur, I don't have to call her room. There is no point because she left her keys when she left with the men.'

'Ah,' he said. 'So my young friends arrived OK then? Tall

young guys, athletic looking?'

The receptionist sent her perfect lashes skywards. 'Hardly, Monsieur. Old men, bad suits, bad manners.'

He tried to get a better description but he was already picturing two of Aubert's men for whom such a description was as good as a photofit. Besides, an American couple were hanging around and it was clear that she'd much rather speak with them.

Barney signalled to Shona that he was going to the gents toilets to clean up and she nodded agreement before heading off to the *Femmes.*

Minutes later, looking almost normal despite sweat-stained clothing which clung to their bodies, they drove the short distance to Barney's building.

As he opened the door and walked in it felt as if he'd been gone for days. He checked his phone. It wasn't yet eleven o'clock.

He pulled two beers from the fridge and led the way to the terrace.

'I'd forgotten how small this place was,' Shona said. 'You must suffer agoraphobia at the villa.'

'Aye, small but perfectly formed,' he said.

He'd forgotten glasses so they drank in big gulps from the bottles, the bubbles exploding all the way down parched throats while they stood staring across the rooftops.

Barney finished first then put his bottle down heavily onto the table and pulled a chair towards him. She sat opposite, cradling the rest of her drink in both hands.

'Right,' he said. 'I'm supposed to be getting a text soon which will tell me how they want to do the exchange. Don't know yet how we're going to play it but I'm open to suggestions. The thing is… I think I might know who they are.'

She sat up, looked sharply across at him. 'Who?'

'Well, no guarantees, but he called me *Mister Policeman.* I've been trying to remember the only other person to have called me that since I came here.'

'And?'

'And I'm pretty sure it was none other than the man who would be president. Henri Aubert.'

'What? You recognised his voice?'

'No. I don't know for certain that it was him. The voice was disguised and if it *was* him then *he sure dumbed down a lot, sister.* But it could have been one of his men who just picked up on the phrase when I was there. But I'd lay money that it was his goons who lifted her from the hotel, so I've got a feeling he might still be close.'

'You've got an idea, haven't you?'

'Well, more of a hope. If it *is* Aubert and he *is* close, I need to find out where he might be. That could give us an edge, a chance to take the initiative.'

'And..? You're going to ask Jean-Luc for help?'

'Shona, I can't. Not yet. Not until we make the memory stick safe. No. Think. How can we find out where he stays when he's in Nice?'

Barney stared at her, his eyebrows half way up his forehead, willing her to come up with something, anything, from her time spent here mixing with the rich and the filthy rich.

'Well,' she finally said, 'he's fairly well known on the party circuit. But he never entertained here, in town, as far as I know. It was always out at his farmhouse. So I've no idea, I'm afraid. I know lots of people who might have been at the same parties but it would take time to phone round. And it'd be a bit hit and miss. But how about... Just a thought, but *you* might know the best guy to ask, who seems to keep his ear to the ground and probably gets to more of these select events than anyone. Jack Thomson.'

Barney looked sceptical. How would a Charlie Chaplin impersonator know where such a high-flyer kept his very private nest? But he already had the phone in his hand and was punching in the number. *Why not?*

Jack answered on the third ring. 'Jack. Barney. Look, got your message about tomorrow night. Sounds great. I'll be there. But listen, Jack, I need a wee favour. You know this guy Henri Aubert, Monsieur Le President? Right. Yeah, well he believes it. But, thing is, I need to get in touch with him, quite urgently. Sorry, can't say why. It's just that he apparently has a place in Nice and I'm trying to find out where it is.'

Barney suddenly stopped and looked at Shona. 'OK, great,' he said into the phone then put it away. 'Well that was pretty impressive. He just said: *See what I can do. Leave it with me.* You know, calm as a hotel receptionist? I mean, who is this guy?'

'Don't be so surprised. I told you; I expect he's better connected than most of his wealthy employers.'

He got up and went inside then returned with a bottle of his favourite malt whisky and two glasses. 'Well, he said, you're doing all the driving. Though you're welcome if you'd like a wee bracer.'

She put up both hands to fend off temptation. 'No, but you carry on. Just remember that you might be launching a one-man assault on a private army soon. As is your way.'

He didn't laugh. Besides, he was too busy swallowing.

They weren't quite in full sun but it was already warm and

Shona helped herself to a bottle of cold water while they waited, pointedly placing a second beside Barney's re-fill.

They both jerked when his phone sounded.

The text said: 'Le Chateau. South cafe. Noon. Alone.'

He checked the time. He had almost an hour. 'Come on, Jack!' he said, then wondered if he should phone the lawyer in hospital. She might know more than she'd said. Maybe she would know why the hell Aubert was so interested in whatever Nel had to say.

Barney's phone sounded again. He put it to his ear and just listened, nodded a couple of times, then said: 'Jack, you're a star. See you tomorrow.'

He turned to an anxious Shona. 'Got it. Would you believe, he's in Rue Rossini, virtually round the corner? Massive top-floor apartment. Slightly more salubrious building than this. But the bastard's actually a neighbour!'

They quickly worked out what they were going to do. Barney doubted that Aubert or his men would bring Maddy to Le Chateau, the picturesque hill which overlooked the Port. It would be too public should anyone start acting up. But the open-air cafe and the area around it were wide open, a good space in which to spot any loitering plain-clothes police types amongst the tourists, impromptu pétanque games and Tai Chi groups. And enough space to get away via various steep-stepped exits to the Old Town or Prom.

What the kidnappers didn't know was that Barney was going to stake out their nearby base in Rue Rossini while Shona followed anyone who left it for Le Chateau.

They didn't have to wait long. Two vaguely familiar men in bad suits emerged from Aubert's hideaway and headed off on foot towards Le Chateau about twenty minutes away, apparently keen to be in place long before the expected arrival of Barney with their prize.

He reminded Shona she was to stay well back and to run if they so much as looked her way, then he watched uneasily as she took up the trail. He tried to turn his attention to the impressive old building he had to get into. It was built like a stylish fortress but one which the owners who shared it had somehow agreed to paint a sort of doll-house pink. He was pleased to have been right though; that they would leave their captive safely tucked up there - just in case something went wrong when Mutt and Jeff went to collect the goods.

Barney felt a surge of adrenalin, knowing that action could again no longer be avoided. But his adrenalin was fuelled by knowledge. What he hadn't had time to share with Shona was that Jack had also provided him with some very useful information. The actor had guessed that something big was on the go and asked if it had anything to do with Aubert's supposed purchase of the Port of Nice. Jack said he'd heard somewhere that the multi-billion-Euro deal was distinctly dodgy, that bribes had been way beyond the usual, that Aubert's political goal of a lifetime depended on it going through. In short, Barney now knew his enemy. And why the man feared any possible risk of exposure in Nel's legacy.

He pressed the intercom button. A gruff French voice answered. The Scotsman had no problem sounding English. He bawled: 'Allo mate! Is Roger in?'

'Go away. You have the wrong place. No stupid Englishmen here.' It could be Aubert but it was hard to tell. Barney leant on the buzzer and continued to shout at the top of his voice, warming to his role as a tourist who'd had a couple of early beers in the sun. Aubert might have switched off his end of the intercom but half the street couldn't help but hear and Barney gambled that the Frenchman would prefer not to attract attention right now.

'Sod you, chum. Just get Roger down here, right now!' He was sure he could be heard on the top floor, even without any intercom. A couple of Frenchmen walked past, looking his way and mouthing something very rude about the British. But it seemed that he had been correct, that Aubert, or whoever it was up there, didn't want any more disturbance. Because the street door buzzed and the lock clicked open. He was in.

His whole flat would have fitted in the marble entrance hall, six times over. It might even have fitted on the first stair landing. But finally he was at the door on the fifth floor.

He hadn't worked out how he was going to get in. But it had worked downstairs and it might work again. He started thumping on a wooden panel in one of the ornate double doors, conscious that the noise would be tremendous inside but even more so out here and the whole way down the marbled stairwell which served the other highly exclusive apartments.

He followed up with his party piece. 'Roger, for fuck's sake, will you stop taking the piss and get your lardy London arse out here, right now!'

He almost laughed when he finished his charade. But he was encouraged by the French curses from within and responded with a few more smashing thumps with his fist.

The door eased ajar. 'Monsieur, please. You have the wrong apartment. Please go downstairs. It's le weekend and you're disturbing everyone.' Barney felt his back stiffen. Because there was no doubting it now. These were the wheedling tones of Aubert and no-one else. The Scotsman kept to the side, out of his restricted line of vision.

'Aw, I'm sorry, mate. This is where he said, honest. It's just that he's got all the beer and the pub's not open yet. I mean, what's a man to do, eh?'

'Monsieur, if you want beer, I have beer. But if I give you it will you please go away and leave the building?'

'Well that's really big of you, man. Yeah, sure. Really sorry and all that.'

Barney had been thinking on his feet. Aubert obviously had the door on a latch but maybe if he had to pass out a pack of beer, he would have to open it wider. Even as he crossed his fingers, he saw the door briefly close, then open more fully. And there stood Aubert, a big pack of cans in his arms like a serving tray. The look on his face was priceless as he tried to make sense of everything before him: the face, the accent... it was all wrong.

'Hello, sunshine. Remember me?'

Aubert was too stunned to protest as Barney moved in and pushed him towards a black leather couch.

'Right, you've got three seconds to tell me where she is. Then I start shouting again. And this time it'll be to the police.'

Aubert seemed unaware that he had the pack of beer on his lap. He freed a hand to point across the room to a door.

But his captive removed any doubt by shouting: 'In here, Barney. The bedroom.'

He found her tied up in a straight-backed chair at the dressing table, a cotton bag over her head. 'What kept you?' she asked.

'Traffic. It's a bastard.'

Maddy stood and stretched. 'Well, what the hell was all that about? And who are these freaks, anyway?'

Barney led the way out of the room. 'Explanations later.' Aubert could only watch, any idea of resistance robbed by surprise. They took pleasure in tying him to the chair at his writing desk. 'Oh, and by the way, Aubert,' Barney said, smiling, 'I know all about the bribes in your Port deal. Don't think that'll be too good a deal now. After we get it in the press, that is. Which should be - what would you say, Maddy, ten minutes?' Aubert's tan had already vanished but now he wore the ashen mask of an old, defeated man. The bluff had hit home.

He could tell that Shona was still walking when she took the call. 'I've got her, Shona. All good. Aubert was on his own. We've left him tied up. On our way round to the hotel to get that stuff away just like we planned. The moment it's gone, I'm calling Jean-Luc and telling him everything. So just let your guys go. We don't need them.'

But he occasionally forgot that Shona did not take instruction well. 'Bugger that,' she said. 'I'm going to keep an eye on them. Just you get Jean-Luc to send some of his men up to the Chateau and I'll point them out. No bother.'

He smiled as he walked with Maddy, who seemed none the worse for her kidnap, judging by the questions she now plied him with. But he was short on answers until they got to the hotel. He stopped at a pair of big red fire extinguishers in the foyer and put his hand behind them. 'It was something a friend told me about fire extinguishers that made me think of it. No-one looks at them, so it's a good place to hide things if you think you could be about to mugged, or worse.'

For the next half hour in her room he merely sat passively on the edge of the bed, watching her fire off the data here, there and wherever, while he fought off the urge to sink back and sleep for a week after what had been the longest morning of his life.

But he still had the hardest thing to do. To face Jean-Luc.

18 - Coming Clean

Jean-Luc remained scarily silent at the other end of the line as Barney spoke in short, clipped bursts; Nel's legacy, Saint-Jeannet, Maddy's abduction.

'Jean-Luc, I can't tell you how sorry I am that I had to keep all this from you. And I promise, I'm going to tell you everything - just not in the office. We have to meet outside. And Jean-Luc, I know I don't deserve your trust but I need you to meet me in Rue Rossini. I've, em, left Aubert tied up in his apartment.'

He heard his friend almost choke. But the Frenchman said nothing and Barney guessed that Fleur Dupont was at her desk a few metres away.

At last the Captain spoke. 'Yes, that's very interesting. Well I think I can do that. Shall we say fifteen minutes?'

Barney gave the address then pocketed his phone and felt the tension ease from his shoulders. He told Maddy where he was going but she was still on her phone and waved him away.

It was a glorious day outside. As usual. Locals were going about their lives, walking dogs, hauling shopping bags, obedient children skipping along beside, dodging pink-skinned tourists wandering trance-like across the street, oblivious to traffic signals. Life as normal.

Jean-Luc arrived alone. Not particularly happy. Barney

produced Aubert's keys and nodded. The Frenchman snatched them away and opened the main door then led the way upstairs.

They found Aubert as Barney had left him, firmly trussed up on the chair. Jean-Luc signalled for him to calm down then surprised Barney by leading the way out on to the terrace. He signed for Barney to sit.

'Right, Barney. Talk.'

And he did, concisely, as if dictating a witness statement in the interview room. He stumbled only twice. The first was when he described his first meeting with Bridget, Nel's lawyer; how Nel's letter had warned of police corruption, a corruption which prevented him sharing Nel's legacy with Jean-Luc for fear that someone more senior might make it disappear. The second was when he confessed to lying about who he was visiting in hospital, that it had been the lawyer and not a friend as he'd claimed. Having started with a lie, he couldn't have admitted to knowing the lawyer.

The Frenchman continued to wear a grave expression. 'And Nel has given you evidence of his allegation about police corruption?'

'No. But I suspect there's something in the data Maddy has just sent out to her newspaper contacts. I just had to get it out quick and be done with it.'

'Yes, this is what you would call a *hot potato*?'

Barney detected a hard humour in the question and dared a tentative smile.

But the Captain needed more. 'So do you have any other confirmation of Nel's claim?'

'Well, nothing hard, but someone pointed out to me just how surprising it was that not one single person was hurt in all these home attacks and not one person had been arrested. And then, for what's it's worth, there's what Serge Leroy said.'

'About how you might look *a lot closer to home?* Yes, I saw that in your report.'

'You remember that? So you think he could be right?'

'I think it's true that he wants to stay in control here. And if he thinks Aubert is in league with corrupt policemen to create chaos and whip up nationalist anger then he'd be very interested in any proof he could get.'

Jean-Luc sat back and seemed to savour the sun on his face. 'Barney, you asked to meet outside the office, to keep this between ourselves. Now I ask you to do the same with what I'm about to tell you.'

Suddenly, it was Barney's turn to be surprised.

'You see,' said the Captain, 'I too have had my suspicions for some time, long before Nel's execution. I have strong evidence that a number of officers have joined an extreme right wing group but until recently I couldn't tell how far up the ranks it went and I daren't raise a complaint until I knew.'

Barney leant in towards him, as if someone might hear. 'You say *until recently.*'

'Yes, until I had a meeting with my Commandant. I was shocked. He told me I needed to decide what side I was on. He really hates the Brits, said they were taking over the whole region; your politicians, journalists, your elite I suppose, all with their holiday homes. He even said that more of those houses were going to burn. But Barney, I have to be very careful before I do anything about this. So if there is anything reliable in Nel's information, it would be good to know.'

Barney nodded and made a mental note to speak with Maddy.

'But first, Barney, we have the little matter of a leading national politician who is tied up in the next room.'

Barney laughed more freely than he might have normally done; it just felt good to be able to be open again with his friend.

'Aye, and thereby hangs a tale. You see, I suspect that the reason Aubert wanted Nel's treasure was that it contains proof of bribery in his attempt to buy the Port of Nice. Or at least that Aubert believes it does. Nel was very well connected, despite his day job, and might well have had the inside track on all sorts of crooked activity amongst the blessed elite of society.

Jean-Luc nodded deeply. 'Sounds about right. But it looks like we will have plenty of time to question our Monsieur Aubert about that. All this information you talk about - this *treasure* - it is safe?'

Barney nodded.

'Good, then let's get him back to base.' Jean-Luc hit a number on his phone. 'I'll get a team to pick him up. But you'll need to get this Maddy woman to come in right away. We have to go by the book on this.' He spoke to police control then stood, pocketed his phone and heaved a great sigh. 'This will be big, very big. It will have a huge impact on the election.' He shook his head. 'This is just what I need. Now I have the full set: a major art theft; insurance fraud, a public execution and now the arrest of one of the most powerful men in the country.'

Barney grinned sheepishly. 'Well, I do my best.' He pulled out his own phone. He had put it on silent for their talk and now saw that he had a message. 'Shit! That's Shona. Apparently she's lost Aubert's goons and she thinks they're on the way back here.' He saw the question on his friend's face.

'Don't ask.'

Jean-Luc shook his head again. 'You can tell me what Shona is doing mixed up in all this later. For now, we just have to wait for my men to arrive. Then we can do a package deal and offer all three a free lift back to the station.'

'That's good,' said Barney, 'because the chances are that it was these two heavies who put the lawyer in hospital.'

* * *

Back at his desk, Jean-Luc felt the need to explain himself to his hard-working assistant Dupont, who was showing distinct signs of feeling left out.

'You will be part of the investigation and it will be one of the biggest the force has ever known. It will make your career - well, if we don't solve the Nel case first. But you just have to trust me when I say it was necessary for me to first meet DI Mains on my own. It will all come out later but you will understand that he wanted to explain to me first how he'd come to tie up the great Henri Aubert - rather than have some random officers turn up and dump Barney in the slammer first then ask questions later.'

He thought she seemed placated but it was hard to tell and besides, she was again busying herself with trying to track down the missing cleaner, Madame Cortes.

Aubert had made all sorts of accusations in the cells, alleging assault, wrongful arrest and vowing to sue the police for a fortune. In contrast, his two foot soldiers seemed struck dumb, having still not recovered from the shock of arriving back at the apartment only to be bundled into a police vehicle beside their boss. They would soon feature in their very own id parade as soon as the lawyer was well enough.

In a sense, the pressure was now off. The case, since it seemed likely to include allegations against a national figure relating to the sale of the Port, would almost certainly be led by heavyweights from up north, though he would try to keep his promise and get Dupont on the team. Any allegation of police corruption would in any case have to be handed to an outside force.

But now, assuming the fires were all about getting Aubert elected, then it would be interesting to see whether they would suddenly stop.

If so, he and Barney would be free to join forces and focus on the remaining business in hand; the missing paintings and the small matter of solving Nel's murder.

By the time he was ready to head home to Tourrettes-sur-Loup, his thoughts were already turning to tomorrow's delights of tending his network of beehives in the surrounding hills. Aubert could stew in the cells until his fancy Paris lawyers could find their way down south. But neither they nor the Serious Crime cops would arrive until Monday. The merde wouldn't start flying until after he'd spent a perfect Sunday in the hills.

But when he got up to leave, Dupont caught his eye. 'That's her, sir,' she said, putting down her phone. 'Cortes. She'd been in San Remo for a holiday. All good and going back to work on Monday.'

'Good news, Dupont. Well done. Best get a uniform outside her house at least until Monday, when we can decide what to do with her. Bon weekend, or whatever is left of it.'

Despite the avalanche of events he was leaving behind, he was pleased to feel a spring in his step.

19 - Find the DI

Sunday, July 13

Breakfast was served at lunchtime on the villa's terrace. A canopy shaded them from the hot sun as Barney and Shona wordlessly grazed on the over-abundance of pastries, cheeses, meats and fruit. They both felt sore all over but were at least well rested. And Barney knew that the precious gift of a free Sunday would give them time in which to process everything they had been through.

He'd invited Maddy Johnson to come over but she'd spent yesterday afternoon and evening being questioned by the police over her ordeal and had already taken part in a reconstruction. The journalist had no choice but to hand over Nel's little present but seemed unconcerned during their phone conversation. 'It's no big deal because it's already with several major newspapers and their top people will be analysing and verifying its contents. We'll all publish simultaneously if it stands up. Meantime, I'll start going through my own copy. For now though, all I want is a large gin and tonic or three and a cool bed.'

They'd left it at that, apart from a gentle reminder from

Barney that while she was welcome to everything in Nel's legacy, she must give him anything relating to Aubert and the whole South of France situation. Anything she got on alleged crimes in the UK would be a distinct bonus, he hinted.

She'd laughed at that. 'Well, I wouldn't go getting your hopes up. We've cast the net but we don't yet know what we've caught. But no sweat. A deal's a deal.'

He remembered the conversation as he looked across at Shona. 'Fancy a spot of fishing?'

She thought for a moment. 'Well you can fish. I'll handle the boat.'

They were soon on their way down to the village. It was being invaded by tourists from a huge cruise ship in the bay and Barney was relieved to escape into the dinghy and pick up the oars.

The *Bonnie Fechter* bobbed on its mooring line as a shuttle craft scurried back to the mother ship for its next consignment of passengers. She fired up the engine and they slipped past the liner's towering hull. Shona had delighted in telling him, that day when he was a nervous landlubber going sailing for the first time, that the big ships came because the water was almost 100 metres deep.

Today, once they were out of the bay and on sail, they were a practised team, she at the wheel, he letting out the jib on command. There was a gentle breeze here on the west side of Cap Ferrat but he knew it could blow hard further out. Not a natural sailor, he found a secure seat on the port side, partly shaded by the mainsail.

The white frothing foam spilled out behind them as they cut a line almost parallel to the cap, heading roughly south under the sun. They had nowhere special to go and Shona was happy to point the boat wherever the wind wanted.

As it happened, the wind for once decided to ease as they came level with the lighthouse at the end of the Cap. Unusually, they were all but becalmed.

He said: 'Oh well, suppose we'll just have to break out lunch.' The sails flapped feebly as if in confirmation.

'For God's sake, man, you've just had breakfast.' But she duly obliged, vanishing into the cabin then reappearing with the hamper.

First out of the hamper was a half bottle of champagne in an ice sleeve. He watched bemused while she removed two fine glasses and filled them.

'What's all this about?' he asked, worried that he'd forgotten a birthday or something.

'Typical man! Our anniversary, of course.'

He panicked. Then he started counting back. They'd only got together about six months ago, in Edinburgh.

'One year,' she said. 'Well, give or take. One year since we met.'

Then he got it. Yes, they'd met here in Villefranche, for the first time, probably just about a year ago, right enough. Not love at first sight but a slow burn.

They clinked glasses, sipped, then kissed, a slow lingering kiss while he and no doubt she tried to absorb the enormous changes in their lives in that single year, appreciating all that they had. Because yesterday it might all have been snatched away.

He broke off to empty his glass. 'Maybe next year, we'll managed a whole bottle?'

She calmly poured the rest of her champagne on his head and he cried out at the shock of the cold and she screamed in laughter.

'Right,' he said. 'You're in trouble now.' He grabbed her and she struggled to escape. One thing led to another. The bottle was knocked over.

* * *

Detective Sergeant Ffiona McLuskey wasn't really cross, more disappointed. She'd tried to reach Barney several times without success and now that her flight had been called, it looked like her arrival would just have to be a surprise, hopefully a good one.

She had better luck with Jean-Luc. She could tell he was outside and it turned out that all that interference on the line was actually a hive of disturbed bees.

He explained that he needed to quieten them down and she waited. 'OK, all good now, Ffiona. Great to hear from you.'

'Hi Jean-Luc. I'm at Edinburgh Airport. Just got told I've to come down to help Barney but I can't reach him so...'

'Ah, Barney, yes. Barney has had a busy time but maybe he won't be so busy now.'

She was intrigued and not a little worried. 'Not so busy now? What do you mean?'

She heard him move somewhere quiet and settle down. Then he gave her the highlights. The arrest of Aubert, the probability that he was behind the *Brits Out* protests and fires, the possibility that Barney's job had just become a lot easier.

'Well, that's just great,' she said, thinking the opposite. 'Looks like I won't be staying long. Which suits me fine, actually. Going like a fair here. But what the hell, I'm just heading to the gate so at least I'll get to see you again and catch up.'

'Ah, but of course, dear Ffiona. But just to make you aware that tomorrow I may be a little busy. We've got the big boys coming down from Paris to teach us locals how to do our jobs.'

She stopped walking, causing a woman and small child to bump into her. Ffiona apologised then resumed walking towards the gate. She had for a moment thought to turn round and walk straight back out of the airport. But orders were orders. Her bosses wanted her in the South of France for reasons best known to themselves and to the South of France she must go. Even if she had to get a flight back tomorrow.

* * *

They had gone on the boat with the intention of fishing. But they never cast a line and instead bought their fish in the form of lunch on the quayside. And now that they were climbing back up the steep steps through the village towards the villa they were arm in arm. He'd remember their anniversary next time round.

All he had to think about now was just how lazy a late afternoon they were going to have and how much whisky he had left.

'Reporting for duty, sir!' Ffiona's words had what was no doubt the desired effect. He was flummoxed, trying to place the voice, the context, the whatever-the-hell was going on. It was Shona who reacted first, running up to the younger woman and giving her a tight hug.

'I'd rather you just salute, sir, if you don't mind.'

'Aye, aye, enough of your cheek, McLuskey. And what kind of uniform do you call that?'

She still had her usual dark trouser suit to match her short black hair but the jacket was draped over her arm and her pale, fine-boned face was in the shade of a floppy straw hat and dark glasses.

'Undercover, sir. On a big case. Called *Find the Detective Inspector*.'

He laughed. 'In which case, congratulations. No wonder you made Sergeant so quickly. Great to see you, Ffiona, really. Though I've got to ask. What the hell are you doing here?'

Shona shushed them before they could get started. 'Barney, bring Ffiona inside. You've got plenty of time to talk. But let's get inside, out of the sun, and have something cool to drink.'

They stayed indoors with the ceiling fans at full speed. Hermione, the maid, had provided snacks and chilled soft drinks. Barney offered something stronger all round but got no takers and consoled himself with a very large glass of his usual malt whisky. For once, he compromised by adding a little ice.

'OK, Ffiona, shoot!'

She sipped her orange juice and shrugged. 'It's all a bit bizarre. You know they'd been thinking of sending me down to help out? So, suddenly this morning, they said to get the next available flight. Well, I naturally assumed things were hotting up - sorry - and you really needed a hand. But now I hear from Jean-Luc that I'm probably wasting my time.'

'You spoke to Jean-Luc and not me?'

'Check your phone, sir. I could never get an answer.'

He looked across at Shona. 'Ah, well, that's probably because we were out sailing. Must have been outside signal range, or something'

'Which is why I tried Jean-Luc. And he told me about this guy Aubert and how maybe the fires might all stop. Which

184

would presumably mean you don't need me?'

Barney stuck his nose in his glass to enjoy the smoky fumes before committing to that special, first swallow. 'Well, I wouldn't go running back to the airport just yet. Let's just see how tomorrow goes. There's a wee bit more going on here than Edinburgh might be aware off. I'll fill you in. But later. Now, if you ladies will excuse me, I feel a dip coming on.'

Barney rose, gave Shona a peck on the cheek, and took his whisky for a walk out to the pool. He heard his two favourite women launch into animated conversation. He imagined Shona's retelling of yesterday's adventures, the constant interjections from Ffiona. Always on duty, it was a wonder she didn't have her ever-present notebook out.

But for now, he was glad to escape to the solitude of an empty pool. He took a long, throat-burning slug of whisky then put the glass down on the glass-topped table and stripped down to his trunks, glad to be rid off his sweaty shirt and shorts.

He slipped through the warm surface of the water then thrilled in the cool beneath. He turned onto his back to idly paddle towards the far end then stopped and just floated there, staring up into the deep blue sky with not a single, blessed thought in his head.

20 - Deadeye Jack

The city away from the tourist hot spots had the feel of a typical lazy Sunday; little traffic and very few people out and about despite the easing heat.

Barney parked their rental outside Jack Thomson's spectacular deco building. They'd aimed to call on the man but it was almost seven o'clock and judging by the buzz coming from across the road, people had already gathered in the pétanque club.

Shona had about ten years on Ffiona and instinctively grabbed the younger woman's hand to pull her across the road. Ffiona laughed but played along.

Barney hadn't known what to expect from the event. He'd assumed that while Jack the showman had given it the big build up, it could turn out to be just a quiet Sunday evening bit of fun. The crowd he found inside said otherwise. He estimated three or four hundred. And there was a distinct air of suppressed excitement. There were few children; this was a mature audience which now formed a human amphitheatre around the *terrain* where the gladiators would engage in battle.

The crowd hushed just as Barney and the girls entered. But attention was focused away from them, towards the little clubhouse. Barney's height enabled him to give a running commentary.

'There's Jack coming out now with another bloke, a young guy who's got a big smile on his face and waving to folk. Jack's either nervous or super cool but he looks pretty stern. Ha! It's like the parting of the waters. The crowds are splitting to let them past. Come on. Let's get closer.'

But the girls preferred to stay on the edge and told Barney to do his own thing. They'd catch up back at the car after the match.

The big Scotsman eased his way through the crowd, using plenty of *pardons* and *excusez-mois* on the way. He wouldn't have got away with it at Tynecastle or Easter Road, Edinburgh's tribal football clubs. Maybe it was the weather in this part of the world but there wasn't the same aggro at big events. Though he reckoned that it might be best if they didn't suss him as a Brit.

At last, he was almost at the front. He was looking down the length of the playing surface towards the clubhouse. Jack and his opponent stood chatting with an official-looking man with an id card hanging on a red ribbon round his neck. Jack seemed unmoved by the occasion, nodding slowly, holding a small bag against his stomach. His young opponent had his head down as if listening intently but might have been more intent on rolling the metal boule back and forth under his foot.

Then the official stood aside, the opponents shook hands without engaging, like boxers touching gloves before they commenced to knock the stuffing out of each other.

The young man, tall and wiry with wavy black hair, was a bit of a pin-up. He threw down the little circle from which he'd have to throw, stepped in then sent out the *cochonnet* with an easy flick of the wrist. The tiny target ball jigged across the gravel towards Barney then settled.

Pin-up held his first piece of artillery in his right hand, palm down. He swung back and through sharply and the silver orb shot skywards. Probably weighing a good three-quarters of a kilo, it plummeted straight down, smashing into the gravel just inches short of the target and clinging to its crater as if to a magnet. A roar of approval from his supporters. A release of tension, renewed conviction that they'd made a good bet.

It was Jack's turn. Barney knew a little about the game but anyone could see that there was no way he could get close because he wouldn't even be able to see his target behind that blocking shot.

Jack stretched as tall as he could on the balls of his feet then suddenly crouched and in what seemed like one movement, fired his missile on a flat trajectory. It struck the boule like a cannonball, sending it flying in a jet of dust. Barney needed *instant replay;* it had happened so fast that he doubted his eyes. He squinted up the length of the terrain to check that it was Jack, soulmate of mild-mannered Charlie Chaplin, who had unleashed that incredible shot with such violent precision.

But Jack had turned away to pick up his next boule, with barely a nod to acknowledge the gasps, then applause, of well over half the crowd. Barney loved to be surprised by people, to find unexpected talents, refreshing reminders that everyone was uniquely special. He smiled and shook his head in happy wonder at the little man.

Time froze after that. The cycle repeated. Pin-up again planted a towering shot to cover the cochon, or pig, as some called the diminutive target ball. And Jack blew it away. But on his final throw, facing the self-same challenge, Jack's missile failed to catch its target full on and glanced off instead, leaving his opponent to chalk up the first score.

The two men ambled up towards Barney for the next end, the young man relaxed and smiling to friends in the crowd, Jack impassive and appearing to stare straight ahead. Barney waved, trying to offer encouragement but Jack was somewhere off in Jackland.

The players battled it out like that for five more ends with Pin-up sometimes taking over the role of dead-eye dick, then Jack. The crowd was loving it. It was clear that the majority favoured the Scotsman but he seemed to be forever chasing the game and finally ended up losing.

But there was a long way to go. And Barney wasn't going anywhere. He got talking to a young couple who told him it was a district final with a lot of betting going on. Jack was the local man and naturally everyone's favourite but his opponent was a rising star and they feared for Jack's chances. They shared their pack of beer from a cool bag and oohed and aahed along with Barney for the next ninety minutes, until suddenly the gladiators were into the decider.

It started much like the first with neither man flinching in the testing plant-and-shoot exchanges. But finally, almost inevitably it seemed, it all came down to the final shot which would decide the match.

Jack stood at the clubhouse end, stooped in the circle, the final boule in his right hand. Barney felt as if they were peering into each other's eyes but Jack had eyes only for his target and Barney could see that he was off somewhere in his imagination, feeding in the calculations, feeling the distance, picturing the required trajectory and preparing the muscle memory to impart maximum controlled force at release. Then, as if he'd thrown a switch, he straightened in that now familiar rise then crouched and fired. Bullseye! His target vanished as if snatched away on a chain and in it's place sat its destroyer. The cochon never moved. Jack had won.

The crowd, so well behaved until now, swarmed onto the pitch. Jack was still shaking his opponent's hand when he was plucked away and hoisted on shoulders. As always on such occasions, someone had a bottle of champagne and Jack was now beaming as he splashed it all over himself. Jack, the carefree, easy-going man he had come to know, was back. But there was no way Barney would even try to get close. The Charlie Chaplin lookalike was again the property of his fans and Barney had no problem making his escape through the thinning knots of disappointed losers.

With no sign of the girls, he checked his phone at the gate. *We're probably at Sandrine's* was the vague message from Shona. But he had an idea where that might be and headed up Boulevard Gambetta.

Sure enough, a few minutes walk away, he found them sitting outside the same little wine bar where he'd joined Jack and Gracie that fateful evening when he first met the lawyer.

Gracie was there again this time too. Shona had remembered her from the Fitzwilliam's party and they seemed to be getting on like, well, like a house on fire.

Barney loved how women could have such a great spontaneous time together and he wasn't surprised that no-one even asked how Jack had fared. Too many stories, too many laughs.

He ordered them another bottle of white and a large beer for himself. 'Better make it a small one, big man,' Shona said. 'Looks like you're the nominated driver.'

Barney put on a hard-done-by look but didn't change his

order. 'Maybe I should get champagne all round to celebrate.'

The three women looked blank.

'To toast Jack? You know, the match? The big event you two ladies came to watch?'

'Shit!' said Ffiona. 'I forgot. How'd it go? He won, I take it?'

'Actually, he was totally amazing. What a guy. I've never seen anything like it. The precision, the focus…'

Gracie was nodding. 'Yes, he was always pretty good at things like that. I remember once we were on a gig at some F1 driver's place in Monaco. Can't remember the name. Lots of them live in Monaco. But anyway, someone brought out carpet bowls and thought it would be funny to get photos of him playing against Charlie Chaplin. But of course Jack's really competitive and one thing led to another. All the guys wanted in on the game and they ended up playing till dawn. Some serious money changed hands that night, I can tell you.'

And then the girls were pressing Gracie for more tales of gigs for the rich and famous. Any faint interest in the night's proceedings was gone. It reminded him of his rugby days, when he would come back, usually bruised and bloody, still high on the battle and the booze. His then wife showed about as much interest as he had managed to muster tonight.

After a while, Ffiona and Shona got into talking about Edinburgh and the places they both knew in their home town, giving Barney the chance to lean over to Gracie. 'So remind me again how you guys met in the first place, you and Jack?'

She seemed to be a couple of glasses ahead of the girls, her lips turning to rubber. She waved a hand. 'I do not wish to make a statement at this time, occifer.' She giggled.

'But seriously. I'm curious. It's just that he seems like a guy with hidden talents.'

'Oh, you can sure say that again,' she said, slurring a little before just about managing to tap her nose with a finger then nodding in agreement with herself. 'More than you'll ever know.'

'But you discovered him, on a beach, wasn't it?'

She laughed and stared into the past 'Well, it's always been great publicity. They always use that. The great Jack Thomson. Rags to riches. Everybody's favourite.'

'Ha! So just a story for the press?'

'Something like that. Ask Jack. He wouldn't like me telling tales out of school.

Barney nodded and sipped his beer. 'Will do. Will do.' She'd made him curious but before he could ask anything else, Shona had her hand on his arm and was saying something about *time to go*. He saw Ffiona watching and he twigged that she was probably the one who thought that. His ever-diligent young sidekick would be well aware that tomorrow was going to be a big day. And that they would need to be on their toes.

21 - Square One

Monday, July 14

Jean-Luc had Barney and Ffiona beside him in the ringside seats behind the two-way glass and they were all sipping their coffees as Aubert's lawyer began. The man presented a document to the two officers from Paris sitting across the table then told them they had to release his man immediately and bring *the rogue Scottish policeman* in for questioning. And then charge him with assault, kidnap and forced imprisonment.

Barney had to give the Paris cops their due. They might be, as Jean-Luc had said, *a couple of self-important twats,* but they didn't seem ready to take any bullshit.

'You're not here to make allegations or tell us how to do our job, chum,' said the smaller one. 'And if anyone's being charged with assault, kidnap and forced imprisonment it's your client. And not that it's any of your business but we have this morning taken a full statement from our Scottish colleague. But he's not sitting here; your client is. So now's the time for him to talk.'

The officer looked to his taller, younger colleague alongside, who took up the action.

'Now, Monsieur Aubert, can you tell us how you know the journalist Madame Madeleine Johnson?'

Aubert, now restored to his elegant best, awaited a nod from his lawyer, an effete-looking type with a starched white-collar so sharp he could cut himself. The politician then sat up straight and raised his chin to speak with the utmost sincerity. 'I don't know this woman.'

'Can you then explain why she says you abducted her and kept her tied up in your property in Rue Rossini?'

Again the consultation. 'I don't have to explain it because it's not true.'

Barney looked at Jean-Luc. 'Really, he's using that old one?'

The Frenchman shrugged. 'He has no choice. We have him, as you say, *bang to rights.* We have her statement and yours. He has nowhere to go except prison. But he'll spend a lot longer inside if we can get evidence of corruption over the Port deal and can link that to the attack on the lawyer. Now that I know about that attack, I can get her statement too and maybe make the connection to Aubert through his goons.'

Barney bit back another apology. The main thing now was to get a result.

There was a sudden shout from behind the glass. Aubert had sprung to his feet and was stabbing a finger at the cops. He was bright red and swearing like a trooper while his alarmed lawyer tugged at his arm.

The cops merely stood up. The smaller one said: 'Interview suspended' and led his colleague out of the room.

Jean-Luc shrugged and suggested the canteen.

Barney saw Ffiona's face but insisted she come. He explained that it wasn't like at home. Here, the canteen was somewhere to enjoy, not a place that reeked of stewed vegetables and chips with everything.

They topped up their coffees and chose three comfy chairs around a small table.

Ffiona was impressed but still not happy. 'Look, sir, this is great but I'm starting to feel guilty. I think it's about time I was thinking of heading back home.'

Barney smiled. 'Look, Ffiona, chill. They sent you out. You go back now and they'll think they've made a mistake and wasted their money. They don't like to admit making a mistake. You need to hang on a bit. And don't worry, I'll find something for you to do.'

Just what that might be, he had no idea. But at a push he could have her chase up some of the house attacks he hadn't got round to. On the other hand, if the arrest of Aubert meant there would be no new ones to investigate, he might be struggling to even find enough work to keep himself busy.

But Jean-Luc seemed to have been reading Barney's mind. 'Now, since you've already met Nel's lawyer, can I suggest you and Ffiona go and speak to her, see if she's up to checking out our two special guests in an identification parade. I would like to meet her too.'

'Good idea. It was on my list.'

'Your list?'

'Well, short list. I need to contact Edinburgh, bring them up to date before they read all about Aubert in the press. Plus I need to see Maddy to find out what the hell Shona and I have been risking our lives for.'

Jean-Luc was nodding his agreement. Ffiona looked interested.

'Good,' said Jean-Luc, preparing to rise. 'I have a few things to check out. But after that, I need to concentrate on Nel's murder. Let's meet up later, once you know how the lawyer is.'

Barney knew he could call the garage for a car but it was already hot out there and he could use some fresh air so he called a velo-taxi. Their young veloiste spoke perfect English and insisted on chatting over his shoulder. *Cabbies, the same all over the world.* But the trip was short and they were soon at the hospital reception. To Barney's delight, he found Bridget O'Brien walking along the corridor outside her private room, fully dressed.

'My God, Maitre O'Brien, they make lawyers tough in Ireland.'

'Ha, not tough enough,' said the lawyer.

Barney made the introductions and quickly explained that Jean-Luc would like her to come in to Police HQ to give a statement and possibly identify her attackers. She was all for it but insisted on going home first. 'I just want to feel normal for a bit. I'll come in later, or maybe tomorrow. I'll call.'

'That's great, Bridget. In your own time. But if you don't mind, could we maybe have a private word?'

They moved into her room, where she sank gratefully into a chair. 'Getting there,' she said.

'Yeah, it'll take time. But speaking of which, I just wanted to bring you up to speed on Saint-Jeannet, where Pieter Nel left his little present.'

She slowly nodded.

He gave her the highlights of Saturday, the drama in the hills, Maddy's involvement, her abduction by Aubert and finally how Nel's legacy had been shared with several newspapers. Barney could feel Ffiona's eyes piercing into him as he spoke.

'The thing is, I think the two guys who attacked you were

sent by Aubert, that he fears something in Nel's stuff that could implicate him over the purchase of Nice Port. So anything you might know about that would be really helpful...'

But Bridget was shaking her head. 'All I know is that there are a lot of questions around that deal. Everyone suspects something but as far as I know, there's no proof.'

'Fair enough. But one more question. Bridget, you told me that you were Nel's original Plan B, before I became the poor bugger with the poison chalice. But by the time he knew that I was coming to Nice, he would have been locked up. So there's no way he could have personally stuck it in a hole in the wall of a ruin at Saint-Jeannet. Which means someone else did.'

She smiled. 'Agreed.'

'So who else knew about it?'

'Barney, I'm sorry, but I was acting in the best interests of my client and he wanted it this way. Full disclosure? It was originally in my safe but like I told you already, he was worried that he might have put me in danger. So when he heard you were coming he saw a way to make me safe - or so he thought.'

'By having you plant it up there for me to collect and almost get myself - and Shona - killed.'

'Barney, I'm so sorry. I had no idea. I know that area well and we thought it was the perfect place, away from any security cameras or cops. So isolated that you could see and hear anyone coming anywhere close.'

It was Barney's turn to smile.

'What is it?' asked the lawyer.

'Well, at least he was right on that front. But OK, let's say he decided, for reasons best known to himself, that he could trust me and not the French Police Nationale. I can think of a thousand places he could have got you to leave it. But I could see in court that he had a devilish sense of humour. I wondered at the time why he had picked me out to pretend to shoot. But now I understand. It was his idea of a joke. He had you put it up there on a clifftop because he found out I had a real fear of heights. It was his last joke.'

She made to speak but stopped herself, seeming to see that Barney was right, as if this did indeed sound like the Pieter Nel she had come to know.

* * *

It was the talk of the canteen. Two off-duty police officers had been treated for burns at the weekend after being caught in a wildfire in the hills. They'd been out hunting when the wind turned and lit up the hillside like a torch. They were lucky to be alive by all accounts.

Jean-Luc didn't believe in coincidences. These had to be the guys who attacked Barney and Shona. It looked like he could now positively identify two of his corrupt colleagues, two traitors who had no doubt been operating under Aubert's orders.

But he was wary of believing everything he was hearing from the next table. Police were no less guilty than the general public of embellishing facts with gossip, after all.

He hurried back to his office and immediately logged into the force database. It all suddenly became clear. The two injured officers were two of the guards from the court building, two who had guarded a staircase on the day of the shooting. They were members of a local hunting club and would no doubt use that fact as cover for being in the Saint-Jeannet hills in the first place. But it wasn't only *their* names which threw Jean-Luc into a black mood. For after identifying this two, it had been logical to then check the names of the second pair of guards. And now he learned that while they weren't in the same club, they did belong to another one, towards the west. France had more hunters than anywhere else in Europe and it was quite possible for the four to have met up at any of the region's many so-called *sporting* events. He wanted to believe what they'd told him, that they really hadn't seen each other before that day. But his gut told him otherwise.

He sat frozen-faced when Fleur Dupont returned to the office. He hated what he was thinking. He had trusted Dupont to check out the four officers. He just couldn't believe that she'd missed it. Had he given her too much responsibility too soon? Was it his fault? And then the thought that made his skin tighten: this could send them back to day one of the inquiry, again having to assume that they were dealing with crooked cops. And this time they had potentially damning evidence.

Dupont was saying something about protection for Madame Cortes, the cleaner, but he never took it in. He had to go through everything in the file, to check every single step they'd taken. It they'd missed such an obvious potential connection, what else might have been missed?

* * *

Ffiona was bending Barney's ear about the drama of Saint-Jeannet even before they left the hospital. He tried to shrug it all off but she was having none it and eventually he promised to tell all, but first they had to find a cafe and sit down.

They settled on one in the massive Place Garibaldi. It was still quiet and the waiters hadn't started setting up for lunch. The fountain at the statue of the great man burbled in the background as they sat in the dappled shade of low, feathery-leafed trees. While they waited for their drinks he pointed out the amazing trompe l'oeil which ennobled the otherwise flat-faced buildings which formed the square.

'Very interesting,' she said, not in the least interested. 'Now give.'

So he gave pretty well everything about the last few days as she sat, her chin occasionally dropping, those expressive black slashes of eyebrows, her personal trompe l'oeil, rising, falling and arching in turn.

He hadn't meant to sound bored but he'd told the story so often that he hoped this was the last. She was sitting back in her chair now, a bemused look on her face. But at least she had stopped hassling him for details.

He pulled out his phone and made a call he'd been looking forward to. 'Hey, Jack. Not too early am I? You probably had a late night.'

'Barney, old chum. How simply spiffing to hear from you. Not too early at all. Just been out for a wee run. Had my shower. Ready to go.'

'I just wanted to congratulate you on last night. That was a hell of a performance. You were, as the kids say, awesome.'

'Aw shucks, it were nuttin' at all.'

'Yeah, well, that's not what I saw. That was some serious precision firing. I've only ever seen that on French TV. Where did you learn to play like that? I mean, the focus, the technique.'

'Och it's just one of those things. But why didn't you come back for a drink? I was looking for you?'

'Oh, there was too big a crowd round you. And I had to meet up with the girls. Gracie was there by the way. At the Sandrine. She was in good form. A wee bit tipsy, but she fairly came up with some stories. You featured actually.'

'How do you mean? What did she say about me?'

'Oh nothing. It was just a tale about you playing carpet bowls in Monaco with some F1 driver. What a life. I was even hoping to hear more about how you two first met up, how you got started. But she went all mysterious. Said I'd have to ask you.'

'Och, that old story. You don't want to hear that. But hey, why don't you come over later. I'm taking a couple of days off. I can maybe pass on a few tips on the pétanque terrain.'

'Sounds great, Jack. But I'll come back to you on that. Got a few things on at the moment.'

He was still smiling when he ended the call. He turned to Ffiona. 'That was Jack, from last night, as you might have guessed. Wants to teach me to play pétanque.' But Barney had a niggle, one he couldn't yet define, one he would keep to himself for now.

22 - Secrets

Maddy couldn't get them into her room quick enough, as if she'd been waiting for hours. She'd acquired two extra chairs and now, introductions over and with the three of them crammed in around the laptop on her little desk, she got straight down to business.

'OK Barney, Ffiona. First, I can tell you that I've heard back from a couple of my colleagues. And you are not going to believe what they've found encrypted on that memory stick.

'At first glance, it looks like this legacy of yours is only about a political plot affecting the South of France. But in fact, there's a much bigger picture.

'You see, Barney, it turns out that this region was only just the beginning of something much scarier.'

She shook her head as if irritated by herself. 'Sorry, I'm getting ahead of myself. First, you need to know that Pieter Nel has somehow been able to produce solid evidence of serious police corruption, including big financial transactions involving senior officers. To cut to the chase, it looks like our dear friend Monsieur Aubert owns half the force!

'And that's not all. Nel's even given us a document with Aubert's signature on it; a manifesto setting out his maniac vision of an independent state within France, a right-wing enclave free of all immigrants. Even immigrants like rich Brits.'

Maddy leaned towards Barney. 'Listen, what you need to know is that Aubert is only one part of a hard right network which has spread throughout Europe.

'If his campaign of terror and corruption of the justice system had succeeded here, you'd have seen chaos like this flare up in at least five other countries within a year. These guys thrive on instability and Aubert was close to showing them all exactly how to do it.'

'Shit, Maddy. Scary stuff indeed. So what do we do about it? What happens now?'

'Now? Now we're going to going to shine the cold light of day on this dark web of fascists. Don't get me wrong. We'll never be entirely free of them. But thanks to you, we've stopped them in their tracks this time. They'll take years to regroup.'

Barney thought for a moment. 'Well, I reckon that anything good that comes out of all this is down to Nel. God knows what his motive was. Maybe he wanted to make amends for his crimes. Maybe he simply hated fascists. Whatever. I guess we just have to be grateful.

'Meantime though,' he said, 'I don't suppose there's any more detail in there about the small matter of Aubert's crooked Port deal?'

Maddy nodded quickly. 'I was coming to that.' She scrolled down the screen of her laptop. 'Here it is. I don't know who Nel hacked to get all this but he's got bank statements which provide an incontrovertible paper trail of massive bribes paid by Henri Aubert, not only to police but to senior public officials he paid to trash rival bids. You've got him bang to rights.'

'Ha! Someone else said that already. Speaking of whom, I take it you can give all this to my colleague Jean-Luc Verten?'

'Just in the process of putting it all together for him, although they've got the original and will no doubt work all this out themselves.

'Barney, I know Pieter Nel trusted no-one in the police but I'm happy to take your assurances about Captain Verten. Though, sorry, but even if he wasn't straight, this is all going to come out in the press anyway, once we've got it all fact-checked and lawyered.'

Barney nodded. 'From one professional cynic to another, no need to apologise.'

As they left the journalist alone to finish her summary for Jean-Luc, Barney felt Ffiona's impatience at again being a passenger in proceedings at a time when the interlocking cases that had absorbed him since arriving in the South of France were all, or almost all, in the process of being resolved.

Yet he still had a niggle.

'Look Ffiona, before you say anything. I totally get how you feel. You need to be busy and here you are having to play catch-up all the time and it's driving you crazy. It must be like arriving late at the movies and only getting the happy-ever-after ending. But there's something I want you to do, something I can't do myself because I'm personally involved. It could be important or it could be nothing. But it's a gut feeling and it has to be checked.

* * *

Barney found Jean-Luc bent over his keyboard, again. The

Frenchman looked up as he entered but said nothing. Fleur Dupont was focused on her screen. She never even looked up. You could cut the atmosphere with a knife.

'Hi guys. I can see you're busy. I just wanted to let you know, Jean-Luc, that Madeleine Johnson is about to send you the bones of Nel's package. It sounds like good stuff. Just what your guys need to close the Aubert case.'

Jean-Luc looked up and grunted.

'And the lawyer, Bridget O'Brien, is getting out today. She'll come in later or, more likely tomorrow, as requested. No bother.'

Getting no more than a nod and an apologetic smile, Barney turned to make his escape. Whatever was going on, he'd no doubt find out in the fullness of time. The truth be told, now that everything was falling into place, he was more concerned about what Ffiona would come back with when they met up later in the Cours Saleya for lunch.

'I'll be off then,' he said, exaggerating a breezy tone. 'I'll be at your slippery friend's bistro for lunch if you're free.' He settled for a pained grunt and left.

He opted to walk despite the heat. But he chose the narrower streets parallel to Boulevard Carabacel and was soon able to cut through into the shaded lanes of the Old Town. The downside of his preferred route was that there was little escape from meandering tourists gawping at stalls, shops and art galleries with all their rich and strange offerings, from unknown components of animal innards to the bizarre creations of man which someone had decided was art.

He got there first and claimed the table he had first shared with Jean-Luc, back when all they had to deal with was a nice simple murder. He suddenly realised that that had been a

Monday too, though a little later in the day. Then, the weekly antique market was breaking up. Today, it was very much open for business. He watched as a couple of mature tourists tried to haggle over a painting. The stall-holder looked up to heaven, mortally insulted. You didn't need to hear the words to appreciate the ritual. He pulled the painting out of the man's hands and made great show of putting it back on his stall. But the woman spoke to her man and suddenly a deal was done. The stallholder was pained; he was starving his wife and children. It was only because this charming couple loved it so, that he would let them have this masterpiece for such a ridiculous price. Talk about performance art. Barney almost resented the arrival of the rarely-seen waiter who'd deigned to serve him last Monday only when Jean-Luc appeared. He ordered a beer and a glass of white.

When Ffiona turned up, the tourists were marching off with their bargain, the wife hugging her partner's arm. The stallholder was counting his money.

'Aw, I don't want any wine, thanks, sir. I had enough last night. But I'll have a glass of water if that's OK.'

'Fine with me. All you have to do is persuade the waiter.'

'Uh, OK.' She sat then pulled out her laptop and placed it on the table.

'This looks serious,' he said, half joking.

'Not sure, sir. Let you be the judge. But first off, lovely Gracie couldn't have discovered Jack. On the beach or anywhere else. Because when Jack arrived here she was still doing repertory theatre in England. She didn't come here until two years later.'

Barney was nodding. 'I knew there was something. They were both so vague. So go on. Where does that take us?'

'Well, there's nothing much to say about Gracie. She came over after lots of theatre and has by all accounts become pretty successful here as a lookalike.

'Jack on the other hand has a very interesting back story. I think you said he'd told you that he'd been an actor too but I couldn't find anything to back that up. No, he's ex-Army.'

Barney peered at her. 'Ex-Army? No, he was only in for a short time after school, pretty soon realised the error of his ways and left, he said.'

'Sorry, not correct. Joined straight from school probably but never came out until shortly before he turned up down here. Started out in what was The Royal Scots. Later the Prince of Wales Royal Regiment, did a couple of tours in Afghanistan...'

'You have got to be joking! He's a slight, wee guy, wouldn't hurt a fly. There must be some mistake.'

But Ffiona carried on. 'Then he was transferred into Military Intelligence. But that's where the trail stops because the MoD wouldn't give me any more without a formal written request. It needs to come from Detective Inspector level or above.'

She checked her screen and turned the laptop round to face him. 'There it is, sir, straight from the MoD. Jack Hunter Thomson, born Auchtermuchty, Fife, and look, here's an old mugshot. And one that's a bit more up to date in a group. But there's nothing since he went into intelligence, for obvious reasons.'

Jack read the information on the screen, scarcely believing, hoping that there had been a mix-up. The Army were famous for it. But the pictures didn't lie. This was Jack Thomson, aka Charlie Chaplin, harmless performer and, he had thought, his friend.

He checked the dates, the incredible, undeniable facts which Ffiona had managed to put together in such a short time. Then he registered the details. He'd left the Army in the same year as he'd claimed to have arrived in Nice. So it all tied in. What Ffiona had failed to mention was something that on the face of it could be totally irrelevant. Jack had indeed served with the Prince of Wales Royal Regiment. But it was with a specific battalion within the famous Regiment - the 5th Battalion The Rifles.

Barney realised he must be showing his shock because Ffiona suddenly asked if he was OK. 'You've done well, Ffiona. And you thought you were wasting your time. This may all turn out to be nothing but I'm afraid it means that Mr Jack Thomson from Auchtermuchty at least has some questions to answer. But first, I need to speak to Gracie. Any ideas on how I get her number - other than asking Jack?'

She pulled back her laptop. Under a minute later her screen was filled by the home page of the Riviera Look-Twice Agency and there at the top were pictures of the Agency's biggest stars - Gracie and Jack. He called and after an initial struggle convincing the receptionist that he really was a personal friend of Gracie's but had lost her number, she finally obliged.

He let the number ring for a long time and was about to give up when a breathless Gracie answered. 'Gracie. Barney. How are you?'

'Oh, fine, luvvie, just fine. You're so sweet.'

'Well maybe not so sweet today, Gracie. You see, I need you to answer the question I asked you last night. I need to know how you first met Jack and when.'

Her voice dropped a tone. 'Are you asking as lovely Shona's man or as a policeman?'

'Both, Gracie.'

'In which case, I'll come clean. It's no big deal. We made up that story about me finding him on the beach and then him having this amazing talent. It was good box office and the press just loved it, so it seemed churlish to change it once we started getting the bookings.'

'You actually arrived here a couple of years after Jack, didn't you?'

'Well, it must have been something like that. But how do you know?'

'It's not important. What I want to know is: if you didn't get Jack started, then who did? As far as I know, he came straight out the Army then suddenly turns up as a star turn on the French Riviera.'

She paused, apparently thinking how to respond. 'Well, like you say, Barney, he was here when I arrived. Nobody had heard of me, but he had already started and it was actually the other way round. He got me started.'

Barney thought about that. 'So we still don't know how he managed this miraculous transformation in his life. He comes out of the Army, presumably with very little money, yet can afford to live here and start making a living as a lookalike. Someone must have helped him, surely.'

She went silent. 'Look Barney, I'd like to help. But Jack is a very private sort of guy. He wouldn't want me talking about his private life. Besides, you might not believe it but he's got a heck of a temper.'

'Look, this is a police inquiry, Gracie. People don't have private lives any more and I don't care if he goes ballistic. So will you please stop being so bloody coy and tell me what you know.'

'OK, OK, keep your shirt on. But this didn't come from me, alright? If you want to know who took Jack under his wing, who's always been a proper father figure to him, it's a guy you might not have heard of. They say he used to be a big-time crook but I've only ever known him as a very successful businessman. Serge Leroy's his name. Some people call him the King.'

23 - Prime Suspect

He hoped it would be enough. He'd downloaded the form from Police Scotland's database and had added his digital signature before firing it off to the Ministry of Defence. All Barney could do now was wait. Having enjoyed a light lunch with Ffiona then seen her back to her hotel, he could now at least wait in the comfort of the canteen with an iced tea; he'd declared the office out of bounds until Jean-Luc and Dupont sorted themselves out.

The next item on his list could be avoided no longer however. It could result in Ffiona's instant recall but it had to be done. 'Bonjour, sir,' he said, hoping the Assistant Chief Constable, old Eagle-eyes, was in a less hawkish mood than usual.

'Cut the French crap, Mains. About time you were reporting in. What's this I'm hearing about a couple of cops getting caught in a wildfire? At first I assumed it was you who'd got lost with your French Captain chappie.'

Barney realised the story about the injured cops must have made the press and only now twigged that the incident was probably what had put Jean-Luc in such a bad mood. He paused to make sure that Eagle-eyes had finished his rant then settled down to tell his own story of the last few days, for hopefully the last time, this time.

For once, the ACC was silent, so silent that when Barney had finished his report, he panicked that they must have been cut off and that he'd have to repeat the whole sodding thing again. But finally his soon-to-be-retired boss spoke.

'Bloody hell, Mains. You've really stirred the shit this time.'

'Yes sir. Thank you sir.'

'But what does it all mean? The Paris police will take over with this Aubert guy and the dodgy cops, right? And they were behind all these fires? Really? Bloody hell!'

'Yes sir, so it would seem. So with any luck, we've seen our last attack on a British home, which will be good news in terms of your retirement plans, if I may say so, sir.'

'What the hell do you mean by that? Who told you?'

'Just gossip, sir. But if you'll permit me to say, sir, you couldn't choose a better place to retire to.'

The ACC snorted. 'Aye well, that's as maybe, Mains. We'll see. But it looks like you'll not be hanging about down there for much longer yourself. Ha! You've gone and done it this time, Mains. Done yourself out of a job. And you'd better get McLuskey back here pronto. Back to auld claes and porridge for the pair of you, my lad.'

'Whatever you say sir, though I understand my six-month secondment was agreed down south? Apparently a lot of interest in London.'

'That's nothing to do with you, Detective Inspector. I make the decisions around here and I'll soon be letting you know exactly what the score is.'

Aye, Barney thought as he ended the call, *once they've told you.*

Then he had to face another unpleasant task. He had to follow his new information, Jack's close links to the King, to its logical conclusion. Whoever pulled off that shot in the courtroom was an ace marksmen. One with a cool head to match. Perhaps the type who could shut out the distractions from hundreds of onlookers and throw a heavy metal ball at lighting speed and with laser-like precision.

But the parallel was too easy. If he was going to present his growing suspicions to Jean-Luc, he had to have a better case than this.

He started to write notes for the report he might soon have to present to one friend when asking him to investigate another.

1 - The night of the Fitzwilliams' party, Jack had made a point of befriending him. Why?

2 - Then when Jack gave him a conducted tour of the King's haunts the actor had pooh-poohed the idea that Leroy had been behind the Fitzwilliam fire. But why would Leroy appear at the party unless to further pressure the hosts into telling him where the paintings really were?

3 - It was Jack who first raised the idea that a certain English hedge fund owner was deep in debt and might have set fire to his own home. A diversion.

4 - And it was Jack who first raised the curious fact that in all the fire attacks, not one person had been hurt or arrested, suggesting that the police were involved.

5 - And then, there was Barney's face to face meeting with the King himself. The man had pointed towards Aubert over the attack on the lawyer and then dropped the heavy hint that Barney should maybe look a lot closer to home, again steering him away from himself and towards the French police.

6 - The bit that struck home most however was how the remarkably well-informed Jack fed him the clincher information at a time when he and Shona were desperate.

Not only did the little lookalike come up with Aubert's Nice address within minutes; he also asked if Barney's interest was anything to do with rumours around the Port deal. All his master's voice. All from the Serge Leroy play book.

Barney felt sick. Like a complete mug. Jack had befriended him and played him like a sucker.

He dearly wanted to go straight to the little man's home right there and then and have it out with him. But he knew he couldn't. He had to wait for the MoD's reply and then he had to share everything he knew with Jean-Luc.

But there was one thing he could do right now. And even as he shot upright he knew it was something he shouldn't even think about doing.

* * *

At first the doorman said his boss wasn't in. He actually said *in residence.* Like the man was a real king. But he read something in Barney's voice which made him change his mind and suggest that he check with reception.

The defence team looked up from their magazines as they sat in the foyer.

'Look guys,' said Barney. 'I know your boss is in and I know he'll want to see me. So can you just call up to him and let me get into that lift?'

Stefan looked confused for a moment then recovered. 'Bonjour Monsieur Mains. Please have a seat and I will see what I can do.'

Barney said thanks but he'd rather stand then walked to the lift while Stefan picked up a reception phone.

'It's OK, Monsieur. You can go. I think you know the way,'

214

he added with a flash of a smile.

Leroy hadn't bothered leaving his terrace to open the lift door, which left Barney to make his own escape then venture out on to the glass ledge. He never even noticed the drop.

'Mr Mains again. Please take a seat. I have the feeling you have something to say.'

Leroy had a glass of what looked like tomato juice on the glass table in front of him and was lounging back with a newspaper in his lap. He seemed relaxed and pleased with himself.

'Reading all the good news, Leroy? Aubert out of the way. Big outside inquiry into the local boys in blue. Your dream ticket.'

'Mr Mains, Barney, please, relax. I'm happy to tell you anything you want to know. But let's not spoil a beautiful day.'

Barney took a breath as he sat to face the man across the table, his back to the view.

'OK, I can do civilized,' he said. 'So tell me how you know Jack Thomson.'

'Ha! Well, that's a long story. But if you've got time,' he said, arching an eyebrow and sending a contour map of a mountain range up one side of his forehead. 'No big secret. Many years ago, I was walking along the Promenade des Anglais when I stopped to watch this funny little performer. It was Jack, doing his now famous Charlie Chaplin act. Well, he made me laugh. It had been a long time since I laughed. I'd come from Algeria, you see. I had no family any more and over the years Jack has become like a son. I helped him get started and...'

'So if you're his great benefactor, why did he and Gracie lie about how she supposedly *discovered* him?'

'Well, I think it was the PR agency who came up with the tale. Wouldn't have done Jack a lot of good to be backed by someone like me, with the reputation I had in those days. Thoroughly deserved, I'm afraid. Still not great PR to be friends with the so-called King. So we tend to keep our relationship private.'

'Look, Mr Leroy, I know that Jack's been feeding me information ever since I got here, information which you've given him to keep me from looking too closely at your affairs.'

The King looked surprised. 'But no. Really, I don't know what you mean. Jack's his own man.'

'His *own man,* who knew where Aubert lived, hinted at the Port deal, pointed me in the direction of Aubert and crooked police. Really, a lookalike performer knows all this?'

'Mr Mains, you can draw your own conclusions but think: who would be among the best informed people in the whole region but a performer who's treated as part of the decor at all these high-end parties where the great and the good have too much drink and speak more freely than they should?'

'So that's really your relationship. He uses his cover as a performer to harvest all this valuable information for you? Nice setup. Makes me wonder what other talents our Jack may have, what else he's done for you?'

Leroy screwed up his face, apparently trying to read some meaning in Barney's. 'Now you've really got me confused.'

Barney stood. 'Yeah, well, I didn't expect a confession. But don't you worry. I'll be back.'

He made to leave but stopped and looked down through the glass floor to the rocks below then looked at Leroy and smiled. 'Nice view,' he said, then walked to the lift.

Stefan was there to see him to the door and to wish him a *bonne journé*e.

Outside, Barney stopped and looked around him, trying hard not to admit to himself what he had just done. He had committed the cardinal sin. He'd let his personal feelings get in the way and made a complete arse of himself. Worse, he'd shown his hand to Serge Leroy and in effect to Jack Thomson. He cringed. *You fucking idiot!*

But there was nothing to be done. He was close to the villa so he might as well walk there and drown his sorrows. Then he could tell Shona everything and let her tell him just exactly how stupid he'd been.

The walk into Villefranche passed in a blur and before he knew it he was sitting poolside with his woman.

'You look like you could use a drink,' she said, peering into his eyes. He nodded. 'Oh, yeah.'

He emptied the first glass before telling her what he'd done. The second was untouched until he'd finished.

'Well, it's not so bad,' she said. 'If you've got enough on Jack, you can just go to Jean-Luc and have him arrested. OK, so you've maybe tipped him off but if he runs, well then, you'll know you're right. And if he doesn't, you can still arrest him. Really, I don't see what you're bothered about.'

He loved how she could simplify complicated issues like that. Even if she had kindly missed out the bit about him being a totally unprofessional arsehole. But hey, he preferred her version.

And he liked it even more later that night when an email arrived from the MoD. It was Jack's service record in detail. But there was only one detail that mattered because it seemed that during Jack's time in action, he'd had a very specialised role.

He'd been a sniper!

24 - OK Corral

Jean-Luc seemed in a better mood this morning. But not much. Barney had wanted to meet somewhere private but Fleur Dupont had called in sick, which meant that the office was as private as he needed.

'Everything OK, Jean-Luc? Sensed a bit of an atmosphere yesterday.'

'Yes, I'm fine thank you, Barney. But why did you want to meet outside? Has there been some important development? Take a seat and tell me everything.'

Barney opened the file on his laptop containing his case against Jack and put it in front of the Captain.

'It's all there, Jean-Luc. But the headlines are this: Jack Thomson - aka Charlie Chaplin - is like a son to the King. Has been since he first turned up here from England years ago. And far from having been an actor back home, he was actually a serving soldier, did tours in Afghanistan. But the clincher, which I just got last night, is what his special skill was in the Army. Jack Thomson was a sniper.'

Jean-Luc was nodding. He read through Barney's take on

everything, the apparently overwhelming combination of details which consolidated the case against Jack as the shooter, the shooter acting on behalf of the King, just as Jean-Luc had earlier speculated.

At last the Captain closed the lid of Barney's laptop and handed it back.

'Barney, I must congratulate you on your work. It is painstaking and solid. I know it must have been difficult for you to do this, to investigate a fellow countryman you have come to see as a friend. But Barney, I have to tell you: you're wrong.'

Barney was nonplussed. 'Wrong? But how?'

'I haven't got all the details yet, Barney, but I am afraid that it is, as the King said, a lot closer to home. We are currently investigating my assistant, Dupont.'

Barney shot to his feet. 'No! You can't be serious!'

'Barney, please sit. What I'm about to tell you is confidential at this stage.'

The Scotsman sank slowly back into his seat, mystified.

'I had my suspicions that everything wasn't right. But it was when I got her to check out the four officers on duty in the court. They supposedly didn't know each other. Said they all rushed upstairs to the gallery right after the shooting, saw a female officer with a gun and assumed she was one of them. Except that Dupont herself knew all these officers through their membership of hunting clubs. She's even in the same club as two of them, out in the Esterel. But she never said a word.'

'But Jean-Luc, just knowing them isn't a crime.'

'No, but having a blond wig and a specialist make-up product at her home which could cover her dark skin is pretty strong evidence.'

'Make-up? I don't understand.'

'Oh, I forgot. You don't know. Our dear forensic guys found a smear of this make-up on the upper edge of the rifle stock, a sort of heavy foundation cream.'

'But Jean-Luc, don't you see? That confirms that it was Jack. He must use greasepaint, or something like that, all the time for his act.'

But Jean-Luc was shaking his head. 'In theory, yes. But as I say, we've matched this sample with the same concoction in her apartment. It is used by some people to cover their dark skin, including some famous people in the music industry, I'm told. And as you know, Dupont has a particularly dark skin. But another thing you may not know... One of the officers said the shooter had a mole on her cheek. He must have thought that this random little observation would help muddy the water. But the fool didn't realise that he'd provided me with a telling clue. You see, once I realised that make-up had been used, I knew that it had not been a mole but a tiny patch of dark skin revealed when part of that make-up had rubbed off on the rifle stock during the recoil of the shot.'

Barney was silent, trying to make sense of all this new information, weighing it against his own convincing case. 'But if she knew these officers, why would she need a disguise?'

'Ah, the disguise wasn't to fool them but everyone else. Because of course, she needed to get down the stairs and outside without anyone recognising her. For what if every officer in the building had suddenly been subjected to the test for gunshot residue?'

'But you must have more?'

'In terms of forensics, no. Just a single date stone she

overlooked after her overnight snack.'

'Date stone? What kind?'

'Ha! As if it matters, medjool. It's a large variety, very popular here.'

Barney wanted to say that Jack loved medjools, but then, so did he and apparently a large proportion of the local population.

'But you're correct, Barney. That's not all we've got. You see, you were right about there being a bad atmosphere yesterday. I had just discovered that the four officers almost certainly knew each other from the big hunts that these gun-happy idiots are always having. Then I took a chance and pulled all the officers' duty schedules to compare against our list of fire attacks.'

'And?'

'An exact match. Every time they were off duty, we had an attack. We've got two of them under guard in hospital now. Burns victims. They're the two who attacked you at Saint-Jeannet, guaranteed. But the other two - and I suspect, Fleur Dupont - have vanished. I think she realised yesterday that I was on to her. But I've had a tip that they might have gone to their clubhouse in the Esterel, no doubt trying to figure out their next move. And I was just getting ready to meet up with a squad out there.'

'But wait, Jean-Luc. Let me get this straight. Didn't you tell me it was Dupont who found the rifle in the fire extinguisher in the first place?'

'Yes, but she knew I was on to that and she just jumped ahead to impress me, win my confidence. Of course she knew where it was all the time. She also jumped ahead with the court doorman. He was all over the place when he was in here.

I suspect he had more to tell and was making her nervous. Maybe she began to fear that he recognised her. But whatever it was, he suddenly became the victim of a hit-and-run *accident*.

'And as for the cleaner, Madame Cortes, whom Dupont was unusually keen to contact, it turns out that she's received death threats to say no more about the bribe that kept her off work and allowed our killer into the court building. They told her what happened to the doorman.'

Barney threw his head back and stared at the ceiling. 'I just can't believe that I got it so wrong. In fact, I still can't really believe that I *have* got it wrong. But maybe.'

'Don't worry about it Barney. You followed the evidence. Just as I have. But you couldn't possibly have the big picture. You see, it was my Commandant who made all this possible, who assigned the officers to their places in the court building that day. Dupont was off duty, given a free run to make the hit. Then my dear Commandant assigned her to work alongside me, where she could follow every single development and manipulate the evidence. I only wish I had spotted her sooner and maybe that doorman would be alive today and his kids would still have a father.

'But Barney, you do get it, yes? That these crooked officers - including my Commandant - were all in the pay of Aubert? Their job was to create chaos and pave the way for the megalomaniac's march to power in the election. The fact is that only they could have staged the shooting. No outsider, not even the King, could have got someone in and out of a building full of police.

'No,' said Jean-Luc, 'this was a hit ordered by Aubert. This was his masterstroke. By pulling off such a daring execution he would send a message that the police were powerless, that the region was descending into chaos and only a strong leader of the right could impose order again.

'At the same time, he would point the finger at the King as a prime suspect. You know I said early on that it would be in Serge Leroy's character to assert his authority so openly, to punish an outsider for daring to carry out a major art heist on his patch.

'But from what I've learned, now that I know about Nel's legacy and the attacks on the lawyer and yourself, Aubert didn't only fear that this legacy could hurt him; he was terrified that the King might get to it before he did. So what better solution than to lay everything at Serge Leroy's door?'

Barney couldn't counter Jean-Luc's scenario. But he just couldn't let go of his own. It was like being given the scientific explanation of aircraft flight but still being left with that undeniable, human doubt that says: *yeah, I get all that, but how can a heavy lump of metal like that actually get off the sodding ground?* It's one thing knowing the facts; belief's another matter.

* * *

Barney remembered the route past Cannes from his trip with Fleur Dupont, that day he went to meet Aubert. How ironic that now, only days later, Aubert was locked up, his dreams of the presidency gone. And that they were on their way to arrest three bent police officers including the selfsame Dupont. As some learned philosopher once said, *it's a funny old world.*

He reckoned it took less than an hour to the car park opposite Las Tayas railway station, starting point for the trail up into the rocks. The all-pervading smell of burning undergrowth hung in the air as they climbed and in the distance, he could hear the faint drone of engines as aircraft continued their relentless shuttle of dousing water from sea to fire.

It wasn't until the pair reached the plateau that Barney got his first sight of the rocky outcrops Jean-Luc had described. And it stopped him in his tracks. Deep red teeth of ancient rock looked to have torn through the scrub and low woods to bask in the blazing sun and now seemed to glow with a life of their own. One in particular had a real presence, standing on its own above the greenery.

Jean-Luc must have seen him staring. 'That's the famous Dent de l'Ours, bear's tooth, literally. Impressive, eh? But no sightseeing today. That's the way we're going but this might turn out to be anything but a nice day out.' The Frenchman handed him a kevlar vest, *just in case.* 'But remember, we need to stay well back out of any action. Leave it all to these guys.'

Barney took in the dozen or so figures dressed all in black. 'Yeah, they look the biz. But I never saw them on the way up.'

'Oh, they were dropped by chopper before we got here.'

Barney bit his tongue. His sandalled feet would have preferred the same mode of travel.

Jean-Luc laughed. 'I know what you're thinking. But there wasn't room. Besides the trail from here is pretty good if I remember correctly. A lot of people come up here hiking.'

For the next half hour the pair followed the squad, all in single file. 'I can't believe I've never been here, Jean-Luc. Why didn't you tell me about the Pic de l'Ours before? It would be absolutely fabulous to come painting here.'

'Good for bees, too, my friend. And no bears to steal their honey.'

Whether from the unreal nature of this hike or the unexpressed tension of the reality, they were still quietly laughing when the squad commander called a halt and came to the back of the column.

'Right guys,' he said, 'that's the clubhouse over there.' He pointed between the small trees which lined the trail and Barney could just make it out, probably less than a hundred metres off to the right. It was a building like an old wild west ranch, complete with covered wooden porch in front. The windows were shuttered, as if those inside were under siege. It lay across clear ground, atop a jutting promontory of red rock, with a very good view of the surrounding countryside. And anyone who approached.

The commander, a surprisingly short and slim guy to be leading such a team, didn't lack authority. 'This is where you stay. OK? Captain Verten, you have the clubhouse number so I suggest you make first contact. Hopefully there won't be a problem.'

It sounded like he didn't fully mean what he said. This was what they trained for.

Jean-Luc already had his phone out. 'Hello, who am I speaking to? Ah, Claude, I thought you might be here. But as you know, it is your daughter I've come to see. Is it OK if I come over for a chat?'

But the Captain pulled the phone from his ear and stared at it in his hand. 'Shit! Fleur Dupont's father. He just told me I wasn't welcome and to bugger off. I'll try him again.'

There was no response. The commander gave a sharp nod then returned to the head of the column. He briefed his gathered men and then accepted a microphone.

'Attention people in the clubhouse. This is Captain Karim

Benchadi of the Police Nationale. Armed officers are about to approach you with a warrant for the arrest of Fleur Dupont and two other serving officers. You are advised to…' He ducked. A single shot. A ricochet from the high rocks to the left of the trail.

He was unflustered as he turned to his men and told them to take defensive positions. He then waved vigorously to Jean-Luc and Barney to get down. They needed no second invitation. Jean-Luc's phone rang.

'That's very stupid, Claude. You should know better after all your years of police service. I don't want to know who fired that shot. But you'd better make it the last.' He listened. 'Man, you're crazy! You want some kind of gunfight at the OK corral or something? You seriously want someone to die over this?'

Again the call was cut short. 'Bastard! He's hung up! Just said if we wanted his daughter we'd have to come and get her.'

The commander had been listening and now signalled to his men. They took up positions along the track, flat on their bellies, automatic weapons locked on the clubhouse. He stood up and stepped through the shielding trees to stand in plain view of whoever had fired that shot. He spoke into the microphone. 'I warn you that any further shooting will be met with an overpowering response. I order all inside to come out and leave any weapons inside.'

His only answer was a second shot. This time the bullet glanced off a rock at his feet and whined into the trees. Captain Benchadi, with impressive composure, turned to take up a protected position on the trail. He looked left and right at his men and raised his right hand, then dropped it. Four single shots rang out, evenly spaced. Each plucked a spray of wood splinters from the four uprights holding up the porch. He repeated the command and a volley of four simultaneous shots rang out, again striking the dry wood of the porch supports.

In the shivering silence, he again stepped into the clear. But this time there was no warning shot. He took the bullet full in the chest and fell backwards. Two of his men dragged him back to safety. Breathlessly, he told them: 'It's OK if they'd wanted to kill me they could have. This wasn't a high-powered rifle. They could see my vest. They knew what they were doing. But this changes things.'

When Benchadi had recovered his breath he rejoined Jean-Luc. 'It's clear ground all the way to the building and they're in a strong defensive position. My men would be sitting ducks. We have to call in support.'

Barney, who had been crouched alongside, listening in, suddenly spoke. 'Gents, I have an idea.'

The Frenchmen looked at him, their faces twisted in a mixture of surprise and confusion and in Benchadi's case, anger.

'Aye well, don't all ask at once.' said Barney. 'But seriously folks, this could work.'

He then told them about Saint-Jeannet, how a freak stroke of luck had saved his and Shona's lives.

'I have to tell you that tonnes of water dropped from a height and in one great deluge like that is seriously scary. We probably only got the tail end of it. But a full load would do serious damage to that building over there.'

The Frenchmen looked at each other but said nothing until Jean-Luc finally broke the stand-off. 'You know, Benchadi, the planes fill their tanks by flying low all along the coast here, probably less than a few kilometres away. One load would do it, for sure.'

Benchadi didn't show what he was thinking but it was his call and he knew it. He looked at Barney, then at Jean-Luc. 'Right. Let me check this out.'

His radio call lasted a few minutes. He seemed to be having a problem explaining what he wanted. But at last he nodded. 'That's it sorted,' he said. 'Ten minutes, give or take. When we hear the plane we're going to fire smoke shells at the building to give them their target.'

Benchadi stood and grabbed the microphone again. 'To the people in the building, you must vacate the premises immediately, unarmed. Should you choose to stay inside, I give you fair warning that you are about to be attacked with overwhelming force. Should you choose to remain, you risk serious injury.'

He repeated the warning twice over the next few minutes, without success. Then, in the distance, Barney heard the aircraft approaching. Benchadi gave a signal and muffled shots rang out from closer to the building. It seemed that two men with the smoke cartridges had crawled within range to deliver their surprise packages.

The clubhouse was suddenly covered by thick black smoke. With no breeze, it just clung to the roof. Any low-flying pilot couldn't miss it and now the drone of the engines drew closer. Suddenly the noise grew to a crescendo. The huge aircraft swooped down in a deafening lunge and fired its fearsome water-bomb straight at the target.

The impact was like a car crash. Barney winced. It had been much worse than he'd anticipated. It was hard to recognise the building. How the hell he and Shona had survived he'd never know. There was no porch any more. Its remains lay scattered all around in great puddles. But the main stone structure stood intact. *Thank God!* he thought. *Please don't let anyone be hurt.*

But Benchadi's men were already inside, shouting their heads off at everyone to drop weapons, to lie down. In the shock of the impact and then this dizzying onslaught there was no shooting. Barney dared to imagine that his idea had not ended in disaster. He got his answer when Benchadi emerged and waved them across.

The devastation was shocking but everyone was on their feet. No injuries that he could see. Just dazed faces and handcuffed wrists.

There was Fleur Dupont and the two crooked officers and an older man Barney took to be Fleur's father, Claude. No-one else. He'd imagined a whole brigade of crackshot hunters inside, just bristling for a fight. But the four now being led out and away looked a sorry sight.

25 - A Niggle

'Yes, you could say they jerked my chain,' said Ffiona down the line. 'But, truth be told, I wasn't sorry to be hauled back to Edinburgh. I was going crazy hanging about with no real work to do.'

'I understand,' Barney said. As he sat at the villa's big dining table, he could easily visualise his sidekick at her desk back in Edinburgh Police HQ with piles of case notes in front of her, an impossible workload, and loving every minute.

'Besides, it looks like I missed all the action again. Was there really a shoot-out at the OK corral?'

'Ach no. It was just a few pot shots. Nobody hurt. No big deal. Jean-Luc got his man, I mean woman, though her old man's in real bother too. It was him doing the shooting apparently. Big supporter of that right-wing nutter, Aubert, it turns out. Don't get it. Why can't folk just leave it to the voters?'

There was a pause on the line. He heard Ffiona thinking and then not being able to stop herself. 'Considering the shower that got voted in down south, I wouldn't put too much faith in that.'

'Oh, don't get started with your politics, Ffiona. Life's complicated enough.'

She laughed. 'Anyway, now that you've cleaned up the South of France, what's the story? Are they pulling you back too? Or have you started to investigate that nice Mr Leroy now too?'

'Leroy, the King? Why do you mention him?'

'Oh it's just that when I was reading all about Aubert's arrest, it said that they reckoned the way was now clear for this King guy to clinch a deal to buy the Port.'

'Really? I didn't know he was involved. But what the hell. It's nothing to do with me. I'm just waiting to hear if I'm supposed to stay on here as planned. Old Eagle-eyes seems to be keeping his head down so I suspect the decisions are being made elsewhere. The thing is, even though everyone thinks it's all over, there's still a huge population of Brits down here and as you know, *crime never sleeps.*'

'But what do you mean: *everyone thinks it's all over,*' she asked.

'No, no, nothing. Jean-Luc's happy. Well, not so happy that an outside force has taken over the Aubert case and has launched a massive investigation into his beloved branch of the Police Nationale.'

'You can't fool me. You've got a niggle.'

'No, really. It *is* all over. Done and dusted. Just waiting to hear my fate. Given myself the rest of the day off. Staying well clear of the office for now. Maybe get out for a wee sail with Shona later.'

'My heart bleeds for you. Sir.'

'Just you get back to work, McLuskey. And no slacking, just because I'm not there to crack the whip.'

'Aye, aye, skipper.'

He was still smiling as he walked out to the terrace.

Shona was dressed for the sea. 'How's Ffiona?'

'Oh, she's in her element back there. Glutton for punishment.

But look at you. I take it we're casting off this evening for a sunset sail?'

'Only if you're up to it, old man. I mean, you've had a busy day. But you can relax now, right?'

He gave his little sideways tilt of the head. 'Maybes aye...'

'Speak, what's bothering you?'

He sat next to her at the table. 'Shona. I know I'm probably wrong but you know how it is when you get an idea in your head and you just can't shake it.'

'Which is?'

'Well, I told you Jean-Luc's case against Dupont. I mean, totally convincing. It's just that while he reckons he's got her for concealing evidence and probably a hell of a lot more, the only thing identifying her as the shooter is what they found at her flat, a blond wig and some greasepaint. Hell, you've got a blond wig. And she could have a good reason for having that makeup. Someone might even have planted it. Either way, that idea of her dark skin showing through the make-up, like a mole - that could apply to anyone with a dark skin or even a good tan. I'm not saying she's *not* the shooter, just that, I don't know... it's just that I hae ma doots.'

She had listened without interruption, like she knew that he had to process things methodically, flush out every single worry and shoot it down.

'OK, so you've got your doubts. I get it. But you're too close to things right now. And you've had a heck of a few days. So why don't we just take some time out. You'll see things differently soon enough and then you'll do whatever you have to do.'

'Ha! I like your confidence. But you're right. It's up to the court to decide. And I haven't got any more evidence than

Jean-Luc has. So, let's get going. At this rate, a sunset sail will turn into a midnight one.'

The evening was still, the sea like glass, the warm air heavy on the chill water as the muted sounds of diners' voices carried from the quayside. Everything was normal, just as it had ever been here in this blessed backwater of the world.

Ready to cast off, she had the motor puttering quietly. It would take them further out, to maybe catch a breeze or even just drift. It wasn't about sailing; it was about being at one with the sea and the red hues of the sun as it hurried to keep its date with the western horizon.

Barney saw it before he heard it; a huge motor cruiser, enormously wide and brilliant white, its twin engines now becoming audible as a sustained low growl of suppressed power as it cut a line across their bow and sent a wake which jolted the little yacht and set the rigging clattering.

'Friend of yours, Shona?'

'No friend of mine. Not a sail in sight. Just a glorified big motorhome. These bloody monstrosities should be banned from the sea.'

'Ha! don't hold back, Shona. Tell it like it is.'

The stern of the intruder comprised a spacious deck where two figures stood looking back at them, a dark-skinned man with Hollywood looks and a smaller man who seemed to be smiling broadly.

The shorter one held up his left hand in front of him in a wave then reached down and lifted a stick, a walking stick, which he raised to eye level, as if aiming a rifle. And he was aiming straight at Barney.

As the vessel eased away, Jack lowered the cane and leaned on it. He seemed to be slowly moving his head from side to side. Then he raised a hand high in a final wave and the engines powered up, churning the water into foam and thrusting the cruiser forward, toward the open sea and into the falling sun.

'You realise who that was?' she asked.

'Yeah, it's my pal, Jack, with *his* big pal, the King himself.'

'Yes, I remember, from the party. Looks like crime pays, right enough.'

'You'd better believe it.'

But for Barney, there was something about Jack's performance with the cane, something beyond the unwelcome memory it provoked of Nel's tragic last act. He just couldn't pin it down. If it mattered, it would come to him in time.

26 - Lunch, No Doubt

Wednesday, July 16

The night sail had been just what he needed. It was so peaceful and silent that, far out off the point of Cap Ferrat, drifting on a sleeping sea in the light of a half moon, Barney came to appreciate just how many thoughts had been cavorting around in his head like demented monkeys.

The engine had brought them back, but slowly, keeping alive as long as possible the illusion that they were the only two people in the world.

He'd slept the sleep of the dead and today was ready for anything.

Except that, as he sipped his wake-up glass of orange juice in the terrace sunshine, one of those damn monkeys started tugging at his thoughts again. That wave from Jack. It just seemed so final.

The number rang out and continued to ring before going to messages. *Shit!* He tried not to show it to Shona but he needed to go into town and check. He could see she suspected that something was up but she said nothing as he, too casually, said he was off into the office to see how Jean-Luc was faring.

He took the train into Nice and walked along Avenue Thiers and back under the iron bridge again to Jack's building.

The gardienne, Madame Charpentier, was sorting mail in her office. 'You come for Mr Charlie?' He remembered how protective she was of him.

'If he's here. Do you know?'

'I don't know but you know the way,' she said, turning her attention back to the mail. Nice to know some things never change, he thought.

All the way up in the lift he asked himself what he was doing here, why he was so anxious to know what Jack had meant by that slow shake of the head last night and whether that wave had meant he was gone for good.

Barney knew the police weren't interested in the little actor; they had their shooter and her accomplices. Game over. But that monkey was now on Barney's back and he needed answers.

He could hear the bell echoing inside the apartment and pictured the immaculate art deco style of the interior, the view from the terrace. But he still heard nothing but that bell. He was about to give up when he heard a shout.

'OK, OK, hold yer horses!'

Suddenly the door swung open and there he was, dishevelled but resplendent in a kaleidoscope of silk kimono.

'Bloody hell, Barney. What time is it?'

Barney was grinning. 'Later than you think, chum.'

'Eh? Well, come in anyway. Feels like dawn to me. Late night and all that. Grab a pew. I'll fix us some breakfast.'

Barney went straight to the terrace doors and stepped out. The clustered domes of the Russian church below were like some elaborate confectionery. The air was almost cool in the shade that still clung to this side of the building. He realised he was relieved to find Jack still here but he was still wondering how to play it when his host finally shuffled out beside him with a tray, back in the costume of the resting thespian. They sat facing out.

'Help yourself to coffee or whatever. Sorry about the welcome, Barney. Never realised the time. '

'Don't mention it. Just thought I'd see if you were up to giving me that lesson in boules.'

Jack seemed surprised then, appearing to remember his offer, said: 'Sure, why not? Would be delighted.'

'Great. It's just that pretty well everything's cleared up now and it looks like I'll have some spare time.'

'Oh yes, I heard, all about Aubert. And the fun and games in the Esterel. You and your friend, that police captain, seem to have been very busy.'

Barney cocked his head and fixed a grimace to his face. 'That's what I don't get, Jack; how you seem to know every damn thing that's going on here.'

Jack sat back, looking surprised.

'I mean, ever since I got here, you've been pointing me in the right direction; hinting at a certain hedge fund owner's carelessness with matches, police involvement in the fires, coming up with Aubert's address, just like that, then a hint about the Port deal. And all the time concealing your close relationship with the King; letting me believe it was Gracie who got you started here. Shit, you even lied about your so-called career in the theatre back home… sniper Thomson.'

Jack had sat stock still, elbows on the arms of his chair while leaning forward to stare at the floor, as if absorbing every word. At last he looked at his visitor. 'I knew you would get all that eventually. I'm sorry. And I know I owe you an explanation. But you've got to believe me, we were only trying to help.'

'Ha! Like I thought. *We.'*

'Yes, OK. *We.* Serge and me. You see, we knew the cops couldn't be trusted and that Aubert was up to no good. But who would listen to the big bad King or a Charlie Chaplin lookalike? And I ask you to forgive me for the Gracie subterfuge but you'll understand that Serge wanted to stay out of the limelight. And it wouldn't have done my career here any good if people knew we were connected.'

Barney laughed. 'Not done you any harm though, has it, your connection? You pick up the scuttlebutt from wealthy drunks at parties and pass it on to your crooked benefactor? Is that it?'

'Well, sort of. But a bit of that scuttlebutt enabled me to tip you off about your hedge fund guy. That was a distraction for us. We wanted you to focus on the cops and Aubert. This Nel business, with him leaving you something, is what really shook things up though. We heard about the attack on the lawyer and guessed that there was something here that had that crazy politician very worried.'

'Nel's legacy.'

'Exactly. And if Aubert was worried about it, then it was something that we wanted to expose.'

'And you knew exactly who would do that for you. Muggins!'

Jack laughed. 'Well, I wouldn't put it like that.'

But Barney had had enough. 'Look, Jack. I don't like being played. And I don't like people lying about their motives - or their past.'

Jack nodded solemnly. 'I can only apologise, Barney. But you know what it's like; when you start in a lie...'

'I need you to tell me why you concealed your time as a sniper in the Army.'

Jack sat back and stared into nothingness. 'Not something I want to remember. You see, I didn't lie about the drink. When I got out of the Army I was a total wreck. The nightmares just never stopped. In fairness, they did their best; put me in a cushy admin job in what was laughingly called *Military Intelligence*. They even got me counselling. But it was only the bottle that really helped. I eventually got discharged. Don't ask me what happened after that. All I know is that I somehow ended up here.'

He looked straight at Barney. 'That part was true. I was a bum, getting by on handouts and drunken performances on the Prom. And I don't believe in fate or destiny or whatever you want to call it, but it was Serge who saved me. You may not believe this, but the man has a good heart. You met some of the young guys he's keeping out of the slums. That basketball team's just one of his things. Me, I must have been one of his first charity cases. He got me straightened out. I asked him once why he'd bothered. You know what he said? *Because you made me laugh.* And when he helped me bring out this little talent I have, I preferred the fiction we'd created around my past.'

Jack gave an ironic little laugh. 'I suspected that at some stage you'd uncover my real life. And,' he said, fixing Barney with a determined look, 'that you might put two and two together over Nel's murder and come up with five.'

Barney stared back, trying to detect something, anything, some kind of a *tell* to reveal whether the man was taking him for a fool and lying through his pearly white teeth.

'Barney, I swear to you: that wasn't me. Your Captain has

the killer. Which means we can all get on with our lives. Yes?' They stayed staring at each other, thinking their own thoughts, until at last the actor's face broke into a smile. 'So are you up for a game or not? Fight it out on the gravel?'

'A game? Oh, boules.' Barney paused. 'Maybe I'll call you to fix that up sometime. For now, I need to get into the office.'

He rose, his coffee untouched.

The little man seemed disappointed but followed Barney to the door.

'I hope you do. Call me, I mean. You know what they say: *You can call me what you want...*'

Barney grinned: *'So long as you call me.* Got it.'

* * *

'Alright Jean-Luc? I expect you were in here before everyone else as usual.'

'Ah, Barney. Well, not that early,' said the Frenchman, stretching back in his chair. But I wanted to be here to make sure everything's processed OK. They're all locked up safe and sound and the boys from up north are taking them into the Aubert case. The only bright moment was when they slapped the cuffs on my Commandant. Oh how I wish I had a picture of his face.'

Barney laughed. It was good to see his friend smiling again. But it didn't last.

'You know, it's going to be pretty strange for a while, with outsiders investigating us to see how far the poison has spread. Everyone is going to be interviewed, records checked, private lives, everything. I don't know how far it went but it has to be done. They'll no doubt want to see me pretty soon too. In the meantime all they'll let me do is look for these damned paintings. But at least now there should be no more fires - of the intentional kind anyway - and we've solved the Nel shooting.'

Barney raised an eyebrow.

'Oh I know you weren't one hundred per cent convinced. But I'm telling you Barney, it could only have been done with the Commandant's help. The case is rock solid, trust me.'

'OK, OK, I know you're right. It's just hard to let go. But I'm going to keep schtum about Jack from now on. I might even have a game of boules with him sometime. But from now on I'm going back to being a humble cop who's only here to mop the brows of my fellow Brits. Mind you, it would have been good to help you wrap up the art heist. I mean, OK, we know it was Nel who carried it out and we know the Fitzwilliams and hedgie were part of it. But those paintings must be somewhere. Then again,' Barney added, eyebrows raised in a question, 'would it hurt them to stay there for another day? Come on. Time for lunch. How about the Cours Saleya?'

Jean-Luc took a big breath. 'Why not? Come on. You're buying.'

By the time they reached the bistro, the Frenchman seemed relaxed at last, having apparently come to terms with the fact that he had been working with colleagues who had cynically betrayed the principles he lived his life by. He was ready to move on and deal with the world as it now would be for months to come, a series of never ending interviews and investigations by officers he had never met. He knew that they had to sweep clean.

Barney's favourite waiter was at the side of their table before they could sit.

'Welcome Captain. Good to see you again. Are you eating? I can recommend the plat du jour. Cod. Very good.'

'That sounds good, Claude. But first, a couple of large beers if you please.'

Claude came straight back with their drinks. They took pleasure in a slow touch of the glasses and then even more with first long gulps. Barney had only just put down his glass when his phone sounded.

The screen said *unknown number*. The text said: *You will find what you seek here.* Then there was an address and a final mysterious line. *Presents have to be given.*

Barney showed Jean-Luc the screen. They looked at each other then rose as one.

The drive to Antibes was trouble-free and they easily found the address given in the cryptic message.

'Nice big house,' said Barney as they stood at the huge double wooden doors. 'Sea view, too. Must be worth a packet.'

Jean-Luc rang the bell and soon they heard someone approach from inside.

One of the big doors swung open.

'Bloody hell!' Barney said. 'Fucking Rufus!'

It seemed that Rufus Burton-Tate was much more than just the architect designing a new home for the hedge fund owner who burned down the old one. So, when he visited hedgie in the nick that time he hadn't been consulting on drawings but on storage facilities for certain elusive works of art.

The man was a pushover, his first weak insistence that they needed a search warrant giving way to protestations of innocence before he caved in and led them to the cellar.

'Stolen you say? You've got to believe me. I had no idea. I

was just doing a favour for a client. He wanted me to look after them for him.'

'Monsieur, I suggest you leave all that for your lawyer,' said Jean-Luc, smiling as he looked at Barney. 'Meantime, I'm calling a van to pick them up. You will be brought in with them to answer a few questions in the comfort of police headquarters in Nice.'

The van arrived quickly from the local police station and two bemused officers started moving the paintings out of the cellar.

'Well, Barney, it looks like you must have made a very useful friend here. Who do you think it was who tipped you off?'

Barney gave a rueful grin. 'Well, I suppose it could have been Jack. He seems to know everything that's going on around here. But it sounds more like the King. Think about it. He said *presents have to be given.* I don't think he meant it in the sense that he was giving us a present. No, he meant that he couldn't keep the presents that had landed in his lap. It would have offended his criminal sense of honour to accept something stolen by an outsider. Besides the arrogant sod is probably convinced that he can steal them back again. Any time he chooses.'

The Frenchman laughed. 'You're probably right.'

'But, Jean-Luc, there's one thing that's still bothering me. About the shooting.'

'Oh, come on, Barney. That's all sorted.'

'Yes, I know. But humour me and I promise not to say another word about it.'

'OK, go for it.'

'Well, you know how your guys found that make-up on the stock of the rifle, on the upper edge, I think you said?'

'That's correct, the *left* upper edge, to be precise.'

Barney thought for a moment. 'Which would mean the transfer of make-up would have been from the right cheek. Which would mean a right-handed shooter?'

'Yes, of course. Fleur Dupont.'

Barney gave a wry smile.

'So that's it, my friend? That's all you wanted?'

The Scotsman slowly nodded. His smile widened. He pictured the scene yesterday evening. He saw Jack aiming his cane, his mock rifle, straight at him.

But the little performer was aiming from the left shoulder, not the right. That was what Barney had missed, what had subconsciously struck him as odd.

The man may have played boules right handed, but he fired a rifle as a leftie!

There was no way he could have fired the fatal shot.

Barney felt the last lingering doubt finally leave him, happy to have been proven wrong in the end.

'Aye, thanks, Jean-Luc,' he said, placing a hand on the Frenchman's shoulder as they strolled to the car. 'That's all I needed to know. Now let's get back to Nice and have a damn good lunch.'

'OK, my friend. But you're still paying.'

Thanks

Thanks for reading Book #3 in the series, *A Killer Legacy.* I hope you enjoyed the tale. The preceding two books are also available and they too can be read as standalones or in sequence.

Below, you can read an outline of the series to date and a bit about how it developed. After that, if you haven't yet read the preceding two, you can check out the opening chapter of each on subsequent pages or on my website at jimmcghee.net.

But in the meantime, if you enjoyed this book, I'd love it if you could take a moment to leave a rating. A brief review would also be much appreciated and would help put the series in front of fellow readers of mysteries. If you have the digital version of the book, these links will take you straight to the review page.

Amazon USA Review Link

Amazon UK Review Link

Thanks again and happy reading!
  Kind regards,
  Jim McGhee

East Lothian, Scotland
Web: jimmcghee.net
Email: jim@jimmcghee.net
Social Media: @bigbarneymains

https://www.jimmcghee.net has samples of all the books - as well as a free story and the option to sign up for occasional newsletters. Meantime, please read on...

The DI Barney Mains Series

Spanning two summers and a winter and set mainly in the South of France, the three books to date can be read in sequence or as standalones.

Book #1 - *The Detective Wakes (January 2022)* - sees DI Barney Mains given a wake-up call one summer in the South of France. He's only there to fly the flag while French police seek a missing Brit, but he finds himself facing political corruption at the highest level and a deadly conspiracy, one which will turn his world upside down.

In Book #2 - *The Major Minor Murders (February 2022)* - his dream of a simple life outside the police is shattered when his criminal brother is accused of murder, a case which leads back to the South of France six months later, into the orbit of corruption and death amongst the super-rich.

Book #3 - *A Killer Legacy* - (May 2022) As you know, it presents Barney with an impossible task. In a South of France which is being torn apart by anti-British protests and wildfires, he must sort out friend from foe and carry out the dying wishes of a killer.

The series is set in an unjust world of haves and have-nots in which Barney nurtures a growing awareness of those who would misuse their power and privilege - the very characters the sometimes leaden-footed cop seems to keep coming up against.

And while murder is never far away, there's always time for a spot of wry humour...

Whatever adventures await Barney, Ffiona and Jean-Luc, the chances are that they will most likely drag the Scottish contingent back, not too unwillingly, to this most beautiful part of the world.

How the series came about...

The starting point for *The Detective Wakes* was the simple belief that everyone deserves a second chance.

For staid Scots DI Barney Mains, that opportunity comes during a simple flag-flying exercise in the South of France.

But his personal journey is in a time and place where the stretching gap between rich and poor is ever more obvious. As the saying goes, the rich get richer and the poor get poorer - and that's been even more true in these pandemic years.

So, a couple of years later, we embark on a voyage of self-discovery alongside Barney in the company of a high-flying young sidekick, a wise French police Capitaine and a multi-billionaire full of surprises in what is (hopefully) a fun, entertaining read, spiced up with the odd murder.

The characters seemed to suggest themselves from the start, the start coming near a place in Scotland called Haddington. I drove past a sign towards a farm. It said simply: *Barney Mains*. For some reason, the two words immediately suggested a fairly boring, older detective.

So, creating a sparky young female sidekick for him in the

form of DC Ffiona McLuskey was an obvious conflict in the making and then in France we just had to have a brilliant Poirot-like Capitaine.

So the characters, including the rags-to-riches Scots-born billionaire central figure, came easily. And while I grew up in the Edinburgh, Scotland area, I have in almost twenty years come to know and love the South of France with its rich variety of settings.

The action of course switches between the UK and France, with some abrupt twists as Barney gets drawn into a shocking plot and suddenly finds himself questioning the very system he's defended all his life.

Far from his old desk in a corner of Edinburgh Police HQ, he finds himself at the centre of world events and facing political corruption at the highest level.

Barney's eyes are opened and he's ready to face the challenges which will confront him in subsequent cases.

And lastly, some useful links...

Check out my website at: https://www.jimmcghee.net

Follow me on Amazon to go to my Amazon Author Page, which lists all the books and has some images and video to illustrate the series: Go direct using this link: **https://www. amazon.com/author/jim.mcghee_-1**

An extract of Book #1 in the series, The Detective Wakes, follows on the next page.

The Detective Wakes

Monday, June 24, Edinburgh, Scotland

Detective Inspector Barney Mains held his usual first-of-the-day coffee and had his usual first-of-the-day thought: *What the hell am I doing here?*

The here was the same tidy desk in the same backwater of Police Scotland's Edinburgh Division, which he had occupied ever since ascending, to the surprise of many (including himself), to his current rank.

But he wouldn't go any further. His inner sense of being in the wrong place all the time had been sussed – now it was only when they were short-handed that he was brought into a live investigation.

Normally, he was desk-bound, tucked away in a recess of the open-plan room, collating evidence gathered by others, doing research, producing reports and occasionally coming up with an idea which was even less occasionally noticed.

The day wasn't helped by the fact that it was Monday, or that the machine-spewed coffee tasted like gritty mud, its only saving grace the fact that it was at least reassuringly familiar.

He switched on his ageing computer. A constant panic over leaks to the press had spawned a steady stream of new, ever more complicated passwords. He had given up trying to

250

remember them and ignored the nonsensical warnings never to write them down but instead kept a growing list in his desk drawer.

As the machine whirred grudgingly to life, he had time to finish his mud while it was still warm enough to be classed alongside primordial soup.

The welcome screen had a new message: Protect your password! Barney opened the drawer, copied the latest line of gibberish into the log-on field and hit return. 'Job done,' he said, closing the drawer.

His inbox had the usual gunk: admin circulars, circulars about circulars, updates from weekend colleagues too lazy to finish their reports before clocking off, but also one marked, unusually, High Priority.

It was from the Assistant Chief Constable's office. This could be it, he thought: voluntary redundancy and a golden handshake to replace his lead handcuffs.

It wasn't of course, but he delayed opening the message long enough to enjoy the fantasy.

He scanned the whole two paragraphs first, seeking out key phrases for some good news. Seeing none, he read it properly from the beginning.

Good morning, Inspector. You will be receiving a visit today from Detective Constable Ffiona McLuskey. She will brief you on a case which is now your top priority. Please complete any ongoing projects immediately or brief civilian staff to process them appropriately.

Ffiona is one of our brightest of the latest intake and this case is an important first challenge. See that you give her all possible help and guidance. From today, you are a team and your superior officers have been instructed to give you both as free a hand as possible. You will be reporting directly to myself. Good luck.

Then he read it again. *F-F-Fiona,* he thought. *How f-f-fantastic. Some high-flying twit with a shiny new degree. No shitty drugs bust in Leith for her. Only the best, highest profile cases for a few years until a door on the top floor gets her name on it. Won't know her arse from her elbow, but if she fucks up, it's muggins who gets the blame.*

Then he thought: *What the hell, might get me out and about for a while.*

He was re-reading the email for a third time when he felt someone loom. He closed the message and spun his chair around.

They say it's all about first impressions, which is unfortunate, because she looked to him like an escapee from Bring Your Daughter to Work Day.

'DI Main?' asked the skinny young girl.

'Mains, like the power and the water. Yes, dear. Who are you with?'

'With?' Then she got the dear and wondered how to deal with her anger.

'Oh, sorry,' he effused. 'You're not... you know, DC, er, McLucky?'

'McLuskey, sir – DC Ffiona McLuskey. Reporting as ordered.'

'Ah, so sorry.' He rose and offered his hand. She looked at it, at him, then decided to risk it. They shook and he noticed the corners of her mouth twitch, as if she had noticed his surprise at the strength of her grip and found it amusing.

He continued: 'I only just read the ACC's email so I was a bit surprised...'

'No problem, sir. Pleased to meet you. And I am so looking

forward to working with you.'

He doubted that. He was the prescribed fall guy. Beyond that, she didn't need him and they both knew it.

Apart from looking hardly old enough to hold a driving licence, she was as thin as a parking ticket and had an offensive overabundance of self-confidence for one so painfully young. The cropped, untamed black hair and matching slashes of eyebrows seemed at odds with her pale, line-free complexion.

And the accent. *What is that? Dundee by way of Cambridge? Odd, whatever.*

'Barney – call me Barney. And pull up a pew. No formalities here.'

'Thank you, er, Barney,' she said, sitting down then crossing her trousered legs and producing a notebook from a shiny new leather satchel.

'So, Ffiona,' he said, enjoying the ability afforded by his rank and his forty-two years to at least set the agenda, 'what have we got?'

She gathered herself, chose a spot high on the wall behind him to stare at, then started as if she was reciting a piece of prose committed to memory during homework.

'... website... billions of pounds... Shona Gladstone...'

Barney was picking up the gist but it was all too tedious. His eyes drifted around the main room they called the Egg Box because of its six partitioned cubicles, some architect's bright idea during the conversion of the Victorian building decades earlier. It felt more like an incubator most days, which is why detectives stayed out – *free range* – as much as possible. Two DCs with nowhere to go were looking his way, giggling like schoolgirls.

'OK, OK, Ffiona, no need for chapter and verse. Just cut to

the chase,' he said, fixing her with his best detective look.

'Sir, I know all this internet stuff can be boring. But it's background you need to know.'

'But why? I don't get it. Where's the crime?'

'Where's the crime? Where's the f—?' she said, more Dundee than Cambridge, just stopping herself in time. 'Sir, I don't know where the crime is. I don't even know if there is a crime. But, sir, you know this. You know what this is all about. You… you're just taking the— Can I speak plainly, sir?'

'I would have it no other way, dear Ffiona.'

'Well you know why I'm here. The ACC has briefed you already?' she asked, clearly beginning to wonder.

'Look, the boss just said I should expect this brilliant young officer who would fill me in on a new case. I know only what you've told me. Really interesting. Thanks so much. But for God's sake will you get to the point. Where the hell is the damn crime?'

'The crime – the potential crime… The fact is that no one has heard from her for almost a week. She's gone missing.'

'Who's gone fucking missing?'

'Shona fucking Gladstone!'

The room went quiet. They were the centre of attention as they sat facing each other, angry eyes locked.

Barney, pleased with having flushed out Ffiona's inner Dundonian and enjoying that all activity had stopped, softened his look and smiled. 'Well why didn't you say so in the first place? We'd better get to work then.'

He still thought it had been a terrible mistake, pairing up high-flying little Ffiona McLuskey with him, big Barney Mains, once described as so low-flying as to be coming in to land. But despite his misgivings, he had to admit that Ffiona's initial briefing, now that she had his attention, was pretty impressive.

Internet entrepreneur Shona Gladstone had already been worth billions when she set up a new website business about five years ago. It basically invited contributions from writers and wannabes, running competitions and attracting hundreds of thousands of short stories, novellas, flash stories and poetry.

Ffiona had to explain that flash writing wasn't flash in that sense, but complete short stories skilfully told in just a few hundred words.

'Sounds pretty flash to me,' he mumbled.

She pretended not to hear and carried on. The website quickly became the most successful site of its kind, apparently due to the fact that Shona had not only the technical and internet know-how, but more importantly the business nous to build her brand and eventually make it as synonymous with writing and books as Google was with searching.

Recently, it was announced that the site had been sold for $5 billion, adding to the status of the young woman – her age varied from twenty-nine to thirty-six in various magazine features – as one of the most desirable singletons in the world.

Barney was mystified as to how any website could be worth such an obscene sum. Even allowing for the fact that it was a major platform for book sales, with no doubt huge advertising revenues, he was left with the distinct impression that it was all a smoke-and-mirrors throwback to the years of the dot-com fiasco.

Shona's money had made up for her plain looks, Ffiona continued, and her fortune was more than enough to make her a prime target. But there was more.

Perhaps not surprisingly for someone so successful at such

a young age, she had made enemies. What was surprising, she told her new boss with a conspiratorial look which made him sit up and smile at her Bond-like raised eyebrow, was how many.

It seemed that while thousands of people were simply over the moon to see their scribblings published online – an ego boost worth infinitely more than mere money – many others, including established authors, were furious about the sale.

She ran a search on Barney's computer and brought up pages of links to stories about Justice for Author Rights, the pressure group which took legal action in a bid to block it. Rightly or wrongly, the authors in JAR felt that it was their writing that had established the site and that they therefore deserved a cut. But the court ruled that the disclaimer box they had ticked as a requirement of their registration meant they had signed away any right to benefit, beyond any modest publication fee or prize they happened to have already earned.

'Not likely that any of them would actually do anything criminal but I think we need to talk to them anyway,' she said.

'I wouldn't dismiss them just like that,' said Barney wisely. 'Some of these writer guys can be serious nutters, you know.'

He thought about adding that none other than their very own Assistant Chief Constable fancied himself as a wordsmith but decided against doing so on the grounds that it might be taken the right way.

Instead, he started scoping out the work. They would have to speak to JAR. But only after contacting Shona's office and arranging to interview her top people.

Then they needed access to the woman's bank and credit-card accounts. From past experience, a record of routine transactions might very well save a lot of bother – their quarry may simply have wanted to get away for a bit, or more likely, gone off and shacked up with some new love interest.

Meantime they should also prepare for the worst and start drawing up a list of the missing woman's main contacts, friends, business associates, staff and, most importantly, the last people to have seen her.

'That might be a bit more difficult,' said Ffiona. 'Seeing as how they're in the South of France.'

Barney paused, remembering the email. He turned to the computer and printed off the High Priority briefing from the ACC. Lifting the single sheet of paper delicately between forefinger and thumb, he said: 'I'm off to see the Wizard.'

***

As he explained later on the flight to Nice, it turned out that he was pushing on an open door. Superintendent Walter Izzard had already been briefed on the interest being shown in the case by the top floor. 'Remember, you're only out there to fly the flag,' he'd said. 'Leave the rest to the French and get your butts back here asap.'

The ACC had then signed off on the flights and personally warned the French investigating team in Nice to expect them.

Barney appreciated that the man's rare enthusiasm was explained partly by the obvious: that the absent Ms Gladstone was not only one of the richest people in the world but also happened to come from the city. What not everybody knew, however, was that she had also once published one of Top Cop's short stories and was therefore deemed gifted with such insight as to be too valuable for the world of literature to lose.

To buy *The Detective Wakes* (or to leave a review if you've

already enjoyed it!) please use this universal link: get-book.at/TheDetectiveWakes which will take you to the book page in your country's Amazon store.

Now, read on for an extract from book two, The Major Minor Murders...

The Major Minor Murders

Wednesday, January 15, France

How the hell are you meant to work in conditions like these? His first-of-the-day moan was a tradition with him, one etched into his psyche during years behind a desk, cooped up in a suffocating room they called the *Egg Box*, back home in Edinburgh Police HQ.

Except that these days, it was recited ironically, his office for the past six months having been wherever he chose to set up his easel, in or around the city of Nice on the French Riviera.

Today it was a spot on the Prom, hard up against the railings above the stony beach. No room for any leg-lifting mutt to leave its unwanted splash of street art. And as far away as possible from all the beautiful lycra people out for their early morning jogs beside an as yet colourless, flat sea.

The early light was fast emerging over the headland to the east as Barney set to work with a speed and fluency he'd only just started to rediscover.

The scene would flaunt its early morning outfit for just a few moments then slip into something new while you looked away. Sometimes you only got one chance.

Which was why he blocked out the bothersome chatter that niggled behind him. *Yes, that's it,* he told himself. *It's coming. Just a few minutes more of this light and I'll have you.*

But the disturbance at his back was now an insistent Scottish voice which he could no longer ignore. Besides, the words seemed to include something a lot like his name. He swung round, brush in hand. And somehow managed to daub a yellowish-green slash across the white throat of a startled young woman. 'My God! So sorry.'

'No, it's OK,' said the young woman, cautiously fingering the moisture on her throat, apparently checking that it wasn't blood. 'But I really need to speak to you.'

Quite tall, decent build. Late teens? He wasn't good at guessing ages of the young. But he couldn't shake the idea that he'd seen her before.

He'd been unconsciously drying his brush on a rag and now folded it to a clean spot and offered it to her.

'Sorry about that. Bet you're glad I'm not a sculptor, ha!'

She didn't seem to find that funny as she hesitantly accepted the cloth in long fingers and started dabbing at the paint. Short fair hair, faint eyebrows almost transparent against the pale, lightly freckled complexion, the face depending for character upon high cheekbones and clear blue eyes.

Barney fought with his memory. 'Have I met you before? And how do you know my name anyway?'

Her face lit up, revealing a lopsided wry turn at the corner of the mouth. She seemed to be relaxing, enjoying the fact that she had him guessing.

'I'll tell you if you buy me a coffee,' she said, faking a childish impishness. But he could see that she was older than her years, whatever they were. And that she was dying to talk.

'Ha! Well, that sounds like a pretty damn good deal to me. Particularly after decorating your neck like that. Come on, I know the perfect place.' He switched his phone back on, for once happy to end his painting for the day, intrigued to discover what this was all about. Then he stuffed the wet canvas, palette and paints into his big cloth satchel and folded the easel into its nifty carrying case, sparing a glance to the headland, now in its full glory.

L'Instant Parfait cafe was close to the famous Hotel Negresco, a couple of blocks along the Promenade des Anglais, yet it remained a modest, welcoming place where Barney had always felt at home.

By the time they reached it, the sun was already producing some warmth and the sea had begun its daily transformation to turquoise and lapis lazuli.

It was a sight of which former Detective Inspector Barney Mains had never tired since leaving behind his old life in Scotland.

Few tourists were around at this time of day and he was able to claim a pavement table under a bright blue parasol. He pulled out a chair for his surprise guest, who sat then let her yellow bag slide from the shoulder of her black puffer jacket to lie against her designer trainers.

Barney ordered an américan and a cappuccino and although she refused breakfast, he added a couple of croissants and jam, just in case. He allowed himself to drift off for a moment while they sat in silence, merely watching the world go by as the palm trees stirred in a tentative breeze. He remembered being told that the narrow roadway between them and the Prom used to be filled by six lanes of endless choking traffic. This morning, internal combustion engines were few amongst the eerily quiet electric cars, bikes and scooters which whispered by.

She lifted her cup the moment it arrived. 'OK, so you wanted to know who I am,' she said, taking a first sip then hastily dragging a paper serviette across her cappuccino moustache. She giggled. 'Don't know why I drink these. Not very ladylike.' Again that contradictory mix of girlishness and a mature turn of the mouth.

Barney suddenly sat up in his chair. 'I know who you are! Sorry. Been a long time. But you must be Ricky's girl. Abbey! My God, you must be what, eighteen by now?'

She sat back, a stern, pugnacious look replacing the wry smile, the striking blue eyes now piercing and defiant.

'So I'm right, then?'

'Yeah, you're right. And the reason you didn't recognise me at first is that you've never had anything to do with us for ten years.'

Years, decades, flashed through Barney's mind. Scenes of boyhood scrapes and confidences shared with his little brother. Four years apart growing up, worlds apart after Barney followed their father into the police and Ricky disappeared from view, lost to Edinburgh's dark side. The last time his baby brother surfaced was indeed a good ten years ago. Convicted on a drug charge. It made the papers. And made Barney's life at work distinctly awkward for a while.

He became aware of her face awaiting his return from the past and as he focused he saw it full of scorn.

'Yeah, that's right. Remember! You and your bloody father cut him off.'

'Hang on. Hang on...' Barney had his hands up against her attack. He sighed as he took a moment to compose his thoughts, to find the words, the conciliatory tone. 'Abbey, I understand. But life isn't that simple. Your dad wasn't always the easiest guy to help back then, you know.' He could see her start to protest and so stopped himself saying more, shaking uninvited images of ancient angry clashes from his head. 'But anyway, that was all a long time ago,' he said, in a bid to change the mood. 'The main thing is: you're here. And I'm really glad that you bumped into me. Really, I am. But now that my niece is in Nice, am I permitted to know what brings her here?'

There was no responding smile but the fury had subsided as she took a quick sip of her coffee, then another, apparently taking some time out. Or more likely, Barney decided, building up to something.

As it turned out, he was right. But he could never have imagined the tale she then told him.

It started in an artist's studio near Edinburgh's picturesque Dean Village. His brother Ricky had by some act of divine intervention been transformed from a good-for-nothing drunk and druggie into an artist apprenticed to one of Europe's most famous artists.

He stopped her at this point, peering into her face. 'Are you sure you're my niece? Because this sure doesn't sound like my little brother.'

Her chin lifted. 'Shows you how much you know. He got straight a long time ago. If you'd kept in touch you'd have known that.'

He could only nod and wait for the rest of the story.

She pushed her cup away and fixed him with a resolute stare. There had been a murder. The great man, Anton Haas, had been shot in the head.

And there was only one suspect.

She angrily threw back her head. 'Ah, there you go. I can just see it running through your mind. You're thinking: *that's better, that's my brother back in character. Now he's finally graduated to murder.*'

He tried to say she was wrong but she was in full flow. 'If you knew anything about him, you would know that he's totally incapable of violence. The cops have just taken one look at his record and decided he's their man. Just like you would have done if you hadn't jacked in the fuzz and swanned off down here.'

Barney was shaking his head. But from what she then went on to say, he had to admit to himself that he would at least have to consider his brother a suspect. Ricky was known to work closely every day with the victim. On Sunday a neighbour heard a shot. The old artist was found dead with a bullet in his head and no-one had seen Ricky since.

She spread her hands, as if coming clean. 'I know it looks bad. I'm not stupid. But the whole idea that he would be capable of killing anyone, let alone a man who meant the world to him... It's just ridiculous.'

Barney could see that she was close to angry tears and so he asked as gently as he could: 'So tell me, what do you think happened?'

She swallowed hard then looked to the sky. 'I just know he's dead too.'

Barney couldn't help but show his confusion.

She leant over the table towards him, tears suddenly forming. 'I'm telling you, whoever killed Amos must have killed my dad too. It's the only explanation.' She seemed to be pushing him to agree whilst also holding back, as if hoping he didn't.

He instinctively reached across to put a reassuring hand on hers. She flinched in surprise but left her hand where it was. 'Look, Abbey, we don't know that. In fact, from what you've told me, there's a hell of a lot we don't know.'

'So you'll help? You'll come back to Edinburgh? I absolutely know he didn't do it, you see. And even if you don't believe that now, you'll soon realise he's innocent once you start investigating.' She pushed her face towards him, the better to deliver the intensity of her final words: 'You've just got to find out what happened to him. You've just got to!'

Barney felt the strength of her emotion, her naive belief in the abilities of an ex-cop she barely knew.

'So you'll do it then? Come back with me.' Abbey's face had morphed into a picture of innocence for her next words. 'I happen to know there are seats on tonight's flight.'

He tilted his head and peered into her eyes, as if seeing her for the first time. 'Oh, you just happen to know that, do you?' He grinned as a burst of admiration ran through him for this headstrong young woman who'd do anything to help her dad.

Barney doubted that he would turn out to be the saviour she imagined but she had at least succeeded in her quest. She'd convinced him that he needed to get back home right away.

* * *

On the flight to Edinburgh that evening, he was relieved that their seats were far apart. No need for conversation. No chance that he could let slip what his young former colleague Ffiona McLuskey had told him when he'd called her from the privacy of his rented studio flat.

Ffiona, already promoted to Detective Sergeant, was one of the force's high-flyers and was never going to completely spill the beans over the phone. But they'd forged a close friendship the previous summer during the Shona Gladstone case.

It was that investigation - or rather the political interference that ended it - which had so scunnered Barney that he resigned on the spot and refused to go home.

He had learned to trust Ffiona's judgement however and

she too reckoned that he should return to Scotland as soon as possible.

Without going into details, she said there was compelling evidence against his brother - beyond the facts reported in the press. She also needed to interview Barney. And he in turn needed to do something about his father, who'd been creating mayhem at police HQ, refusing to leave until he got some answers. Officers had no choice but to lock him up until he cooled down.

Barney's mood darkened as he gazed blankly from his window seat into the deepening night, the events of the summer telescoping into the uncertain present.

Had he been living a fantasy these last six months? Was he about to be kicked in the teeth by harsh reality; be shown the error of his misguided ways and get sucked back into *real life* in Scotland?

Maybe things had changed. Maybe self-serving careerists and accountants no longer ruled the roost in Police Scotland. 'Aye, maybe,' he muttered out loud, not believing a word of it.

Besides, all he needed to worry about right now was his father, who appeared to be losing the plot. And his brother, the murderer.

To buy *The Major Minor Murders* (or to leave a review if you've already enjoyed it!) please use this universal link: getbook.at/TheMajorMinorMurders **which will take you to the book page in your country's Amazon store.**

About the Author

Jim McGhee's a former award-winning environmental journalist.

Based in East Lothian, near Edinburgh, Scotland, he spends much of each year (in normal times) in the South of France, the main setting for the DI Barney Mains series, with tolerant wife Jean and rampant Irish Terrier, Jack.

After a full-on career as a campaigning newspaper reporter, he and Jean launched their own recruitment company in central Edinburgh and for twelve fun-packed years worked closely together alongside their brilliant team - without spilling a single drop of blood.

The Alpes-Maritimes and Var departments, on the other hand, have provided a host of dramatic locations just perfect as inspiration for the odd spot of fictional gore.

Locals, blessed with scenery ranging from unspoilt mountain villages to the classic palms-and-marinas coast, claim that they can be swimming one moment and ski-ing a little over an hour later. It's a claim not yet put to the test!

Besides, when not writing or travelling en famille, Jim's more likely to be off on a hike in the hills with his ever-ready buddy, Jack.

Please feel free to get in touch with comments or questions to: jim@jimmcghee.net

Or on social media to @bigbarneymains

Happy reading!

Printed in Great Britain
by Amazon

33876569R00158